A CHARM OF FINCHES

Recent Titles by Sheila Newberry

TILLY'S FAMILY

PAINTED SKY

A CHARM OF FINCHES

Sheila Newberry

This first world edition published in Great Britain 1998 by
SEVERN HOUSE PUBLISHERS LTD of
9–15 High Street, Sutton, Surrey SM1 1DF.
First published in the USA 1998 by
SEVERN HOUSE PUBLISHERS INC., of
595 Madison Avenue, New York, NY 10022.

British Library Cataloguing in Publication Data

Newberry, Sheila
A charm of finches
1. Farm life – Fiction
1. Title
823.9'14 [F]]

ISBN 0-7278-5354-6

All situations in this publication are fictitious and
any resemblance to living persons is purely coincidental.

Typeset by Palimpsest Book Production Limited,
Polmont, Stirlingshire, Scotland.
Printed and bound in Great Britain by
MPG Books Ltd, Bodmin, Cornwall.

For The Homesteaders, all nine of you, who helped us grow, pick and eat all the apples, pears, plums – and nuts!

Acknowledgements

My love and thanks to John, who refreshed my memory of the distant time we grew 'fruit and nuts' and who helped generally with the research.

To the gypsy friends and neighbours, whose way of life we respected, of thirty-odd years ago . . .

‘I had a little nut tree,
Nothing would it bear,
But a silver nutmeg,
And a golden pear.’

Bibliography

The Deaf Advance, by Brian Grant. The Pentland Press, Edinburgh. This was an inspiring book, by a dedicated voluntary helper for the British Deaf Association.

The excellent factsheet of the Kentish Cobnuts Association, rightly proud of the end product!

Part One

1888–1902

Chapter One

The dappled-grey wooden horse still rocked gently as the small girl slid to the ground. Jerusha let go of the coarse mane, made from real horsehair like the luxuriant, sweeping tail. Rather fearfully, with her fingers, she explored the carved face, the flaring nostrils, painted bright red, the shining glass eyes under their fringe of rigid eyelashes. This was a well-used toy but too stiff and unyielding to be cherished. Not unlike Valentine, her mother's cousin, who had recently come to stay with them and who had decided in her imperious fashion to act as her tutor, telling Kathleen, Jerusha's mother, "She's a bright child, but she needs to stop all that daydreaming and to begin the discipline of learning . . ."

"Just what she said about me, when I was your age," Kathleen consoled her daughter later, when she kissed her goodnight. "She came to live here, to look after me, when my mother died and stayed until I went off to boarding school. She seems very stern, I know, Jerusha, but she really cares about us in her own way. You'll realise just how much later, when you're old enough to understand . . ." Jerusha had been named for the grandmother-she-never-knew and also for her godmother Valentine, for that was her second name.

Valentine sat now in the long-backed chair, writing a letter, frowning as she dipped her pen in and out of the inkwell in the writing slope balanced on her knees. Even her wiry hair resembled the rocking horse's, being streaked black and grey and wound into a bulky plait round her head. Or so Jerusha imagined. Like the rocking horse, Valentine occasionally featured in the vivid dreams which wakened her, trembling and sweating and calling out for her mother in the night, though, until now, it had always been Nimsie, her young governess, who came to reassure her.

The rocking horse stayed firmly in place in the centre of the nursery, which had a faded, hand-painted frieze half-way down the walls, depicting nursery rhyme characters. Jerusha's favourite was Little Jack Horner, for he grinned triumphantly as he brandished the giant plum on the end of his thumb. She knew she would have screamed just like Miss Muffet because she was afraid of spiders too . . . The leaping coals in the fireplace were guarded by burnished brass mesh and the windows by bars. There were books in abundance on the shelves but Valentine had soon banished the clutter of sawdust-stuffed toys into the cupboard, even the Noah's Ark with its beautiful animals carved in Switzerland, her Christmas present from her mother's great friend Oliver last year. Jerusha's favourite doll, made in Germany, with its expressive wax face and dark wig, matching her own hair, which had been passed down to her from her mother, lay forlornly on her bed. Valentine had decreed that the doll would be ruined if it was played with every day. "It cost a pretty penny when it was new . . ." What was the point of toys if they were 'just to be looked at?' Jerusha wondered in bewilderment.

Jerusha Carey climbed on to the ottoman under the window and gazed hopefully down upon the deserted square below. Her living quarters were on the third floor of this square Georgian house. The branches of the spindly trees along the pavement were scarcely visible. The November fog today in London was thick, foul and choking. She eased one hand cautiously between the bars and rubbed ineffectually at the condensation which clouded the glass, making a squeaking sound.

"Don't do that, Jerusha," Valentine said sharply, without looking up from her letter. She had a deep, almost masculine voice. "It is most irritating."

Nimsie, Jerusha thought wistfully, would have delighted in kneeling beside her, drawing funny pictures with her finger. Window pictures, they called them. She missed Nimsie very much. One day she had been here, the next gone. Valentine had somehow been involved with that and also with the departure of the other servants, apart from Libby the maid, for in such a big house some help was essential. Her mother, too, was out so much these days and she never said where she was going or when she would return. Jerusha's lower lip trembled because she had an irrational fear of her mother leaving her, but she would not cry in front of Valentine. She knew she would be told not to be so silly; after all, wasn't she almost seven years old?

Just when she was about to come away from the dismal view,

she heard the muffled clopping of a horse and glimpsed the beaming, yellow lantern of the hansom. The cab driver assisted her mother down and carried her parcels to the door. The gate clanged behind him, then the cab moved off and was soon swallowed up by the swirling fog.

To Jerusha's delight her mother came straight upstairs and she rushed to the door to greet her. Valentine put aside her writing with a little sigh. "Wait for her to put the parcels down first, Jerusha—" But she was already hugging her mother, breathing in the damp, choking smell of London on a foggy day, observing close-to the beads of moisture on Kathleen's plaid woollen cape with its fox fur trim, but not noticing her mother's bedraggled hair under her extravagant hat. When Kathleen kissed her, laughing at her welcome, she felt the chilliness of her mother's pale cheek, but now she inhaled the familiar fragrance of her perfume, of her face powder and she shut her eyes at the sheer pleasure of being loved.

"A miserable day to be out shopping! Let me just go and divest myself of my coat and hat, darling. I'll ask Libby to bring us tea, *then* I'll show you what I've been buying." Kathleen cried.

They ate hot, toasted muffins, dripping with butter on yellow plates. There were special little teatime knives for cutting and spreading, with matching handles. Tiny pronged silver forks for scooping up dainty portions of shop sponge, oozing raspberry conserve and cream for, as Valentine reminded them, the untrained Libby could not be expected to cook more than three simple meals each day. It might be tea in the nursery, but good manners must always be observed. In fact, Kathleen and Valentine semed to be taking all their meals with Jerusha now.

Jerusha drank hot milk from the delicate glass engraved with translucent fairy figures playing pipes. She was not yet allowed to drink tea, although Kathleen, winking at her and pretending not to notice Valentine's disapproval, dropped two sugar lumps into the milk. Her mother understood. Hot milk didn't taste nearly as sweet as cold. She was careful with the glass because that too had been her mother's as a child. Kathleen had been born in this house, staying on here even during her brief marriage to Edwin Carey. The furniture and furnishings were just the same as then, but now rooms were shut off, contents shrouded in dust sheets. The servants had done all that before they left, on Valentine's orders. It was all very puzzling and unsettling for Jerusha.

"How did you get on with your reading this morning, Jerusha?" Kathleen asked.

Even as she opened her mouth to answer, Valentine said, "She is very precocious in that respect. I hope she won't addle her brain any more with those frivolous picture books. The old primers, the ones I used with you, stress the importance of grammar, of composition. The content of the story at this stage is less important. In my opinion a child learns to read too quickly, to skim rather than scan the pages where the story is too stimulating." How prim she sounded, how old-fashioned, to Jerusha.

"I'd much rather read my own books!" Jerusha surprised herself. She thought that the coloured pictures in the books she and Nimsie had shared together at bedtime made the story come alive, enriching the words. The print was too close, the words too dull, the black and white plates too small in the old textbooks which Valentine had restored to the bookshelves. Reading was not nearly so enjoyable with her cousin, but nevertheless she was learning fast and improving at the disliked arithmetic too.

"*Jerusha*!" Kathleen exclaimed at her rudeness.

"It's all right, Kathleen, she'll change her mind soon enough. The classics, she will discover, rarely have pictures." Jerusha could not know that Valentine was not displeased that her young relative had shown a touch of spirit. That should be encouraged in the weeks ahead for there would be a great many changes in her life to cope with . . .

"Can we look in the parcels now?" Jerusha asked, sure that there would be a surprise or two for herself.

"Wipe your hands on your napkin, then," her mother smiled, "and ask Valentine if she will excuse you from the table."

There was a dress for Jerusha in plum-red velvet, with a full, short skirt to show off ribbed wool black stockings and shiny boots with tiny, tight buttons which, without Nimsie to do the honours with the button hook, would no doubt cause much frustration. She tried on the matching hat, a miniature of her mother's, wide-brimmed with the crown adorned with ruched velvet roses, but with narrow elastic to tether it under her chin which Jerusha knew from experience would snap cruelly and pinch her neck. Only ladies made use of dangerous hat pins.

"You look very pretty!" Kathleen assured her. "The hat will cheer up last winter's coat."

"Pretty like *you*?" Jerusha asked anxiously. She must pretend pleasure at these new clothes, but she hoped there would be something more exciting in the remaining neatly-tied brown paper package. There was also a large, white, cardboard box, but surely that must be Kathleen's?

"Of course," Kathleen said, lifting her up so that they saw themselves reflected together in the mirror over the fireplace. They were indeed alike, with pointed faces, lustrous, dark eyes and thick, shining, black hair. Jerusha's already hung to her waist, caught back tightly with a wide blue ribbon. Her mother was petite, slight, and Jerusha was small for her age. They smiled at each other. Kathleen set her down. "I wanted you to look smart, on my birthday tomorrow, when we take lunch with Oliver."

"I've made you a present. Valentine helped me, but it was my idea," Jerusha told her, excited, because now she knew that her mother would not be leaving her behind tomorrow when she went out. "I'm glad I'm going to meet Oliver at last. He sounds nice." She wasn't sure if he was another cousin, but she did know that he wasn't nearly so old as Valentine. Kathleen had told her that she and Oliver were much of an age, and she had been barely twenty years old when Jerusha was born. Oliver never called at their house, few men did, for Kathleen and her daughter were on their own, since Grandpa died two years ago. Grandpa had been engrossed in his failing business and had lived in another part of the house. Jerusha had really seen very little of him. She was not yet curious about her lack of a father. How could she miss what she had never known? The only photograph displayed on her mother's dressing table was of her maternal grandparents. It would be some years before she learned from Valentine that her father's family had disowned him and severed all ties with Kathleen and her baby daughter.

"I always have lunch with Oliver on my birthday," Kathleen told her, with a sidelong glance at Valentine, who, seeming to show little interest in her purchases, had resumed her writing. "He is a very kind man, quite ordinary really, but I'm sure you will get on well with him. He wanted to meet you long before this, but I didn't feel you were old enough to eat in the hotel until now."

"I certainly wouldn't call him 'ordinary'," Valentine observed, showing that she was listening after all.

Puzzled, Jerusha looked from one to the other. Then she asked, "What's in that parcel, Mummy?"

"Something I couldn't resist buying for my favourite daughter!"

Valentine commented at last, "Not *too* expensive, I hope, Kathleen, as things are—"

"Oh, Valentine, it's just a pretty trifle, and anyway, the clothes were necessary. Jerusha had nothing to wear on special occasions—"

"You don't have to justify yourself to me," Valentine said drily. "But remember you asked me to come here because you were desperate—"

"You know how grateful I am for your help and advice!"

Jerusha, puzzled, looked from one to the other. "Can I look now?" she asked uncertainly.

"Of course you can, darling! Here, let me untie the string . . ."

The Japanese paper parasol was light, painted with birds, flowers and tiny ladies in kimonos, flirting with fans.

"Don't put it up in here, they say that's unlucky – but keep it to remind you that the sun really *will* shine again one of these days!" Kathleen told her daughter.

Jerusha hid her disappointment. She wanted to open out the parasol, to twirl round with it. There was nothing else to do with her present, pretty indeed though it was. "What's in your box?" she asked instead.

Kathleen hesitated, looking defensively at Valentine. "Would you like to see my new outfit, Val?" she asked.

Valentine shrugged, but she watched as Kathleen lifted the lid of the cardboard box and parted the rustling top layer of tissue paper, revealing a garment carefully folded. Heavy ivory satin, embroidered with seed pearls. Even that brief glimpse told them that this was an outfit for a very special occasion. Kathleen did not take it out, but replaced the lid. "I *had* to have it," was all she said. Then she piled up Jerusha's new clothes on top of the box and went out and down the short flight of stairs to her bedroom.

Valentine folded her letter, slid it into an envelope and sealed it firmly. "I must catch the afternoon post, Jerusha. My friend will have been waiting for a letter. I shall tell Kathleen where I'm going on my way down. You can look after yourself for ten minutes, can't you? You really have to learn not to cling to your mother as you do."

As Valentine closed the door, Jerusha climbed on to the wooden horse and set it rocking fast. Why did Valentine have to come here and spoil everything for them? She and Kathleen had been so happy here, the two of them together.

Chapter Two

"How clever you are!" Kathleen admired the long strip of french knitting which Jerusha had painstakingly made, winding wool round the four nails Valentine had fixed to the top of an empty cotton reel, showing her how to slip the loops one over the other with a pin. It was tedious work but eventually the rainbow-coloured tube had grown to the desired length. Valentine had promised to teach her to knit next, saying she must never sit 'with idle hands.' That was an admonition her mother had obviously forgotten from her own childhood, as Valentine pointed out.

"You could tie it round your robe," Jerusha suggested. She was snuggled up happily in bed beside her mother. Libby had just brought in breakfast for them both, on a tray. A few cards had arrived in the early post, the usual ones from her mother's old school friends. Like Jerusha, Kathleen had been an only child. There were aunts in Ireland, but they did not keep in touch; Valentine was the only family member whom Jerusha could recall meeting.

"What a good idea!" Kathleen said. "Now eat your boiled egg up and try not to get too many crumbs in my bed. Then you must go back to your room, wash and get changed into your new outfit, while I have a bath."

"What did Valentine give you?" Jerusha dipped her spoon in the egg which Libby had decapitated. The tray cloth was crumpled; the poor girl was rushed off her feet, the ironing basket was overflowing. It would not have occurred to Kathleen to help with household tasks, she wouldn't have known where to begin, but she was an easy employer to please and would not have dreamt of grumbling at her maid.

"Oh, I don't expect much from *her* today, she has been so generous in other ways . . ."

* * *

The organdy pinafore was to keep her dress clean until it was time for them to leave for their luncheon appointment.

"You can finish that page of sums while you are waiting," Valentine said firmly.

Jerusha cleaned her slate to buy a little time. The slate pencil was attached by a plaited string, which had become knotted. The minutes ticked by while she unravelled the knots. Valentine cleared her throat meaningfully. Jerusha sighed and reluctantly opened up the arithmetic book with its perplexing problems.

Kathleen came for her at last, also wearing a velvet dress but in a darker shade of red than Jerusha's. The creamy lace insert which modestly covered her throat was matched by the double layer of frills showing below her cuffs. Being so slender she really had no need of the constricting whalebone stays which nipped her waist in cruelly and gave the illusion of a fuller bust. The exaggeration of her arched back and bustle meant she had to lower herself carefully into a chair.

"They say the bustle is going out of fashion," Valentine said pointedly. She wore much simpler, more comfortable gowns, made to her own designs by her local dressmaker back in Limerick.

"I'm glad I haven't got a bustle, but I'd rather not wear a hat either," Jerusha said with feeling.

Kathleen, now lacking a lady's maid, had compromised with her hair, putting it up as best she could and crimping her fringe with sizzling tongs. She held her hat in her lap, tapped her toes, while Jerusha removed her pinafore and thankfully put her work away.

"I suppose you expect me to make sure the child has fastened her boots and buttoned her coat correctly," Valentine added, when Kathleen refused to rise to her sarcasm.

"If you would be so kind, Valentine. Oh, and I would be grateful if you could pin on my hat for me, I had enough trouble with my hair."

"Oliver will think you look *beautiful*," Jerusha told her.

"I've no doubt he will," Valentine added drily. "He always did, as I recall."

Then Jerusha glimpsed a flash of silver on her mother's wrist as she put out her hand to straighten a ruck on her daughter's dress. She couldn't prevent herself from giving a little shriek. "Oh, why do you have to wear that today?"

"Because Oliver gave it to me a few years ago for another birthday, Jerusha. I really can't help it if you don't like my bracelet. You mustn't be so silly." Kathleen actually sounded cross.

Jerusha recalled vividly going downstairs to the drawing room on that previous birthday evening. Kathleen had been reclining languidly on a sofa piled with cushions. Nimsie whispered that her mother was suffering from a bad headache. Maybe something she had eaten at lunchtime had upset her. Little Jerusha was greeted by outstretched arms, drawing her close for a kiss. "Did you miss me, darling? Has it been a long day without me?" On her wrist was a coiled, solid silver snake, with red eyes winking at her malevolently so that she screamed, "I *hate* it, take it off!"

She had not even been five years old then, of course, but she couldn't remember her mother wearing the bracelet since.

"The child is far too imaginative," Valentine said. "No wonder she has nightmares, Kathleen."

It was not nearly so foggy today, but there were wisps of it lingering about and there was a chill wind, whipping up leaves and scraps of paper for the cab wheels to catch and grind. Kathleen looked dreamily excited and she cuddled Jerusha close to her under the cover the cab driver had fastened over their laps for protection against the elements. They were driving to Regent's Park, for the hotel was nearby.

There were wide steps leading to the double doors of the great hotel and a doorman to greet them deferentially and escort them inside. To Jerusha the thick, deep rose-coloured carpet into which their feet seemed to sink appeared to go on endlessly past the reception desk. Kathleen spoke to someone there and then they were escorted to the dining room, where the crystal bowls suspended from the ornate ceiling glowed with incandescent light despite the early hour. They crossed another sea of carpet, past people already lunching, to a table in an alcove where Oliver was waiting. There were flowers in a cut-glass vase in the centre of the table and pale pink napkins by each place.

He rose instantly to his feet. "It's good to see you again," he said. "So, this is Jerusha! You are just as I imagined." He had a soft voice, but there was no shyness about him. He had a warm, wide smile. Jerusha instantly responded to it, smiling in return as she regarded him curiously.

He was not very tall and stood ramrod straight, with his head held high to compensate for his lack of height. His thick, dark hair was centre-parted, and flopped over his forehead, giving him a boyish appearance, especially as he was clean-shaven. He was pale-skinned, as if he spent much time indoors. When he put out his hand gravely for Jerusha to shake, she stared openly at his long, tapering fingers, the beautifully-manicured nails and the heavy gold signet ring on the third finger of his right hand. His handshake was warm, but he took care not to grip too tightly.

"I am pleased to meet you, Oliver," Jerusha answered belatedly, remembering her mother's coaching, then she added spontaneously, "You're not ordinary at all! You look very grand to me. You must be *awfully* rich!"

He wore an elegant grey frock-coat over a waistcoat fastened by tiny pearl buttons, with a matching pearl-headed pin in the gold stock displayed below the high wing-collar of his shirt. Surely even Valentine would consider him a dandy, Jerusha thought. No wonder her mother had bought her these new clothes to impress him!

"Jerusha!" Kathleen said, shaking her head, but both she and Oliver looked amused. "Oliver's father owns the hotel. Oliver is expected to look smart – you see, he is the manager!"

He pulled out their chairs in turn, settled them at the table. Jerusha sat beside Kathleen and Oliver seated himself opposite. This time Jerusha remembered that she was expected to keep quiet while they were eating, but her mother hadn't said anything about not listening – anyway, how could she do otherwise, when she was sitting so close to them both? The soup was difficult to eat without slurping, which Nimsie had neglected to reprimand her for, and which was definitely something Valentine frowned upon.

"I found your last letter disturbing, Kathleen – there was not time to reply before seeing you today—"

"You think I shouldn't go to him?"

"I think it would be wiser if he came home to see you first. How do you know your feelings for him will be the same as they were seven years ago?"

"He *can't* come – you know the reasons, Oliver . . . He says he is making a go of it out there, that the money I sent him was a godsend . . . And I know I still feel for him as I did, even though you – and Valentine, of course – are convinced he will always let me down . . ." Kathleen sounded agitated.

Oliver shook his head slowly. "What about the house?"

"I already have a prospective buyer. Valentine will see to it all. There should be a little left, after all the bills are settled. My father was quite heavily in debt when he died. Valentine sighs heavily regarding my own imprudence, of course."

"And have you made proper provision for—?" He paused. "Ah, here is the fish. You like fish, I hope, Jerusha?"

She didn't, but she dutifully agreed, and wondered just how much she would be able to leave, to conceal with the old nursery trick of squashing unwanted food under her strategically placed knife and fork at the end of the course.

While she was concentrating on this, the conversation continued, but in a more restrained fashion. The snatches she did absorb were puzzling, but since Valentine's arrival, in particular, she was becoming aware that grown-ups did this deliberately when children were in earshot.

"Valentine will make the arrangements, see to her settling-in, before she goes home. She will feel much happier if she knows you will keep an eye on – things – here."

"I will keep in touch, discreetly, I promise."

"And you will write to Valentine, regarding this?"

"Again, I promise."

"It must be the best, well, it's the only way, until I know exactly how things are working out, Oliver. You see, he never wanted that – tie. I have to persuade him otherwise."

"I feel sick, Mummy . . ." Jerusha made a choking sound. The sauce with the fish was too rich for her unsophisticated palate.

Then Oliver was wrapping his napkin round her neck to protect her new dress, and her mother was hurrying her to the ladies' powder room, where she promptly brought up the fish she had forced herself to swallow. It was fortunate the attendant was there to help with the mopping and sponging-off, for Kathleen had not dealt with this situation before – Nimsie had cheerfully accepted that she was expected to cope, even with the nightmares,

When they returned to the table ten minutes later, they found it had been cleared.

Oliver looked concerned. "Do you feel better? I'm so sorry, Jerusha, but I haven't lunched with such a young lady before and had no idea that a different menu might be required! I have ordered soda water for you, which the waiter assures me will settle your stomach nicely. And coffee for you and I, after the usual toast to you, Kathleen. Now, I think we have been talking too much, and Jerusha will think I have forgotten it is your birthday, eh?"

"I am wearing the bracelet," Kathleen smiled. She displayed it on her wrist, folding back the lace ruffles.

"I hope you will like this as much. Happy birthday, dear Kathleen." He handed over a small jeweller's box. "And, of course, there is a present for you, too, Jerusha, to set the seal on our friendship."

While her mother pinned the delicate filigree brooch to her bodice, Jerusha carefully unwrapped her own gift, a fine copy of *Alice in Wonderland* with the beautiful pictures protected by shiny, thin, paper leaves. Would Valentine approve of this? She didn't care, for although she had read it before, this edition was one to treasure always.

Back home, Jerusha curled up on the ottoman and turned the pages with great care. This time she was only half-aware of the low voices, as Valentine questioned Kathleen about their meeting with Oliver.

"Yes, I put it to him. He kindly agreed at once to share the responsibility with you, as you live so far away. I really do appreciate that you have made a new life for yourself, Valentine, with your friend, researching and writing together – you always had a passion for the academic life. Yes, Oliver will be a rock, as always."

"Good. I shall never understand why you chose the other one. Yet I, of all people, should recognise how single-minded the women in our family are when they are in love. Your father never ceased mourning your mother; he had no idea of my feelings for him. But I can't really believe you can leave like this—"

"Shush! Not *today*. Not on my birthday, Valentine . . ."

Chapter Three

Several official-looking gentlemen called during the next week or so. They merely glanced into the nursery where Valentine, who was called upon to talk to them on each occasion, had insisted that Jerusha continue with her schoolwork on her own for a while, and to 'mind her p's and q's', in other words not to speak unless she was spoken to. So she sat at the table practising her writing with careful curls and loops and, hopefully, not more than a blot or two. Valentine actually praised her industry.

When there had been no more visitors for a week or two, the cabin trunks were brought out from the box room, dusted off and lined with paper. Valentine undertook the packing of her mother's clothes, carefully folding and rolling, even pressing garments when required.

This activity did not really disturb Jerusha, for the smaller, shabbier trunk which was still labelled with her mother's maiden name and destination, *Copper Leas School, Chalfont*, was also being packed, with her own things. This must mean, she thought with excitement, that her mother was planning a winter holiday! It wouldn't do to ask, and spoil Kathleen's surprise. Valentine had already said that she was going back to Ireland in the New Year, so it would be just the two of them again.

Jerusha could respond generously, on hearing this news. "I'm glad you'll be here for Christmas Day, Valentine, 'specially as that's my birthday, too!"

"It's going to be a Christmas to remember!" her mother cried happily.

Neither of them heard Valentine mutter, "And so it *should* be."

Before Christmas, Libby bade them a tearful goodbye. She had a new place to take up, in the country, not too far from her own family, which would be very nice, she explained to Jerusha, for she had missed *them* a great deal.

"We are going to Oliver's hotel for Christmas, at his kind

invitation," Valentine told Jerusha, "It would be short shrift indeed if we stayed here."

Jerusha wasn't sure what short shrift meant, but she was pleased about seeing Oliver again so soon. He had made quite an impression on her, which would have surprised him, had he been aware of it.

When they drove away on the afternoon of Christmas Eve, Jerusha had no idea that she was leaving her first home for ever, or that she would set the wooden horse rocking in the nursery no more. Like the furniture and household effects, it was destined for the auction rooms. The only toys she took with her were the doll, the parasol and the Noah's Ark. And just one book, the *Alice*.

There was a roaring fire in the great fireplace in the main lounge area at the hotel. A Christmas tree, following the tradition started by the Prince Consort for the nine children of his marriage to the little, now long-widowed and reclusive Queen, was decked with coloured baubles and scarlet ribbons, but no candles, for as Oliver remarked, "There is always the risk of fire, for they are difficult to secure safely to the branches."

Jerusha wore her new frock, of course, thankfully minus the hat. She had opened her presents first thing in the luxurious room which, to her delight, she was sharing with her mother. Valentine had come through the connecting door from her room to pull a chair up by the double bed and share in the excitement.

"Your hair looks like my horse's tail this morning, Valentine," Jerusha observed, "All long and flowing—"

"I suppose you expect me to toss my head and stamp my hooves, eh?" Valentine replied drily, but the crinkles around her eyes betrayed her amusement at the very idea. She seemed to have shed her schoolma'am role here. Jerusha decided that she quite liked her after all.

Kathleen's main gift to her daughter was a mother-of-pearl-backed brush and comb set, with a matching hand mirror. "Something you can keep and use for always, my darling. The diary may seem a little dull now, but you will enjoy looking back on it when you are older."

"Thank you! Best of all, Mummy, I like the little dolls, because they look like you and me – and all these spare clothes to dress them up in – what fun!"

The mother and daughter dolls, perhaps six and nine inches tall, were jointed and exquisitely dressed in matching fashionable outfits trimmed with white fur and with tiny real buttons. Jerusha checked their underpinnings: "Oh, look Valentine, they have drawers, and petticoats, and stockings – and garters!"

"I have bought you some more new clothes, for yourself, useful ones, I'm afraid," Valentine apologised. "I'll keep those to give you later, you won't find them in the least exciting today. Paints and sketch books never come amiss, do they? Here you are! And I thought you might like to have this for your birthday. I was given it by a favourite aunt when I was seven."

Jerusha unwrapped the writing slope, noticing that the inkwell had been rinsed clean, but when she lifted the lid she discovered that the box inside had been filled with paper and envelopes, pens and pencils, even stamps.

"Thank you, Valentine! Are you sure you really want me to have it?"

"I'm sure, Jerusha. I hope you will treasure it as I have, and write many letters – the first one to me, of course! That little book is for addresses; I have written mine inside. Mind you always write neatly – no scribbling or drawings."

Kathleen said softly, "Here is my birthday gift, with my love, darling, always." She fastened the fine silver chain, which had tiny clasped hands suspended from the centre instead of a pendant, round her daughter's neck. "There, now we are linked together for *ever* – your hand in mine!"

They didn't see much of Oliver, for he was too busy, until they were settled in the lounge and tea was served. There was seasonal music, played in the background by a trio of ladies dressed in green cloaks with garlands in their hair. The tunes were muted and restrained, for the elderly residents of the hotel slumped, snoozing in their jealously-guarded easy chairs, mouths agape. They had partaken of a gargantuan lunch and in some cases, too much port wine or brandy. Jerusha giggled at the spasmodic snoring. "I think *we* are the only ones awake!"

"May I join you ladies for mince pies, cake and tea?" asked Oliver gallantly. He handed neat parcels to Valentine and Jerusha, an envelope to Kathleen. "Happy Christmas – and a very happy birthday, too, Jerusha!"

"Perfume – this is much appreciated Oliver!" Valentine exclaimed.

Kathleen did not open her envelope. "I can guess, Oliver, what this is; really, my dear, haven't you done more than enough, inviting us here—"

"I can never do enough for you, Kathleen," he said quietly.

"*Fudge*! Thank you, Oliver! Can I open it now? Would you all like a piece?" Jerusha asked.

"Don't make yourself sick again, will you?" Oliver smiled.

Kathleen stood by the bed, looking at her sleeping daughter, who had carefully arranged the little dolls, now in their night attire, on the pillow beside her. She still wore the chain with the linked hands, round her neck. She looked almost like a little dark-haired doll herself, with her pale face and sweep of eyelashes.

Tears came all too readily to Kathleen's eyes. Valentine had exhorted her earlier to tell Jerusha the truth, to prepare her for their separation. She had promised to do so tomorrow.

"I will send for you as soon as I can," she whispered. "You are too young to understand why I have to leave you, but one day you may forgive me. And I hope you will never love any man as unwisely as I love your father, your weak, untrustworthy, charming father . . ."

"I thought, when you packed the trunks, that you were going to take me with you on holiday . . ." Jerusha looked bewildered. They were sitting in their hotel room; Valentine was there, but she sat at a distance, not saying anything yet.

"Darling, it's *so* difficult to explain! I am going abroad to see your father, Edwin. He left England before you were born – there was a terrible misunderstanding with the merchant bank where he was employed—" She looked helplessly over at Valentine.

"It was more than a misunderstanding," Valentine stated bluntly. "However, you are not of an age to be told more, Jerusha. Your father will probably never return to this country; it would be unwise for him to do so. It is very natural for your mother to want to see him again, to find out if he is at last prepared to make a home for you both in the future. In the meantime, you are to go to your mother's old school, where she was happy and I am sure you will be too."

"Thank you, Valentine," Kathleen said gratefully. "Jerusha, Valentine has very kindly promised to look after your welfare while I am away. She will keep in close touch with the school, with you and with me."

"And so will Oliver," Valentine put in.

"Please don't go away, Mummy!" Jerusha wept. "Oh, why can't you take me with you? I don't want to go away to school—"

Kathleen looked beseechingly at Valentine again.

There was a knock on the door. Valentine rose, opened it and took the tray from the maid. "Ah, coffee for us, and hot milk and a mince pie for you, Jerusha. Come on, cheer up, you will find as you grow up that life is a journey, an adventure, and that there are many twists and turns on the way. You have to learn to accept disappointments, I am afraid, and now you must believe that Kathleen is doing what she considers is the best thing for you. You need to mix with other girls of your age, you will soon make friends and learn to be independent."

Jerusha was not to be consoled. It was all too much to take in. "Will you take me to the school? When are you going away? Oh, please, not yet?" she beseeched her mother.

Kathleen dropped sugar in Jerusha's milk. She did not look at her daughter as she told her, "Valentine is taking you to Copper Leas next Sunday. I shall be leaving tomorrow, the boat sails from Tilbury in the late afternoon. Oliver is to see me off. I think it is best if you stay here with Valentine. You would only upset yourself, me too . . . We must make the most of today, together."

Chapter Four

Jerusha sat quietly beside Valentine. Two days of sobbing, two nights broken by frightening dreams when Valentine had shown how very kind she could be, had left her drained, exhausted. She was ready to accept what lay ahead. There was not the excitement she would normally have experienced on a train journey into the country. Those excursions had been on summer days with Kathleen and Nimsie, carrying the picnic basket.

She wore the school clothes Valentine had provided: a sensible, dark serge dress with detachable white collar and cuffs, concealed now by a heavy coat, also in navy blue, with brass buttons and a wide belt. Her hair was tightly braided and the tam o'shanter was pulled down on her head at the regulation, unflattering angle.

"You are not supposed to wear jewellery of any kind," Valentine worried, when she was dressed.

"I *won't* take my necklace off! I promised Mummy I would *always* wear it!"

"Tuck it under your bodice then and keep quiet about it."

Oliver had accompanied them to the station, waited with them for their train. He looked tired and unsmiling himself. When the time came to say goodbye, he took both Jerusha's gloved hands in his and raised them to his lips. "I shall come to see you at the school from time to time – I promise. And from now on, we two will always meet up on Kathleen's birthday to celebrate, wherever you are – that's another promise."

When the train stopped next, the only other passenger in their carriage, an elderly lady, departed. The station was almost deserted. "People are staying put in this cold weather, I suppose." Valentine gave a little shiver. "Of course, we are between Christmas and New Year, too, not much reason now for travelling."

The train moved off again, belching steam and gathering speed. The fields they passed were deserted, except for a lone labourer pruning a hedge, tossing twigs and raking dead leaves on to a bonfire, which was smouldering and smoking. The man did not seem to notice, or maybe he was indifferent to the great engine thundering by.

"I imagine he is working while he can, before the snow comes: it is cold enough for it, look how heavy and grey the skies are, eh?" Valentine looked rather worried. She was returning to London in the late afternoon.

"Where are all the animals?" Jerusha spoke at last.

"The sheep may already be lambing – did you see those stone shelters? At this time of year the shepherds sleep in them, taking care of their flocks."

"But it's *much* too cold for lambs to be born, Valentine—"

"It may be, but this is the time of year they always choose, it seems. It was snowing when *you* were born, seven years ago!"

"That was in London. I don't think I shall like the country much in January," Jerusha said in a sad, little voice.

Valentine opened her bag, held out a square, flat parcel. "Open this now, that is what Kathleen wished."

It was a photograph in a simple brass frame. Kathleen, dressed as she was the day they lunched with Oliver, smiling at Jerusha. Across one corner she had written: '*With love, always, Mummy*'.

"You are allowed a photograph on your locker, and she thought you might like this one, Jerusha."

"Oh, I *do*!" Jerusha whispered. After a while, she added, "Do you know what my father looks like, Valentine?"

"Seven years ago, when I saw him last, at their wedding, he could have been considered handsome. You don't take after him, for he was very tall, fair-haired and blue-eyed with rather a weedy moustache, but then he wasn't much more than a callow youth – but more intelligent, or maybe less, bearing in mind what happened at his business soon after, than he appeared to be. Your grandfather definitely did not approve of the marriage, I'm afraid."

"You don't like him one bit, do you, Valentine? And I don't think *I* do either!" How could she, when he had taken her mother away from her? Boarding school had never been mentioned previously. In fact, Kathleen had discussed with Nimsie only recently the merits of day schools in the area.

"Then you already have more good sense than your mother, Jerusha. I hope you will eventually grow up to have a stronger character than Kathleen, more like your grandmother, my cousin, but you really *will* have to learn not to cry so much, you know."

Great beech hedges hid the house from the road. The drive beyond the stern iron gates was long and winding. They had been met from the station, driven through wooded countryside, and now they sat in the open trap, bowling smartly along, holding on to their hats as the wind whipped and hurried them on. Despite the rug over their knees, they were chilled to the marrow.

The house was gabled, old and rather run-down. Their feet crunched over thinning gravel, then climbed the steps to the front entrance. Inside the echoing hall, with worn woodblock floor, there was a strange smell. "Chalk, children, cabbage and *cats!*" Valentine murmured, taking out her handkerchief and blowing her nose, as they stood there, stranded, with Jerusha's trunk beside them, and the hand baggage leaning against it. A grandfather clock ticked sonorously, its arrowed hands moving far too slowly on its yellowed face. The place was silent, dark, unwelcoming.

"I don't like it." Jerusha whispered. She meant both the smell and the house.

They both looked up in relief as they heard someone coming down the sweeping staircase.

"I am so sorry to keep you waiting, Miss Ryan. So this is Jerusha! How like Kathleen at that age she is! Do follow me: I will have your luggage brought up directly. I am Mrs Drew, Jerusha. I look after the girls who are unable to go home for the holidays. The Principal, Miss Murray, will be returning from her holiday shortly before the rest of the pupils arrive next weekend. You should be well-settled in by then, I'm sure."

Mrs Drew's appearance was instantly reassuring. She was motherly and plump, with a round face, creased with much smiling, untidy grey hair and what looked suspiciously like gravy stains on the front of her dress which surely must mean, Jerusha thought instantly, that she liked slurping too!

"I will take you to your room first, then while you make yourself at home and meet your room-mate, Miss Ryan and I will go to the sitting room and have a little chat. You will stay for lunch, Miss Ryan, I hope? Plain school fare, I must admit. It seems silly for you to go to a hotel, when you are not intending to stay overnight. Here we are, Jerusha," Mrs Drew ushered them along a corridor, opened a door. "This is Millicent. She arrived earlier today. This is her second year with us. I am sure you will find you have much in common."

It was a small room, with a fireless grate filled with pine cones, and a single window under the eaves. There were two iron bedsteads, side by side, with narrow flat mattresses, a locker by each bed and a walk-in cupboard with hanging space, shelves for other clothes and a rack for shoes. There was a spartan washstand in a corner. Jerusha couldn't help thinking of the warm bedroom she had vacated this morning at the hotel, the brass-railed bed with shining knobs, the soft mattress and puffy pink eiderdown.

The child sitting on the bed farthest from the door had obviously been crying. She sniffed spasmodically, clutching a battered peg doll to her. When she saw them, she stuffed the doll under her pillow. She had gingery hair, sharp features, and her reddened eyes and nose added to her unattractive appearance. She looked more angry than bereft.

Jerusha stood there awkwardly, near to tears again herself, now that Valentine had been spirited away so quickly.

"That's your bed," Millicent said at last. "You should put away anything personal inside your locker; we are supposed to keep the room tidy. That shelf is for books, between us. We are told not to use the chamber pot in the washstand except for emergencies. We have to wash in here, morning and night, but there is a bathroom with a WC and we can have a bath once a week. What's your name?"

"Jerusha Carey."

"Have your parents gone abroad too? Mine are missionaries. I was born in Africa and I don't like England one bit, it's much too cold, and I don't see why I must stay here and go to school. How old are you? You're *very* small." she added disparagingly.

"I'm seven, just – on Christmas Day. My mother – has gone to see my father, in Trinidad. I'm not quite sure where that is. They'll send for me soon. I won't have to be here long." Jerusha needed to convince herself of that.

"D'you really believe that? My parents are supposed to tell me the truth, being religious, but they don't *explain* things, and I think they care more about the little heathens than they do me! Well, is there anything you want to know about this place?" She rose, and Jerusha saw that she was much taller than herself, a lanky girl who was obviously fast outgrowing last year's clothes, for her bony wrists protruded from her cuffs and her skirts hardly skimmed her knobbly knees. Not very friendly either, but what Valentine would approvingly call 'spirited'.

"What are the teachers like?" she ventured nervously.

"Not too bad. Mrs Drew sort of doubles up – she teaches geography and she looks after the girls after school and at the weekend. Miss Murray is quite fierce, but you won't see a lot of her, because she is mostly in her study downstairs, except when she's teaching the older girls. The food's all right, I suppose, but there's too much stodge. Still, it'd take a lot to fatten *me* up."

"*Fish* – do you have fish very often?" Jerusha asked.

"I should say we do. Herrings mostly, cheap and cheerful, so Mrs Drew says, because the fees here are about the lowest you can get, otherwise *I* wouldn't be here, of course. Missionaries are always poor. Why, don't you like fish?"

"Not much." Jerusha admitted miserably.

"Look, don't worry about it, there are a couple of girls who will eat anything *you* can't, from the main course; mind, you have to give them your pudding too, as a reward for helping you out. But it's easier if you learn to swallow it all, you won't feel hungry then. And you can always fill up on bread, there's always plenty of that."

"Come and look out of the window. See the lake, over there to the left? We boat out there sometimes in the summer, and if it snows properly now, we *might* be allowed to skate on it, if it ices over. If you don't have skates, and not many of us have, you can always glide along pushing a chair! Now, I think I had better take you along to the sitting room, there's a good fire there to thaw out by. The bedrooms are always freezing in winter, to discourage us from moping about in them, Mrs Drew says."

Valentine and Mrs Drew sat comfortably close to the blaze in shabby chairs, with their feet stretched out on a somewhat threadbare carpet, talking, while half-a-dozen girls sat round a games table at a respectful distance, playing snakes-and-ladders. There were bursts of suppressed laughter, curious glances at Valentine.

"I understand that the fees will be paid by Jerusha's other guardian, Mr Oliver Browne and that we are to contact him in the first instance regarding any problems which arise?" asked Mrs Drew.

"Yes. Mr Browne would then get in touch with me, if necessary. I live in Ireland, as you know. I hope to come over to England again at Easter, and will visit Jerusha then."

"I find it difficult to understand why Kathleen has chosen to abandon her daughter in this abrupt manner. She was always an impulsive girl, of course—" kindly Mrs Drew worried.

"Which resulted in an unwise marriage. Jerusha has never met her father, Mrs Drew. Whatever Kathleen hopes, I think it is probable that she never will. Kathleen will be forced to choose between the two of them."

"I can promise that the school will make every effort to provide the stability that poor child sadly needs. Ah, here is Millicent, and Jerusha. Come here and get warm, children. You see, you have made a friend already, Jerusha!"

Jerusha was not so sure, and she thought that Millicent probably felt the same.

Back in London, at the hotel, Valentine told Oliver about her day. She had joined him in his study after eleven o'clock for a nightcap. She cared nothing for the impropriety of this. Anyway, she was more than thirty years his senior, she smiled wryly to herself. She knew it was unlikely that she would sleep much that night, even though she was tired. She was getting too old for all this rushing about, she thought. Jerusha had actually clung to her, weeping silently, when it was time for her to leave the school. She still seemed to feel the tug of her arms. It reminded her too much of the time she had left Kathleen at the school.

"It is for the best," she said aloud to Oliver now. "If I had taken her home with me, well, she wouldn't have fitted in to our way of life. I had my turn at mothering, with Kathleen. Seven years of it. I must have failed there somewhere—"

"You mustn't think that," Oliver told her firmly. "I was the one who introduced her to Edwin, after all, but at the time I was as bedazzled by him as she was. Nothing so dull as following obediently in his father's footsteps like me, for Edwin. He was so ambitious, so arrogant, yet so charismatic. He said he would make his name known to many, and in an ironic way he did. I have felt responsible for Kathleen and her daughter ever since . . ."

"There is rather more to it than that, isn't there, Oliver?" Valentine asked shrewdly, sipping her brandy and lemon.

He sighed. "As you say, Valentine, rather more."

Mrs Drew brought an extra blanket for Jerusha's bed. "We can't have you shivering all night, my dear. Breakfast at eight, as we are still on holiday – make the most of the late rising, eh? Lights out, no more reading. Good night, both of you."

Under cover of the bedclothes, Jerusha held the little dolls her mother had given her. Outside the snow fell steadily; in the morning she would see a great stretch of white from the window.

In the other bed, Millicent turned over, cleared her throat. "Are you awake, Jerusha?"

Jerusha nodded, then realised that as the room was in darkness, Millicent would not see. "Yes," she whispered.

"If you feel lonely in the night," said prickly, awkward Millicent, whom Jerusha had thought forlornly was unlikely to become her friend, "remember I am here. I know what it's like you see, to be – *left behind* – it's the same, every time. I don't suppose I'll sleep much either. If you feel like crying, put your head under the covers. All right?"

"All right," Jerusha said, and she tentatively stretched out her hand across the space between their beds, and instantly, like the silver hands round her neck, she felt a comforting clasp.

Chapter Five

The whole school was still stunned by the sudden death of Miss Murray. To most of the girls she had been a rather aloof presence, though as they progressed through the school they discovered, in turn, that she was a brilliant teacher. Mrs Drew was the mother-figure they all turned to in times of adolescent angst. Having written to the parents and guardians of the pupils, she called an extraordinary meeting of her girls in June, a few weeks short of the end of term.

The big room was flooded with sunlight and Mrs Drew sat with her back to the windows, with the sixty or so girls, aged from seven to seventeen, grouped informally round her.

Jerusha gazed out of the window at the lake sparkling now under a cloudless sky, but where she had daringly skated one severe winter urged on by Millicent; at the lawns, sprinkled with daisies, for funds were always short at Copper Leas and there was only one elderly gardener and a lad to cope with several acres. Over the past five years Jerusha had come to think of the school as her home. She was cloistered there, safe. The anguish of the abrupt parting with her mother would always be with her, but because she had been so young when Kathleen left, sometimes it all seemed part of one of her bad dreams. She had had no contact with her mother since, which was not uncommon at this school. The letters she wrote every week were to '*Dear Valentine*' and she looked forward to her cousin's visits at the end of each term. Valentine stayed at the local hotel and took her out on educational excursions, usually to London to the museums and art galleries, where they would be joined by Oliver. He also came to the school now and then and took her out for lunch, and as promised, always on Kathleen's birthday on the tenth of November each year. When she was with Oliver, her friend Millicent was included in the invitation, for school rules decreed that no girl should go out on her own with a gentleman of any age, if he were not a blood relative.

Despite being two years older, and very different in temperament, Millicent had proved a staunch ally. At fourteen she was still head and shoulders taller than Jerusha, just as she had been at the start of their friendship. As with any school, there was an element of bullying, nothing serious, but Jerusha had been grateful for her protection, until she learned, with Millicent's encouragement, to stand on her own two feet. She was still a quiet girl, given to reveries, but she was a determined survivor, that was plain.

"And so," Mrs Drew concluded regretfully, "I am afraid the school is to close at the end of term. Those responsible for you at home must soon make arrangements for your transfer to other places. You will understand that I cannot carry on without Miss Murray. We founded the school together almost thirty years ago. I shall miss it – miss you all, too . . ."

"My parents are due home any minute; my father is to take up a living in Oxfordshire. I imagine that my schooldays are over." Millicent was realistic. "They could only just scrape the fees for Copper Leas."

"But you were hoping to go on to college, Millicent, to train as a teacher—"

"I can still become a pupil teacher, I suppose. It's not an impossible dream. What about you?"

"I – I don't know. Valentine will decide, of course."

Two days later, Jerusha was called unexpectedly into Miss Murray's study, where Mrs Drew was now reluctantly ensconced.

"Ah, Jerusha, do sit down. I have mixed news for you, I'm afraid. Your guardian, Miss Ryan, writes to say that the companion with whom she lives has had a stroke. Much as she would like to have you with her permanently in Ireland, she is now fully occupied with caring full-time for her friend. She writes: 'It is certainly not the case that I no longer feel responsible for Jerusha's continued happiness and welfare, or for her education, but having discussed my predicament with her joint-guardian, Mr Browne, we have decided that it would be best for Jerusha to return to London, to live in a suitable foster home, to attend a good day school for girls, under Mr Browne's supervision, until she is of an age to be independent. Naturally, I will continue to keep in close touch with Jerusha's progress . . .' Is that all clear to you, Jerusha?"

Jerusha nodded. She was not sure what she was expected to say. She only knew that her hard-won security had been shattered. She had prepared herself for the move to Valentine's home, the parting with Millicent. Now apprehension swamped her.

Mrs Drew pressed her hand, kind as always. "I'm sure it will all work out. Nothing is ever as bad as it seems at first sight." She sighed sadly. "I know from experience that when things have been ticking along nicely for a long time, the rug always gets pulled from under our feet. We all have to pick ourselves up, and make a new start."

Jerusha travelled with Millicent to London and they bade each other a tearful farewell, promising to write often. They had exchanged presents: Millicent gave Jerusha writing paper for her box and Jerusha brought out the Noah's Ark, which they had often played with when they were younger. "I don't suppose your parents will frown on that, as Noah is in the Old Testament. Your little brothers will give you a good excuse to play with it again!"

Then Millicent's parents whisked her away, and Oliver, who had met the train, was instructing the porter to load her luggage on a cart, and escorting her to a waiting cab.

"I am taking you back to the hotel tonight so that you can relax, and tomorrow we will talk about the arrangements that have been made. Cheer up, Jerusha! I promise you an excellent lunch, and absolutely no fish!"

"Thank you, Oliver," she said quietly.

He tucked her hand firmly in the crook of his arm, just as if she were grown-up, and smiled at her. "I shall be glad to have you nearer, to see more of you, I must say."

As they walked off together Jerusha thought, he's comforting me, reassuring me that all will be well, in his own way. This is the closest I have ever been to Oliver, arm-in-arm . . .

When Oliver had gone, leaving Jerusha in her new home, she guessed rightly that she would shortly see another side to Mr and Mrs Masterson. They had been far too gushing in their welcome. It was all too good to be true. The well-furnished town house in an exclusive part of Knightsbridge, so convenient for Hyde Park; the newly-decorated guest bedroom for herself, with a study annexe, the splendid drawing and dining rooms, shelves full of books, and the mention of horses out to livery and riding in the park. Jerusha would like that, wouldn't she? Also, the school she was to attend was a mere ten-minute walk away.

The Mastersons assured Oliver that the allowance for their care of Jerusha was not a major factor in their response to his carefully-worded advertisement in *The Times.* They looked forward, they said, to a lively young person in their home, for they regretted not having been blessed with a family themselves.

"We are going to get along splendidly, I'm sure! You need have no qualms about leaving your ward with us, Mr Browne," Mrs Masterson beamed. She was a tall woman, sparely built, it was easy to imagine her in the saddle, in impeccable riding clothes. She held her head high, and Jerusha, looking up at her as she spoke, at the flaring nostrils, was instantly reminded of the rocking horse in her long-ago nursery. She gave her own head a little shake, reproving herself silently for making such a comparison. What had kindly Mrs Drew once said? 'Save your imagination for writing essays, Jerusha . . .'

Mr Masterson, like his wife, was probably in his late forties. He had disposed of his business interests abroad, he intimated, when he had inherited this house. His main interest in life now, like his wife's, was an equine one – in his case, horse racing. There were many framed prints of racing scenes on the walls of his study. He had a round, ruddy face, a bulbous nose and a waxed moustache. Despite his hearty laugh, his patting her on the head – as if she was a pet dog, Jerusha thought, wanting to duck – she knew instinctively that this was someone she distrusted.

There was something not quite right here, she told herself, as she unpacked her clothes and hung them in the wardrobe. Then it came to her. She recalled the last weeks in her grandfather's house. Of course! Despite the size of the place, there were apparently no servants here, apart from one who was presumably the cleaning woman. She had answered the door to Oliver and herself, calling out: "Your visitors are here, Mrs Masterson! I'm off now, see you tomorrow!" Then with a cheerful wink at Jerusha, she was gone, closing the door behind her.

Mrs Masterson, Jerusha thought, did not look the type to stoop to cooking or anything more strenuous.

Her suspicion was correct. When she came reluctantly downstairs to the dining room she found the table laid frugally and haphazardly and Mrs Masterson pouring tea.

"Sit down, Jerusha, it's cold cuts tonight, I'm afraid – do help yourself." Her tone now was curt, no longer ingratiating.

Mr Masterson could at least carve and he cut extremely thin slices of roast beef and arranged two on each plate.

"Thank you." Jerusha said. She looked at the bread. She seemed to hear Millicent's voice clearly in her head. '*Bread*, Jerusha, fill up with bread when you're hungry, there's *always* plenty of *that*!'

"I meant to send Essie out for another loaf," Mrs Masterson said. "Will one piece be enough?"

Jerusha sobbed silently under the covers that night. I don't like them, I don't trust them, I think they've fooled Oliver, but I can't tell him that, not yet anyway, for he was so pleased to think he had me nicely settled again. At least I shall see him more often now I'm back in London, and I'll be well away from here at school all day. I'm old enough to cope with this on my own now, but I'll still miss Millicent, championing my cause!

What exactly had Mrs Masterson said, after dinner? 'You will be accustomed to rules and regulations, Jerusha, having been at boarding school. Breakfast will be at seven-thirty sharp each morning, weekends included, for I always go riding at nine o'clock. Essie, our general factotum, will clear and wash the dishes. You will make your own bed and keep your room tidy at all times. You will, of course, have your studying to keep you occupied in the evenings, so you will retire to your room after dinner. Sometimes we will have guests, and we do not wish you to interrupt when we are entertaining. Essie will be here when you return from school, and will keep you company until we come home. Your guardian was insistent on that point because we are both out a great deal. This is why we preferred an older foster child. You are to sort your linen each Sunday evening, after your weekly bath, then place it, neatly folded, in the basket in the scullery for Essie to deal with on Monday mornings."

"I'm sure we shall get along very well, if you stick to all that," her husband added, not unkindly.

"Do you understand?" Mrs Masterson persisted.

"I understand," Jerusha said.

"You are a very lucky young lady to have this chance of a proper home. Not many abandoned children are so fortunate. You remain a big responsibility for your guardian. Do you understand?"

"I understand," Jerusha repeated.

The worst thing of all was to have to face the truth at last. Her mother had indeed abandoned her that Christmas when she was only seven years old.

Chapter Six

Jerusha had found a new friend and comforter. Essie Bronski was lively and lovable, with a highly-rouged face and a mass of hennaed hair piled carelessly on top of her head, caught here and there with crinkly hairpins which she tended to shed because she was always rushing about. Her dark, almond-shaped eyes reflected her Chinese blood, a mere eighth as Essie gurgled, for as she soon enlightened Jerusha, she was a woman of many parts. Her mother had been half-Russian and as for her father, when drunk, Essie recalled fondly, he had certainly raised his voice in incomprehensible song and whirled his little daughter round in wild, foreign dances.

Those meeting Essie for the first time might well find her own exuberance, her bouncing, plump figure disconcerting, but to Jerusha, unexpectedly enfolded in those great arms and hugged to Essie's unrestricted bosom, when she returned from her first day at her new school, there was comfort and reassurance, and within a very short while she happily became aware that there was mutual, fast-growing, easy affection. Most important of all, despite her intuition that in this house it was not only cold cuts most days, but what amounted to cold charity, she was learning to laugh, for Essie had that effect on all she met.

"Come in, darlin', had a good day?" Essie cried that first time. "Let me give you a hug! Don't look so sheepish, I always grabbed my boy when he came in from school! Mind you, he learned to dodge me later, as boys do, when they're growing into their boots . . . Expect you're hungry, eh? Not much in the larder with old Mrs Meanie in charge so I got you a nice, fat bun at the baker's. I only had to smile and I got it half-price as he was about to close! Eat it up, and don't leave any crumbs – that one's got an eagle eye!"

"Surely you can't like working here, Essie?" Jerusha asked curiously, through a mouthful of sticky bun.

Essie sat down on a kitchen chair, which gave an ominous creak.

"'Course I don't, but I haven't been here long, and now you've come, well, I'll stick it."

"Oh, I'm *glad*!"

"You need someone to keep an eye you, and that someone's me! I'm an artiste, but needs must when the stage don't beckon, I say."

"What did you do, Essie, on the stage?"

"Well, when I was slimmer I was an acrobatic dancer, double-jointed you see, but I can do all sorts – sing a bit, get the audience going, joining in, like – statues, that's posing behind a screen, a tableau, you have to keep very still for that and nowadays old Essie wobbles . . ." They both grinned at the picture that conjured up.

"D'you miss it?"

"I should say I do. I try to keep supple, mind, but it's mainly a cartwheel or two these days. However, I still got my gentlemen friends, my admirers, you could say, from the old days and I dress up and dab on the scent, and go out on the town with them now and then – but don't get me wrong, 'cause like me, they're mostly past sixty!" She lowered her voice. "Madam's got a friend, too, the toff what owns all the horses. Sometimes he sneaks in here when Sir is following the field. You'll be wise to keep out of her way then. Mind you, there'd be all hell let loose if her husband tried the same. She's a jealous one, all right. Sir likes a little flutter, not only with the horses but cards, so he's not here most of the time. I thought I should warn you what they're like, darlin'."

Jerusha wasn't quite sure what Essie was hinting at. But she knew how glad she was to have made a real friend already. The girls at school today had seemed very superior and cool towards her and there were far more of them than there had been at Copper Leas. She wondered unhappily if they were whispering about her because she hadn't yet acquired her new uniform. That was something Valentine usually saw to, on her visits. Oliver had asked Mrs Masterson to take her shopping shortly. "Please send the bill to me," he had said.

Her fellow pupils at Copper Leas had ranged from the intensely academic to one or two with learning difficulties. Today, she had sat a stiff entrance examination in English and maths. The former had been no problem, as she wrote fluently, but she had been unable to complete the second paper for she had absolutely no knowledge of trigonometry. Her bag was heavy with books for home study.

"Like your new school?" Essie asked, peeling potatoes at the sink for dinner.

"I'm not too sure, Essie. I didn't want to leave Copper Leas, but I had to, you see, because the school was closing – the headmistress died and her deputy didn't want to carry on."

"Green, some of these spuds. Madam'll say I've cut too much off 'em but it can't be helped, eh? Miss your pals from the old school, I reckon?"

Jerusha nodded. "'Specially one. Millicent. She was my friend from the very first day."

"You can still meet up, can't you?"

"We're too far apart, and she's older than me, her parents are not very well off, being clergy, and she has to go to work."

"Never mind, darlin', you can keep the friendship going with letters to and fro, that's my advice."

"At least I've got *one* friend in London—"

"Me, darlin'?" Essie beamed.

"Yes, you of course, but—"

"Would your other good friend be Mr Oliver Browne, I wonder?"

Jerusha looked surprised at the use of Oliver's christian name. Had that wink been directed at both of them, the day Essie answered the door to them? "You *know* him, Essie?"

Essie didn't say whether she did or she didn't, she just murmured, "I thought so . . ." and poured cold water on the potatoes. "You'd better get upstairs and get your head down over them books. Madam's key'll turn in the lock any moment."

The German doll languished in her trunk, but Jerusha had hung the parasol on the knob of the cupboard door in her room. For the first time since Valentine had given her the photograph of her mother, she did not set it out on her bedside table, but tucked it away under clothes in a drawer. She couldn't explain why, even to herself. The little dolls, in their now frayed clothes, she hid under her pillow, so that she could feel for them in the middle of the night. This action suddenly reminded her of Millicent the day they met. She felt the tears well in her eyes at the memory. *Alice in Wonderland,* the reading of which had so often helped her to escape from reality when she felt sad in the days after her mother's departure, was, as always, to hand, by her bed. These familiar things reminded her of how it had been.

Jerusha still wore the linked hands round her neck. Once, she had broken a link, and another time the hands themselves had become loose and were in danger of becoming lost. Practical Millicent had busied herself with tweezers and nail file and mended the necklace for her. As she touched the silver hands she thought: I must write to Millicent . . . The other possession she would never part with was the writing box Valentine had given her. But first, she must tackle her homework.

Downstairs in the hall, Mrs Masterson took off her riding jacket, hung up her whip and pulled off her gloves. The boots would have to wait until her spouse arrived home and exerted his strength at pulling them off. That was practically all he was good for. She smiled at the thought of how he had been cuckolded this afternoon. Then she frowned. The child would have to be fed. Essie would have left the potatoes simmering. There should be just enough of the beef left. She herself cared little for food, but she did enjoy the several glasses of wine she imbibed each day with her lunch, particularly when someone else was paying. It was a nuisance to have to provide dinner for their boarder, particularly when the girl lunched each day at school. But she must show willing, otherwise tales might be told.

Oliver called a cab for his visitor. What he had learned this evening had disturbed him. The Mastersons had been recommended to him by a patron of the hotel and he had had no reason to doubt that their reasons for fostering Jerusha were other than they asserted. However, it appeared that this gentleman was a close friend of Mrs Masterson, rather than her husband. And Oliver certainly had not suspected that the Mastersons were short of money. Their home, their possessions had belied that.

He had tried to find a place for Jerusha similar to the house where she had lived with her mother and grandfather. A home with caring foster parents. It seemed that he had succeeded in the first respect, only to fail in the other.

He went back upstairs to his rooms. The hotel was quiet now the busy summer season was past. The porter wished him goodnight. Oliver thought wryly that old Fred Head must wonder why it was that he only entertained older women in his private domain. Particularly one as flamboyant as Essie. At least, he had made one wise move. She was the vital link between himself and Jerusha. As for Valentine, he accepted that she was now forced, through no fault of her own, to pass on to him the full responsibility for Kathleen's daughter.

Did Kathleen, dodging from place to place with Edwin, as unreliable as ever, really care anymore? Last year when he had managed to take a few weeks off he had travelled by steamboat to Port of Spain, Trinidad. That was in June, the beginning of the wet season, but the temperature in the shade was still around 90 degrees. The soil on the island was extremely fertile, not only was sugar cane grown there, but coffee, tobacco, coconuts, oranges and bananas. There was a fine harbour and a colourful population. He had seen some gracious colonial houses but Kathleen and Edwin were now forced to live in the poorer part of town.

Oliver did not stay with them, in fact he had no wish to meet up with Edwin again. He had been shocked by Kathleen's haggard looks. She was so thin and her eyes had a haunted look. He had braced himself to tell her bluntly that he could help no further with the settlement of her husband's escalating debts. Edwin had gone from one failed venture to another and was now involved with the clandestine export of rum, which had been diverted from legitimate shipments. Kathleen confided unhappily that any profits were drained away by his addiction to the product. Oliver had soon deduced that for himself.

To please her, he went with her on a tour of the island. It was indeed a most beautiful place to live and work, which must be some sort of compensation, he felt, for her continued exile from her home country. Was that why she had brought him here, to prove a point?

They stood side by side, close, but not touching, marvelling at the extraordinary natural phenomenon, the pitch lake at La Brea, some sixty miles from Port of Spain. The asphalt covered an area of about 90 acres in a depression immediately to the south of a 140 foot high hill. From the summit the ground sloped gently toward the sea and the banks were covered with coarse scrub.

"Sometimes you can catch a glimpse of humming birds," she told him.

Oliver watched the slow movement of the asphalt. He had learned that prehistoric trees surfaced from time to time, but later vanished again. It was an eerie sight. He supposed it was an analogy of his finding Kathleen only to lose her again.

Jerusha's education, her welfare, from now on must be his first concern.

"Won't you please write to her?" he asked, as he always did.

"It's too late for that," Kathleen said dully. "She must forget me. Maybe you should, too. That's the best, the only thing . . ." She leaned suddenly against him, clinging to his arm, as another torrential downpour of warm rain began. "We must run for shelter—" she cried, and as she tilted her head towards him, her eyes were again as luminous as her daughter's.

Oliver could never forget her. He was sure of that.

Chapter Seven

Until just before her fifteenth birthday, some two years later, Jerusha really was not unhappy at the Mastersons. Essie was responsible for that. In the school holidays it was fun being with Essie all day and going out on different sorts of outings to those she had enjoyed with Valentine while she was at Copper Leas, though these were educational in their own way.

The first time she went to Essie's home she really had her eyes opened to how poorer folk lived. Until now, she realised, she had been cocooned from all this. Being hungry at the Mastersons bore no comparison to starving in the slums.

They boarded the horse tram and clattered up the winding outside stairs to sit on top and view the world. '*Nestle's Swiss Milk, The Richness in Cream*' the advertising on the side of the tram proclaimed. As they jolted along to meaner streets, and Jerusha looked down on children actually in rags, she wondered how many of them even drank milk, let alone cream.

Essie, squashing her with her bulk, squeezed her hand. "We can't put all this wretchedness to rights ourselves, darlin', but we can all try to do a little bit, eh? My way is to go along to one of the London settlements when I can, not that I've so much spare time now I'm working full-time, and to encourage the children in a bit of dancing and gymnastics—"

"London settlements?" Jerusha queried, puzzled. She'd never heard of them.

"Your education's lacking, darlin', eh? There are all the new evening schools, and, of course, I believe they're very worthy, but there's a real need too for recreation, and these youngsters at the settlements enjoy themselves and learn a lot at the same time. Sometimes, on a Saturday afternoon, we take a party to see the sights, like the Tower, Westminster Abbey, the South Kensington Museum, or for a walk in Greenwich Park. Ladies play a big part in running the settlements, I like that. Take Browning Hall, in

Walworth. Not so many years ago, Walworth was a comfortable place, with well-to-do folk living in nice houses and green fields all around. But when the middle classes moved out to the suburbs for the purer air, like, and travelling to the city got easier, everything got run-down, and only the poor were left. So that particular settlement came about, with money put in by rich folk that care, but with ordinary people running it, day to day. There's an infants' school, Sunday school and services, of course, but religion's not rammed down their throats; a crèche, a stock of good, old clothes for the needy, cookery classes – and there's those ready to advise, on the law or nursing, like—"

"But can't they do something to improve the way people have to live and work,?" Jerusha interrupted.

"Those who run the settlements believe that'll come, in time, when the young people they help now learn to help themselves. Their ideas are the way forward, Jerusha."

"You've given me a lot to think about, Essie—"

"Good," Essie said.

The pavement outside the cheapjack shops was strewed with a miscellany of goods. Shopkeepers standing in their doorways touted loudly and coarsely for passing custom.

"Here we are, this is our stop," Essie said, heaving herself up. She lifted her skirts a fraction as she stepped down into familiar territory. The streets were very dirty hereabouts.

They turned a corner, walked briskly down a side road, then turned left along a narrow alleyway backing on either side to stony yards, the rear of tall terraced houses with sooty brickwork, primitive privies – no mistaking the truly dreadful smell. There were pathetic heaps of dusty coal, bottomless buckets and other household debris cast aside. Standpipes leaked water and washing hung, limp, grey and tattered from high-hoisted lines. It was a dull day, but little sunlight ever filtered through to this area. There were children everywhere, undersized and underclothed, in boots with flapping soles.

"You wonder sometimes how they survive, but they do," Essie murmured in Jerusha's ear. "Little blighters are usually cheerful and you don't often hear 'em complain. You should see 'em in winter, when it's raw cold – they're all runny noses, sores and chaps. It was hard bringing my boy up here; he left when he was sixteen to pursue his career. He's doing very well for himself, gone right up in the world, he has. He wanted me to move on, too, but I was born here and here I intend to stay."

Essie's back room was poky, with bare floorboards, apart from the odd hooked rug and the minimum of furniture, but to Jerusha the freshly whitewashed uneven walls hung with bright prints, the flowery curtains and cushions on the chairs, the gaudy parrot perched on the curtain pole squawking a welcome, even the moth-eaten cat scratching energetically in the easy chair spoke of one word: *home*.

"Reckon you'd rather be here, in my little house with me, eh, darlin'?" Essie said perceptively, seeing the wistful look on Jerusha's face.

Jerusha was growing up, not much taller than she had been at twelve, but rapidly becoming a young woman. Mrs Masterson watched her covertly, suspiciously. What was sauce for the goose certainly was not sauce for the gander. She saw her husband look approvingly at the girl when she wore a new dress sent to her by her relative in Ireland. The soft material revealed gentle curves hitherto hidden. No need for corsets, Valentine insisted, just think of all those swooning maidens, so unnecessary, all that ridiculous tight-lacing and damaging to the insides into the bargain. Jerusha mustn't become a martyr to fashion like Kathleen.

All that *hair!* Mrs Masterson thought. Even if it was primly braided and hanging in a rope down her back. Those big, dark eyes, dreamy and innocent. Mrs Masterson herself possessed large hands and feet and was forced to buy men's riding boots. She tightened her lips at the girl's delicate-looking hands, her small, neat feet.

Jerusha was unaware of all this attention. She concentrated on her schoolwork, determined to do well. She had failed to find another Millicent among her classmates but academically she could hold her own. Valentine had written to congratulate her on her good end of term examination results:

> 'I am very proud of you, Jerusha. I am afraid that the situation here is just the same. My friend requires constant care. One of these days we will meet again . . . Meanwhile, keep in touch, won't you? I do so look forward to your letters.'

It was Christmas, and the Mastersons were to host a lavish party on Christmas Eve. Outside caterers had been engaged but Essie had decided, to their displeasure, to take three days off. She would need it, she said, after being expected to tackle all the party washing-up. A few days earlier, she had daringly suggested that Jerusha might stay with her and share her Christmas, but she was told in no uncertain terms that this was not suitable. At least, she thought, Jerusha would be spending Christmas Day and Boxing Day at the hotel; she had had a word in Oliver's ear after her own rejection. He would send a conveyance for the girl mid-morning. She was bound to fare better at the hotel, Oliver was always so generous. Anyway, Essie suspected that the Mastersons would be suffering hangovers after the party – the wine merchants had delivered enough boxes to ensure that, she thought.

"The hall floor needs a good scrub over, Essie, kindly see to it," Mrs Masterson demanded, on the morning of the party. "I am going for my ride now. I will be back for lunch. You can see to that. Mr Masterson will attend to the caterers when they arrive, but if they knock on the front door they are to be sent round to the trade entrance."

Essie made a face at her retreating back. The door slammed. Madam sensed these things.

She filled her bucket with hot water, added a knob of soda, put on her heavy-duty apron and sighed as she reached for cloths, household soap, the scrubbing brush with fierce bristles which really hurt if you pricked your hands inadvertently on them.

She thought fleetingly, wistfully, of her former working life. Reduced to charwoman! *Little Essie Bronski*, *The Amazing Acrobat,* the girl with the flaming hair and the highest of high kicks . . . She wasn't sure how much longer she could stick the job, or the arrogant Mrs Masterson. But then she thought of Jerusha, and she kicked the mats aside because Madam wasn't there to see and swept the hall ready for its swilling.

"Stay upstairs," she called up to Jerusha, who was tidying her room. "It'll be all awash down here, in a minute."

Mr M was still reading the papers in the breakfast room. She might as well make a song and dance of it, she thought, her good humour soon restored, as always, with Madam safely out of the house.

She bent to her scrubbing, humming her favourite music hall ditties. She failed to hear Mr Masterson coming up behind her, treading carefully on the damp floor in his slippers. Her rounded behind was irresistible.

It was only a pinch, but Essie was instantly outraged. She scrambled to her feet, picked up the bucket and threw the filthy contents at him. He stumbled back, his feet slipped in the wet, and he landed on his own backside. The look of utter surprise on his face made Essie's annoyance evaporate and she was laughing helplessly even as she gave him a hand up.

He thrust her aside. "Consider yourself instantly dismissed!" he raged.

"D'you think I care?" She wiped her eyes on her apron. She always cried when she laughed. "All right, but what about my wages?"

"Mrs Masterson sees to all that—" The damp was seeping fast through his trousers. He clapped his hand to his behind.

"Oh, yes, and that means I'm not due 'em until I finish late tonight, so get out of my way – *please!* And if you know what's best for you – if you don't want to tackle the dishes yourself – you won't say anything to Madam about this, will you?"

He pushed past her without another word, and went upstairs to change.

She would have to tell Oliver, as soon as she could. Jerusha mustn't stay here without anyone to keep an eye on her welfare, Essie thought, as she wrung her cloth out. She shouldn't have succumbed to temptation, dousing the fellow like that, even if he deserved it. She consoled herself with the thought that Sir obviously liked women with a bit of flesh. Surely that ruled young Jerusha out . . .

Jerusha was certainly not included in the party plans, although the Mastersons could hardly refuse to let her share in the meal. Immediately afterwards she went up to her room.

It was already nine o'clock. She decided that she might as well get undressed, but she didn't feel like getting into bed. At least there was a good fire going in the grate, Essie had made sure of that, and then heaved upstairs a full coal bucket to the hearth. The Mastersons were, of course, unaware that she was enjoying such a luxury! In fact, she was so blissfully warm for once that she did not bother to cover her nightgown with her robe, but pulled up a chair to the fireplace and became absorbed in a book. She kept the lamp turned low because she did not want Mrs Masterson to look in on her and reprimand her for not being in bed asleep, athough the noise from downstairs made sleep impossible in any case.

She stoked the fire at eleven o'clock, yawning at last. She needed to wash the coal dust from her hands, to visit the bathroom. She opened the bedroom door cautiously, tiptoed along the corridor.

She was twisting the knob on the bathroom door when she felt a heavy hand on her shoulder. She was spun round to face Mr Masterson. He had been drinking all day, following his clash with Essie, the knock to his pride.

"Hello, little girl, where did you spring from? Where have you been hiding since dinner, I wonder?" His breath was hot, reeking of strong spirits and rich food, as he bent over her.

Her scream put an abrupt end to the carousing downstairs. Alarmed, he pushed her back against the closed door, inadvertently banging her head. She shut her eyes in terror and pain.

"Whatever did you want to do that for?" he said thickly. "You shouldn't wander about dressed like that unless you want to draw attention to yourself—"

Jerusha screamed again, even more loudly. His hand went over her open mouth. Instinctively she sank her teeth into his palm, drawing blood. The next thing she knew, Mrs Masterson was there, propelling her furiously back into her room.

"How *dare* you, Jerusha! Your guardian will hear about this! Get straight into bed. I shall be coming to see you again later, you can be *sure* of that."

Perhaps an hour passed, there were the obvious sounds of the guests departing, the slam of carriage doors, finally the front door. Jerusha waited in fear and trembling for retribution.

The bedclothes were pulled back. "Turn over," Mrs Masterson said in a tight, cold voice. Jerusha's nightgown was unceremoniously removed, tossed aside. The horsewhip lashed her bare back, once, twice; a brief pause, then it cut cruelly into her flesh a third time. Jerusha bit her pillow to try to stem the agony of the beating.

"That will teach you, I hope, not to try such a thing again – with my husband, too. After all we have done for you!"

Jerusha would not turn over while she was still there. After a few minutes, she felt the covers replaced, heard retreating footsteps. With violently trembling hands she put on her nightgown, inside out.

The grandfather clock downstairs chimed midnight. It was Christmas Day and her fifteenth birthday. Jerusha had never felt so alone in her life. When the weeping began it was as if it would never stop.

Some long time later, she suffered the terror of her first asthma attack. As she struggled for breath, she tumbled out of bed on to the floor, then crawled towards the door. It swung open, and Essie was there, candle in hand.

"I was just finishing up in the kitchen when I thought I heard a thump up here. Is this to do with all the commotion earlier? Let me help you back to bed, darlin'. Don't worry, Sir and Madam are dead to the world, after all that drinking. Has this ever happened before?"

Jerusha managed to shake her head. Essie's arms were around her, supporting her and the wheezing was lessening. She winced, spoke in a husky whisper, "Essie – my *back* . . ."

The bleeding had stopped, but her nightgown was stuck to the weals. Essie could say nothing. She was too shocked. She gently sponged the place until she could ease the material free, fetched more hot water from the bathroom, anointed Jerusha's shoulders with ointment, covered the cuts with lint, held in place with a bandage, all of which she had taken from the cabinet. She mixed up one of Madam's headache powders in a tooth glass, and encouraged Jerusha to sip it.

"There, darlin', lay on your front and try to get some sleep. I'm going to pack up your things *right now,* and I'm staying here with you, then I'm going with you to the hotel in the morning. You won't have to speak to them despicable people again, I'll deal with them, I promise you, and you won't never have to come back here, *never*!"

Chapter Eight

At the hotel, Essie put Jerusha straight to bed. The warmth, the relief, made her sleepy. The fact that it was Christmas Day, also her birthday, didn't really seem important.

"I'll be with you, darlin', 'til the doctor's been, then I must go home and pack my own bag and give my Christmas dinner to her next door, I was going to share it with her any way, old misery-martin though she is. Poor old girl's not got two farthings to bless herself with. I'll be back in time for lunch, I hope, but I've got to tidy myself up, put on my finery like, if I'm to look right for staying in the hotel. You don't mind sharing your room here with me, do you?"

Jerusha stretched out her hand to her friend. "Oh, Essie, I'd love you to!"

Oliver looked helplessly at Essie. They were in his study. He had not liked to disturb Jerusha, for she had slept the day away, having been prescribed a sedative by the doctor, hoping not to be called out again on Christmas Day.

"I really should inform the police, Essie. I dread to think what could have happened if you had not been around. I blame myself for allowing her to stay on there. You told me soon enough after Jerusha's arrival that I had made an unfortunate choice, after all."

"No, Oliver, you mustn't think like that. Things really haven't been bad until now – she and I are real pals and I hope I made up for what was lacking there. He's a fellow what likes to – well, *touch*, but no more'n that, I reckon. He was a bit het-up what with me having a go at him earlier on, and then he got blind drunk and Jerusha was in the wrong place at the wrong time, you see. Also, *you* may not have noticed, but she's a young woman now, Oliver—"

"I hadn't thought of her like that."

"No, to you, she's your beloved Kathleen's child, and you've done all this for her for her mother's sake."

He nodded slowly. "Of course you're right, you always are, dear Essie. But what am I to do with her now? The hotel is not a suitable place for her to stay indefinitely, there would soon be speculation regarding our relationship, innocent though it is. Father would not countenance that. He thinks I am a fool to expend so much time, such a slice of my income, on Jerusha, as it is."

"He's a hard man, but I suppose that's why he's successful. Oliver . . . Why don't you let Jerusha live with *me?* It wouldn't cost you more than her food. I've got my allowance, and I won't need to go out scrubbing any more, I'm certainly not like those greedy Mastersons, eh, and I'll look after her as if she was my own. What do you say?"

"I say, let's ask Jerusha tomorrow what she thinks, but I believe we both know what her answer will be. What *would* I do without you, Essie?"

"That'll never come up, darlin', for I'll always be here."

Oliver seems different somehow, Jerusha thought. Of course, he's as kind and concerned as always but it's as if he's realised that I'm not a little girl anymore, that I can make my own mind up about my life from now on.

They were taking tea together, the three of them, on Boxing Day in the hotel lounge. Jerusha wore her new dress because the fine material did not chafe her sore back. Her face was pale, her eyes shadowed, but she had washed her hair that morning after she had bathed, as if intent on cleansing herself from the recent trauma. Her hair hung silky and loose, dark against the moss-rose colour of her dress. The silver chain was her only jewellery. Oliver looked long and searchingly at her, then turned his face away, almost as if he found the sight of her painful.

As they had that last Christmas with her mother, the ladies in their green, their garlands, looking just the same, played sweet music in the background.

"Have you considered Essie's proposal?" Oliver asked at last. He had not touched the food on his plate, but Jerusha, in contrast, had felt surprisingly hungry.

"I have, and Oliver, *of course* I'll live with Essie! But," she paused, a little nervous as to how he would react, "I want to leave school, Oliver. I'm quite old enough, and I want to earn my own living now, pay for my keep. Millicent had to go out to work when she was fourteen and *I'm* a year older than that! You mustn't blame

Essie for telling me, because I made her, but I know now what you have done for me all these years. Valentine has been so good, too, but it was *you* who paid for my schooling, my clothes, even those beastly Mastersons . . ."

He toyed with his napkin, cleared his throat. "Legally, I remain your guardian until you are of age, unless you marry earlier, when you would need my consent, but in any case, Jerusha, I will never sever my ties with you. I promised Kathleen that." He looked directly at her now and she recognised the worry in his eyes. "I must contact Valentine and ask if she agrees to what you suggest. But, I shall raise no objection. The only assurance I require from you is that you will always come to me if you are in need, in trouble. Is that a promise you can make, Jerusha?"

She nodded. "Yes. Thank you for being so understanding, Oliver. My mother should have married you, I think, as Valentine often says. I suppose I sort of think of you as a father—" she added impulsively, then she blushed as she observed the acute embarrassment, pain this had caused. Oliver was such a private person, she had been unaware until this moment, she realised, of the depth of his feelings for her mother.

"I would rather you thought of me as your friend," he said quietly.

Jerusha thought, he's right. *Fathers* hug you, don't they? Indulge you. Oh, I know *all* fathers, or mothers, aren't like that, but that's what the word conjures up for *me.* Essie is the only person since my mother to hold me close. Valentine loves me, I know it, but she finds it hard to unbend; even Millicent was a, well, *fierce* kind of friend, and Oliver is always so polite . . .

"That's settled then!" Essie grinned broadly. "We've got a lot to talk over, Jerusha, but today let's just celebrate you leaving all your cares behind, and the start of a new life!"

Chapter Nine

Jerusha was absorbed in her work. She flexed her right hand now and then when she experienced the inevitable writer's cramp. For days on end she might copy a single letter painstakingly. When these copy letters had been signed and returned to her, she had to fold and insert each one in the pile of envelopes before her, which she had previously addressed and matched with the appropriate letter. Then would come the final touch, the stamping. There were often more than fifty to do and it was tedious work but she was determined and did not complain; the most she allowed herself was the occasional yawn or sigh. Her life was orderly, she felt secure and loved. That was enough right now.

She sat at the big table in Essie's parlour, now her workroom during the day. It was a relief to emerge from this room into the back kitchen and to relax with Essie at the end of a long working session. She was grateful for Essie's kindness in finding her the work, even though it was spasmodic, and courtesy of one of Essie's gentlemen. "As ladylike an occupation as I can find you, Jerusha my darlin'. At least I can keep a motherly eye on you most of the time, you being unused to the ways of the wicked world."

There was a lovely portrait on the sideboard which affected Jerusha every time she glanced at it. It was of a young mother with a pretty, glowing face, gazing tenderly on the tiny baby in her arms. Essie and her son. She had guessed that immediately, even before Essie said. It was a studio portrait of course, the artificial backdrop portraying a much more luxurious setting than Essie's little house.

"Just the one child," Essie told her one day, when she saw her looking at the photograph. But she did not say, and Jerusha did not ask, if she had been married or if she was long-widowed. They were both entitled to their secrets, their privacy, despite their fondness for and usual frankness with one another.

Because of Jerusha's occasional asthma attacks, she spent more time in the parlour than in Essie's back room. "Feathers and fur flying in here," as Essie said. The cat was put aside at mealtimes, or when the hip-bath was brought in by the stove.

Essie never met her gentlemen very early in the evenings she went out, which was just as well, as she remarked, for she had plenty of time to 'apply the greasepaint.' Later, she would sweep up the street in her smart costume and extravagant hat and cheerfully greet her neighbours on the way. She was well aware that most of them wrongly suspected her intentions, her destination. "Why should I spoil their fun?" she laughed to Jerusha, knowing she was the subject of much gossip. Then she would hail a cab at the corner and go 'up west.' She never returned home before midnight.

Jerusha would make her way upstairs to bed long before that, opening the door set back in the recess by the stove. She slept in the little room next door to Essie. Sometimes she would be asleep, sometimes not, but Essie always came in to say goodnight, leaning over her bed so that the scent she applied so lavishly almost overwhelmed her, and leaving some chocolate or turkish delight on the little cane table for Jerusha to sample next day.

"A lovely show last night," Essie would say, starry-eyed. "And not only a box of chocolates, we had a late supper, oysters no less, and I gave him a bit of good advice and sent him off smiling home to his wife. Oh, and he gave me this new perfume – bought it last week in Paris he said, with me in mind. Like it?"

Jerusha enjoyed her own evenings out with Essie at the settlement. Best of all she looked forward to the varied speakers who climbed the platform, each a specialist in his or her own field. There were the charismatic gospel preachers, of course, the scientists with their colourful lantern slides, the opera singers, musicians, poets, writers, it was all very stimulating and her imagination was fired. Music in particular was considered most important for enriching the spirit. The audience was hushed during the performances but enthusiastic when it was time to applaud, with much stamping and whistling.

The girls from the biscuit factory, pale-faced and tired after a strenuous day, became lively and energetic at Essie's gymnastic sessions. They changed into the loose calico smocks and baggy bloomers provided by the settlement, lifted their fluttering silk sashes high in a complicated drill and giggled like the thirteen- or fourteen-year-olds they were, as the elderly lady pianist, with complete disregard for her arthritic hands and wry-neck, played galloping music with her foot pressed down hard on the loud pedal. Jerusha joined in, soon becoming as unselfconscious as her companions. She often thought that Valentine would have approved. Like Essie, she had a pronounced social conscience. The difference being that Essie pursued her causes with a great sense of fun.

She also benefited from the games played outside on summer evenings in the garden behind the settlement buildings. Both boys and girls played a keen game of rounders or cricket, their determination and rivalry very different from the way the girls at Copper Leas had played, but that now all seemed a long time ago to Jerusha. Rather to her surprise, she realised that it was already over two years since she had come to live with Essie and four years since she had left the school.

When Jerusha actually managed to swipe the ball with her bat, there was a concerted yell of, "*Run!*" When she tumbled face-down on the grass, twisting her ankle, before she had completed her run, no one rushed to pick her up, instead she heard the disappointed groaning from her team. She scrambled to her feet and limped on. These children never gave up, nor must she.

Jerusha was not Essie's first protégée. There was a young dancer called Violet Mendez, one of a succession of lodgers, whom she had encouraged when her own career was waning. Violet had been performing with an acrobatic troupe in Europe for some years. Now she was back in London, appearing as principal dancer in a musical show. She had 'made it', to Essie's pleasure.

"I'd love to see Vi again," Essie said, when she learned of her friend's success. Vi obviously felt the same, for shortly afterwards Essie received an affectionate letter enclosing two complimentary tickets for the Saturday matinée.

"We'll make a day of it, Jerusha," Essie cried, "*Dress to impress*! Walk past the neighbours like the Empress of India! We'll make a real entrance at the theatre, eh? And after the show, I'll take you backstage to meet young Vi – she's *really* done well for herself!" She could have added that young Vi was a credit to her old dancing teacher, too.

Outside, in the London streets, the August sun beat down relentlessly and there was hardly a surge of shoppers. Inside the theatre – barely half-full in such weather, which was disappointing to Essie – when the lights were dimmed, the spotlight beamed on dazzling, sequined costumes, on fairy-tale scenery and on an amazing, supple dancer in particular whose diaphanous dress left nothing to the imagination. Jerusha's eyes were wide, her cheeks aflame, but she was spellbound by the music, the singing of the chorus and most of all the erotic dancing.

Later, Jerusha stood back shyly, while Essie embraced Vi, now wearing the briefest of flimsy underwear, in her dressing room. "You were wonderful, Vi, we have enjoyed ourselves, haven't we, Jerusha? Quite took me back to the old days . . ."

There was a tentative knocking on the door. Essie smiled, as Vi reached for her dressing gown. "An admirer, darlin'?"

Vi concealed her disappointment admirably. A tall, burly man stood there, clutching a bunch of wilting roses, obviously home-grown and clumsily wrapped in brown paper. He had a nice round, ruddy face, dark-jowled although he was freshly-shaven. His hair was thick, short-cut and dark brown, with a sprinkling of grey. He could have been any age between thirty and forty. He wore an unfashionable suit and his voice had a pleasant country intonation. "Daniel Applebee. I wrote to you, Miss Mendez – you said—"

"I said, *do* come backstage and have a chat next time you are at the theatre! Well, come in, Mr Applebee; may I introduce my friend, Essie Bronski and her friend, Jerusha – Carey, did you say? Mr Applebee has *so* enjoyed the show, it seems, this is the *third* Saturday matinée running he has attended—"

The door had been left ajar and was now pushed open. Daniel Applebee, Essie and Jerusha were instantly aware that *this* was the visitor Violet had been hoping and waiting for, as she rushed instantly into his arms. When Violet emerged from her passionate embrace with the handsome young man, she apologised somewhat breathlessly. "This is my husband, Jules, just over from Paris – we haven't seen each other for over six weeks. He has brought our little girl, she is with her nurse at the hotel. Mr Applebee, I'm so sorry to send you away, but I do hope to see you again one of these days. Essie, Jerusha, you will excuse me, and understand, I hope?"

They made their embarrassed farewells. Outside the theatre, Essie saw the disappointment, the uncertainty on Dan's face, the roses still clutched tightly in his hand, and spoke to him impulsively. "You wanted to say something to Violet? You hardly had a chance—"

"I thought – I might – I wanted to tell Miss Mendez how much I—" He cleared his throat nervously.

"How much you enjoyed her performance? She's a *wonderful* artiste, isn't she? Of course, she wanted to rush back to her hotel, to spend precious time with her husband and her baby, before she returns for the evening concert. You don't think of them as ordinary folk, family people, d'you? They seem so special, so magical up there on stage, with the lights on them and all. *I* know. I used to be an artiste myself – *and* a doting mother! Come up from the country, have you?" she enquired kindly.

"Yes, from Kent." He looked rather nervous now, and Essie guessed correctly that he was wondering just why she had engaged him in conversation. She would wonder herself afterwards why she had persisted, but as things turned out later, she was glad.

"Don't mind me, I talk to everyone! Come to London today? Found somewhere to stay? It's not easy, I know, despite or perhaps because it's such a big, busy place, eh?"

"Yes, and no. Please, can you recommend anywhere?" he asked awkwardly.

"Staying here long?"

"Overnight. I have to get back. I am a farmer, in a small way that is."

"Why don't you come home with us and have a nice cup of tea and a bite to eat, oh, don't worry, Jerusha can chaperone us! And anyway, I'm the mother of a well-grown son! Then we can talk about where you might go tonight. You don't want to finish up somewhere dubious, now do you?"

"No." He admitted, "I'm afraid you have just described the hotel room I ended up in last Saturday night."

"Come on then, at least we've been properly introduced!" Essie laughed.

Jerusha, flustered, for Essie never brought her gentlemen friends home as a rule, fetched out the bone china cups and saucers, and obediently made green tea, in deference to Essie's exotic forebears.

Perry the parrot screeched a greeting from his usual perch high on the curtain pole, and Essie left the parlour door wide for Jerusha to carry the bamboo tray through.

Jerusha glanced at them as she arranged cakes on a plate and waited for the tea to brew. Essie was removing her tight shoes, wriggling her toes with relief. She had plumped down on the sofa, still wearing her hat, her face glistening, for it had been so enervating out.

Dan sat solemnly in the high-backed chair. When he thanked Jerusha politely as she handed him his tea, she noticed that his hands were rough and calloused, which meant he was a practical, hard-working man. She wondered if he noticed in turn that her own fingers were deeply inkstained, the result of a lengthy session of copying, despite her best efforts with the pumice stone. Then, she saw that his deep-set eyes were surrounded by criss-crossed skin, the sign of someone who usually smiled a lot. She had no idea then that he was so much older than she was, and anyway, his age was unimportant, for she had taken to him immediately. She smiled at him and instantly he responded and she saw that she was right about the laughter-lines.

She would have blushed even more deeply if she had known what Dan was thinking. If he had been poetic, and that he was not, he might have mused that a man could happily drown in the depths of those amazing dark eyes. She was not strictly pretty, with her rather sharp features, but she had beautiful hair and such pale skin he thought immediately that she was in need of some good, country air. Bemused, he knew that she was the stuff of his dreams, a young woman to respect and care for, even though this really should all have come about twenty-odd years ago . . . He had probably been naïve in imagining that he might find someone to court and marry in London, but fate had been kind to him after all.

Much later, Essie said, "It's getting dark. Why don't you stay here for the night, Dan? The sofa is quite comfortable, and I've plenty of spare blankets."

"I'll fetch them," Jerusha said, and she blushed again, because she knew *she* wanted him to stay, that she would be glad to see him the next day.

Chapter Ten

Jerusha Carey was three months short of her eighteenth birthday when she met Dan Applebee. He was twice her age, but as Essie observed intuitively to Oliver when next they met, around the middle of October, "Dan's a real country innocent, quite as unworldly as Jerusha is. She won't come to any harm with him. He's the kind you can trust, Oliver."

Oliver was still concerned. "Are you sure she's not really looking for a father figure, Essie? The fact remains that he is far too old for her, and that she has no experience of being escorted by young men of her own generation. You say you believe his intentions are serious? I must get in touch with Valentine, soon, I think—"

"It might be better if you wrote, maybe cabled to Kathleen first," Essie advised. "There's the birthday lunch coming up in November. Why don't you invite Dan, too, then you can form your own opinion."

He raised his glass to her, smiling ruefully. "Words from a wise woman, Essie."

Jerusha and Dan walked hand-in-hand in Southwark Park. There were rival tub-thumpers drawing the crowds this Sunday morning, with autumn leaves crisping underfoot and a watery sun trying to belie the wind catching at skirts and coat-tails and tugging at bonnets and caps. The social democrat declaimed his stirring message, crying of troubles at home and war inevitable in far-off South Africa if the conference at Bloemfontein failed. The young Wesleyan minister offered a short sermon and stirring hymn singing. Both were well aware that even on the Sabbath their listeners had limited time and interest. The Sunday street markets would eventually draw them away, with their equally colourful language and cheap and cheerful household necessities for the hungry body rather than the soul.

Jerusha wore a short cape over her dress. The ribbon in her hair exactly matched the dark blue of the woollen material. She wore a knitted tam o'shanter and gloves which she had made herself.

Because she was so small and slight and looked so young, Dan, glancing down at her, felt a momentary pang. Did he really have the right to tell her how he felt about her? He said instead, "What d'you intend to do with your life, Jerusha?"

They sat on a seat and looked at one another.

She said slowly at last, "I believe I'd like to be married and have a real home, and one day, a family, of my own. Much as I love Essie, I'm still not independent, you see. I never go anywhere on my own, I work at home, but I suspect that is on my guardian, Oliver's, instructions. He feels responsible for me because he made certain promises to my mother. At one time I thought, if she sends for me I'll go to her at once, forgive the past, but I think it's too late for that now, Dan. I'm not the little girl she left behind any more . . .

"Tell me about your home, Dan, the countryside. I miss all the trees, the flowers and the fields that I loved when I was away at school in Buckinghamshire. That's why I enjoy coming to the parks so much, I suppose."

"I was born in the village where I still live. My father worked for a Mr Pepper on his farm. When I was thirteen, I joined my dad. It was a mixed farm, dairy, cereal crops and orchards. The Peppers had a daughter a few years older than me, Polly – she's still a great friend – oh, nothing romantic, we weren't sweethearts as our parents fondly imagined us to be. Anyway, Polly fell for someone else, and her son is almost grown up now. When Poll's parents passed on, she didn't want to farm herself, she's restless, likes to go further afield, she says. But she's a fine businesswoman all right, and she supports herself and her son Bart with her goods-carrying. When she inherited her fifty acres she sold most of the land and the farmhouse to a neighbouring farmer who'd always had an eye on it, and she pensioned off the workers. But for me she had another proposition: she'd move into my old cottage, where I lived by then on my own, and she'd give me the down-payment on the smallholding opposite which had been long-deserted. That was six months ago, and," he squeezed Jerusha's hand, "*then,* dear Poll said it was about time I found myself a wife and a helpmate! She speaks out, does Poll."

"Oh . . ." Jerusha murmured.

"It's a lovely part of Kent," he continued. "They call it the Weald. The land means everything to those of us who live and work there. I never thought I'd own my own patch of it, and if I'm truthful I can't say it's wholly mine yet, of course, for I have to find the money for the mortgage each month, but when that's paid off, well, I'll have the right to call myself a fruit farmer. Got a great deal to do to get the place in order – old trees to prune, new ones to be planted—"

"Then, like your friend says, you need a strong, young wife to help you, encourage you, don't you?" Jerusha said. "What about me, Dan?" Over the years she had lived with Essie she had learned that the direct approach was best, but even so, she surprised herself with her boldness.

"But you were born to a different class of folk, Jerusha, you've never got more than ink on your hands. Farming's a hard life, and you're not exactly a strapping girl, are you?" He looked worried now.

"I can learn. I'm willing to. And I don't believe all that rubbish about class. I don't agree with all that social democrat over there is spouting either, but *that* part makes sense. Where I live *now* is *much* more a home to me than the grand house I was born in. When my mother was hard up, she couldn't face it. She ran away from her problems to worse ones. My father is not an honest man like you. Essie doesn't care about being poor and nor do I. You and I get on so well together, don't we? I thought – I thought you might feel, well, *romantic* about me!" She trembled at her own audacity.

"Maybe I'm too old for romance, Jerusha," Dan said ruefully. "But I *do* know I love you. You *might* call it romantic if I say I was smitten right away, the day we met, even though I'd come to London just to gaze on another beautiful girl! I reckon your guardian will object, that he'll say it's much too soon and I'm not good enough for you."

"Well, you'll have your chance to ask him, Dan. He wants to meet you. I'm to bring you along the weekend after next to the hotel, when we celebrate my mother's birthday as we always do."

"I'm *so* happy, Essie," she said that afternoon, after Dan had left to catch his train back to Kent. "Dan wants to marry me, you see—"

It was hard to shock or surprise Essie. She continued with the washing-up, passing the dishes to Jerusha to dry. She didn't even point out that Jerusha had only known Dan for six weeks. She said merely, "You love him, darlin', d'you?"

"*He* loves *me*, Essie, and I – well, I feel so comfortable with him, I just *know* we'll be so happy together, I can't explain it . . ."

"Then that's all that matters, darlin'. I'll put in a good word for you both with Oliver, I promise. But I can't tell you how much I'll miss you, 'cause I've thought of you as my own!" She wrapped her wet arms round Jerusha and hugged her close.

"You'll soon find another lame duck, Essie. Dan won't let me down, leave me ever, Essie. I'm sure of that." Jerusha hugged her tightly in return. "He's strong and good just like *you*."

Jerusha walked determinedly towards the table where Oliver was waiting. Dan, looking diffident, was a step or two behind her. When Oliver got to his feet to greet them, she realised suddenly how short he seemed compared to Dan. The two men were around the same age, but so different. Dan almost crushed Oliver's hand in his grip.

"Do sit down," Oliver said cordially.

To Jerusha, now familiar with the more masculine odours of cheap household soap, tobacco and honest toil, linen worn two days running, the way Oliver dressed, even the perfume of his expensive hair oil, struck her today as fussy. She hoped Dan would not feel intimidated by one who had never had to work with his hands and who had always apparently had life easy.

They ate their lunch almost in silence. When it was time for the toast to Kathleen on her birthday, Oliver withdrew an envelope from his jacket pocket. "For you, Jerusha. Please read it now . . ."

'Dear Jerusha,

It seems strange to be writing to you after such a long silence between us. I know from Oliver that you have grown to be the woman I wish I had been myself.

I won't try to defend my actions in the past except to say I bitterly regret having deserted you, but that one day I believe you will understand and forgive me for loving unwisely.

Oliver writes that you wish to marry. I trust him implicitly as always where your welfare is concerned. It is to be his decision, when he has had the chance to meet your friend.

If you are to wed, who am I to say you are too young? I wish you every happiness, always.

Think of me sometimes,
Your loving mother.'

"She intimated in my letter, what she wrote to you," Oliver said, looking searchingly at her as she folded the letter and put it away in her bag.

Jerusha stretched out a hand to Dan, and he held it in his warm, comforting clasp. "I would take such care of her, sir," he said quietly.

"I believe you will," Oliver observed. He sighed, raised his glass. "To Kathleen – and also to you both."

Chapter Eleven

The only stipulation Oliver made was that they should wait until after Christmas, and Jerusha's birthday. Essie had a request of her own: "You'll get married from my house, darlin', won't you? And I know that Oliver wants to give you away and to host the reception at the hotel—"

Jerusha looked at Dan. He nodded. "Of course." She knew that he had been hoping that they could be married in his village church, with his friends present, but she also knew that he appreciated all that her own friends had done for her in the past and that he would go along with their wishes because he was taking her away from them.

Dan proved unexpectedly obstinate in one respect. He wanted to take Jerusha out and to buy her wedding outfit himself. He had some savings and he intended to show that he could provide for her. In fact, he wished to contribute to her trousseau, too.

"You should be wearing a lovely wedding gown," Essie lamented, when he had gone back as usual to the farm at the end of the weekend. "That's not a lucky colour to be married in, either, darlin'."

"I don't need a lucky colour, Essie. Marrying Dan is luck enough for me." Jerusha hung up the expensive sage green serge costume with the velvet trim on collar and cuffs and such shiny, round horn buttons. Dan had been really rash! They had purchased it in one of the most expensive dress shops in the West End. There was a beige satin blouse to go with it, soft, toning kid gloves and elegant little boots. A new style for a new woman, and a new century, for it would be 1900 when they married. She would ask Essie to go with her to choose her hat. She didn't like to think she had disappointed her friend. "A simple wedding, Essie, that's what we both want, in your little church round the corner. I turned down Oliver's suggestion of something grander, didn't I?"

They had agreed to spend their wedding night in the hotel, but had decided firmly that they would return the next day to Kent. "I haven't even seen my new home yet, Essie, even though I feel

I know every corner of it and am sure I will love it just as much as Dan does. And, don't forget, Dan needs to work and the farm won't run itself: he says he's taken off so much time already while he's been courting me!"

"Courtship is important, Jerusha, you'll come to realise that. Married life will *soon* bring you down to earth, my darlin'!"

Essie's neighbours turned out in their best clothes and packed the church pews. Essie's hair, even more startling in colour today was piled so high her hat had to perch on top, like the decoration on a lopsided, layered cake. With the thought that a double dose of green might cancel out any bad luck, Essie wore emerald green silk, with a ruched, heavy black velvet opera cape, to guard against the January chills. The strong smell of mothballs was not quite masked by her perfume. "One of my gentlemen gave me the cape – I was waiting for the right occasion to wear it."

The bells which had rung in the new century now rang for Jerusha and Dan, as they emerged from the church smiling happily. The Boer War was already a harsh reality and British soldiers were dying, fighting against those who knew every inch of the alien terrain. Queen Victoria was in what would be the last year of her life. It was only two and a half years since the Diamond Jubilee when every part of the British Empire was represented in the great and glorious procession which wound its way from Buckingham Palace to St Paul's Cathedral.

They had not even kissed properly Jerusha thought shyly, though Dan hugged her close, of course, when they parted each weekend, then chastely kissed the top of her head. Wise old Essie had, last night, talked to her of certain things and she was grateful to have been so enlightened. "When you're young, both of you, you learn easily together, darlin'. It all seems to come natural. When a man's older than his bride, he often brings a bit of experience, like, to a marriage. D'you understand me? But sometimes a man who's been a batchelor longer than most, has been that from choice, until he surprises himself and falls in love."

"And you think *Dan's* like that, Essie?" Jerusha ventured.

"Don't expect too much, darlin', and you won't be disappointed. You're marrying a nice, kind chap who worships you and will look after you as you deserve. Think of the one your poor mother married and wasted her life on. Dan won't let you down."

* * *

"I wish Valentine could have come, that would have made it perfect," was Jerusha's only regret as just the four of them sat round the table: herself and Dan, Oliver and Essie. The best man, a colleague of Oliver's, for Dan had sheepishly said that his closest friend was Polly Pepper, had politely excused himself as the hotel was very busy with another wedding party, a large gathering, contrasting with their own. Jerusha didn't mind, because she was with those she cared for most, who were important to her.

Her few possessions were packed, including Valentine's writing slope, but she made her mind up to write to her cousin as soon as she was settled in her new home. She would write to Millicent too, for she realised with a sudden pang that she had neglected her correspondence with her old friend since she met Dan, and hadn't even told her about her forthcoming wedding. Perhaps it was because she knew Millicent was averse to the idea of marriage and was concentrating on her teaching career.

The food was wonderful, the champagne went to Jerusha's head. She was laughing as she embraced Essie, when it was time to part, and Essie whispered in her ear, "I should forget what I said, I don't think you need worry, darlin'!" Then she dabbed her eyes. "I'll miss you so much – but I'm coming to see you off on the train tomorrow!"

Oliver came back into the lounge. "There's a cab waiting, Essie."

"Thank you. Goodnight, Dan, you're a very lucky chap."

"I know." He was laughing and relaxed, too.

Only Oliver was quiet, seemingly preoccupied. "You'd like to go to your room soon, I expect?" he asked. "I'm afraid I must return to my duties now."

"It's been a *wonderful* day, Oliver, and *you've* had a great deal to do with that!" Jerusha cried. For the first time since she had known him, she flung her arms round his neck and kissed him on his cheek.

Oliver held her close for a brief moment. "Always keep in touch," he said gruffly.

"I will, oh, *I will!*"

It was more than a room, it was the bridal suite. More champagne awaited their arrival, in an ice bucket. They smiled happily at each other.

"I think you've had quite enough of *that!*" Dan said.

She put her face down to the bowl of hothouse flowers. "Oh, these smell beautiful, Dan!"

"*You* look beautiful, too," he told her. "You don't look tired at all—"

"No, but I'm ready for bed," she said artlessly. "We've got so much to talk about . . ."

"I'll have to shave, I'll get changed in the bathroom. I won't be long," he told her, lifting his bag from the chair.

She took off her jacket and skirt, then the blouse, and hung them in the walk-in wardrobe. She giggled. "You'll be lonely in there until Dan's suit comes to keep you company!"

She sat down at the dressing table. When Dan comes back, I'll take a bath, for I suspect things are even more primitive at Dan's – our! – house than they are at Essie's and it might be some time before I can indulge in such luxury again. Oh, these lovely soft hotel towels, the scented soap, the lotions and potions . . . I mustn't overdo it, like dear Essie!

Her reflection smiled back at her in the triple mirror – three views of her face, with her hair in unfamiliar curls, pinned by Essie into an elaborate style. She brushed it out, then braided it tightly. She must try not to get it wet in the bath. Should she be discreet like Dan and re-emerge from the bathroom in her nightgown? She still wore her new silk petticoat over her bust bodice and underthings.

When Dan came up behind her, resting his hands lightly on her bare shoulders, she gave a little shiver, aware that he would see the scars etched deeply across her back. For what seemed a long time he said nothing. Then he touched the marks fleetingly and for the first time since they met, for he was such an equable chap, he displayed anger. "Jerusha, my dear girl, *who* could do such a thing to you?"

She was crying now, she couldn't help it. "I'll tell you Dan, one of these days, *not now*, please. I don't want to spoil a perfect day . . ."

There was just the bedside lamp burning on her side of the bed when she returned. She extinguished the light, slipped in beside him. She felt the warmth of him, through the fine cotton lawn of her nightgown.

His embrace was gentle, that first kiss brief but reassuringly affectionate. She lay contentedly in his arms, her head resting against his shoulder. Waiting, unafraid, because she trusted him.

"You're so young, Jerusha," he murmured. "We hardly know each other really – we mustn't rush our loving . . ."

Chapter Twelve

Polly Pepper was waiting for the train from London to steam in. She was a tall, strong, good-looking woman with prematurely silver hair cropped short for, as she said, she hadn't got time to fiddle about in the mornings for she worked hard every day excepting Sunday. She had swept out her cart, usually so full of boxes and barrels, for she collected and delivered over a wide area, and improvised some seating. Even the horse had been curry-combed and his plaited mane and tail were threaded with red ribbons, for wasn't he to pull a bridal carriage of sorts?

Her son Bart, tall, gangly and ginger-haired, lounged sulkily beside the cart and she rightly suspected that he was longing for a cigarette. He had been a sly smoker since he was eleven, but she hadn't yet caught him. He had been born on St Bartholomew's day, fourteen years ago, not that there was anything remotely saintly about him, she thought ruefully. Dan had been a staunch ally when her shocked elderly parents railed against her when they realised she was pregnant with Bart.

Now, she wondered how she would get on with Jerusha. Although there had never been any romantic feelings between herself and Dan, they had always enjoyed a close relationship, both only children, thrown together because at that time they were the only youngsters in the vicinity. They were alike in many ways, but differed in that Polly was ambitious whereas, until she pushed him into becoming his own boss, Dan had been content to be a farm worker. Perhaps she had also pushed him into marriage, in a way, she thought wryly. She just hadn't envisaged him bringing home such a young bride . . .

"Here they come," Bart said, in his newly deep voice which still made her start when she heard it because now he had entered adolescence she had the strong feeling that her troubles were really about to start.

The cheerful porter pushed his trolley towards them, bearing a battered trunk with several peeling labels and Dan's new suitcase.

Dan and Jerusha followed some way behind. Dan, beaming and proud, still in his wedding suit, carried a portmanteau. The bride was obviously travelling light.

"Load up," Polly told her son. She stepped down from her seat at the front, looped the horse's reins over one arm, and waved her other hand in greeting. "Hello!" she called.

"This is Jerusha, Polly," Dan said, and she could see the pride on his face.

Polly looked down at the slight figure, warmed instantly to the shy smile directed at her. Jerusha held out her hand. "I've heard so much about you, Polly—"

"Nothing bad, I hope!" Polly replied, ignoring her hand and bending to kiss her instead. "Because I want us to be friends!"

When she straightened up she knew that she had pleased Dan with her instant acceptance of his wife. Jerusha was indeed very young, but Polly would do all she could to help her settle in her new life, she'd already made up her mind about that.

"Like a hand-up?" invited Bart, giving Jerusha just that. He dusted the wooden seat ostentatiously with his bare hand. As she sat down nervously, for to her it all seemed rather precarious, he said cheekily, while his mother was talking for a minute to Dan, "Life won't be nearly as boring for me now, with a pretty girl like *you* living opposite!"

He hadn't said anything that Jerusha hadn't heard while she was at Essie's, from bold boys of his age, but she knew instinctively that she did not like him, that even at fourteen years of age he was not to be trusted.

Jerusha and Dan stood outside the ramshackle house, weatherboarded as so many houses were in Kent, once painted white but now peeling and chipped. She saw ivy trailing round the doorposts and a step worn down in the centre where muddy boots had been scraped over many years. There were outhouses grouped around the dirt yard and a track leading to the orchard beyond. To one side of the track there was a large barn. "I call it the woodshed, but much more goes on in there than the chopping of wood! I keep the farm implements, store a lot of other things in there, too, including all the rubbish the previous owner left behind," Dan told her.

It was a bright January afternoon and although the trees were twisted and bare, Jerusha exclaimed in excitement at the sight of so many. "What are they, Dan – apples and pears?"

"Plums as well, Early Rivers, Victorias, a precious greengage or two, wild damson, a few cherry trees, all to be pruned – you'll have to learn fast! And I hope you'll want to make a flower garden at the side of the house next spring. There's a nice rose bush or two and plenty of bulbs will be coming up soon among the long grass around the trees. We could do with a couple of geese, or some sheep to graze that."

"*I had a little nut tree*," she quoted fancifully, imagining silver and gold fruits.

"Now *that's* an idea. We might plant some cultivated hazelunts, Kentish cobnuts, of course, filbert-shaped. There's an area we could clear that's bounded by wild hazels, you need those for fertilising—" He was so eager to please her.

"Oh . . ." Jerusha said, blushing at his use of the word.

Dan continued. "And we must get you a few chickens, nothing like fresh eggs—"

"Dan, well, I hadn't thought to tell you, because there wasn't any need, you see I haven't had an attack in ages, thank goodness—"

"What are you trying to tell me?" he teased.

"I suffer from asthma, Dan, if I get upset or worried, so that's not very likely now, is it, because I'm so happy being here with you, but sometimes feathers or fur set it off—"

"No chickens then!" he said easily. "Or sheep. I'll have to sharpen the scythe instead! And I'll sort out the pillows on the bed. Mother always had the flock-filled ones because the feather ones made her wheeze, too. We'll have to get our eggs from Polly, as I do now."

"I want to be a proper country wife," she worried.

"You *will* be! Come inside now, don't you want to look over your palace? I hope you won't be *too* shocked when you step inside! There's the privy, oh, did you notice the pump, just round the corner? That's where our water comes from. There's a stream runs through our field beyond the orchard, so there's no need to lug buckets up there to water the land. The field is a short-cut to the main road, but not much use when it's rained hard and it's all muddy. You'll probably prefer to stroll up the lane to the village proper, us being really in the sticks here, and meet all the neighbours on your way!"

"I love it *all*," she assured him, after her inspection.

"Shabby old place, and no new furniture, Jerusha. I'm afraid we'll have to sleep in my parents' bed."

"I don't mind, not one bit. That bookcase in the parlour, Dan, all those books—" She had resisted the temptation to start browsing among them right then. Her *Alice* would be able to take pride of place at last. Perhaps Kathleen's portrait might find a space among the stern pictures of Dan's family, too.

"Ah, my dad was a bit of a self-taught scholar, and he encouraged me to read. Mostly the sixpenny classics, but there's some nice books he bought when they sold up the Manor in the village about thirty years ago."

The stove in the kitchen gave off a comfortable heat; Polly had seen to that earlier, to ensure a warm welcome. The table was covered with a snowy, well-darned cloth, ready laid for a meal for two. There was a pot of stew bubbling steadily on the hot-plate, potatoes ready to be boiled, a pudding, tied in a cloth, in the steamer. Polly had thought of everything, for upstairs she had smoothed starched sheets on the bed and hung towels on the washstand.

But most important of all was the full, singing kettle, with boiling water ready to pour in the teapot. Tea, not Essie's kind, which Jerusha had never quite got used to, but brown, strong and refreshing. Dan demonstrated how he liked it by making it himself.

When they sat down to eat, Dan said solemnly, "I like to say grace, Jerusha, at my own table; Father always did." And Jerusha obediently bowed her head, recalling Miss Murray reciting the same prayer in her clipped, clear voice each mealtime at Copper Leas. She hadn't heard those simple words said since.

Later, "Don't unpack your trunk until tomorrow," Dan advised. "After all the excitement. I think we'll benefit from an early night!"

The flock pillows were not very comfortable, but she appreciated Dan's thoughtfulness. There were candles to light you to bed here, she discovered, and in the bedroom under the eaves, they chose a corner each to discreetly undress and climbed into bed simultaneously from opposite sides. It's *cold* up here, Jerusha grimaced to herself, snuggling close to her husband under the layers of covers. She felt a trifle apprehensive, but she told herself that was to be expected. Now they were at home, making love would happen quite spontaneously, surely.

She slid her arms round his neck, waiting for him to kiss her. He whispered of his adoration for her, expressed his contentment at being with her. Then he put her gently from him, wished her happy dreams and turned away. He was soon asleep, but Jerusha lay awake for some time, wondering . . .

Chapter Thirteen

As she had throughout her short life so far, Jerusha learned to adapt to her new circumstances, and shortly, to accept what seemed unlikely to change. She was cherished, she was sure of that, and she, in turn, loved Dan unreservedly. The disparity in their ages was unimportant. He was easy to please and it was his pleasure to spoil her in little ways. In years to come she would realise that he had treated her like a beloved daughter.

Dan did all the heavy work around the place, but in early March they planted the young nut trees together. From the start they were known as 'Jerusha's trees'.

Jerusha had already enjoyed the sight of the catkins which appeared on the wild hazels, heralding the spring. She wrote often to Valentine and Essie of her daily discoveries, but only now and again to Oliver. After all, he had relinquished his role as her guardian and they had not yet really established a new relationship. Still, she had promised that she would meet him at the hotel as always, on Kathleen's birthday.

> *'The hazel is a native of Britain, and the nuts have been eaten for, oh,* thousands *of years! It will be at least three years before I can pick the first nuts from my little plantation – as Polly (Pepper, our neighbour) says I should call it!*
>
> *Polly showed me how to make perfect porridge, well, the sort Dan approves of, so thick it sticks to your ribs. He says the thin stuff I made first of all is gruel, and only for invalids! In the autumn she has promised to supervise my first attempts at preserving and bottling all the wonderful fruit.*
>
> *When we have the house as we would like it, you must visit, if possible, dearest Essie, but I know it is difficult for Valentine to get away. I'm not sure if we will ever be grand enough to entertain Oliver!'*

"Roses in your cheeks now, and blossom on the trees," Dan whispered in her ear one day, catching at her slender waist with his hands and hugging her close, her face pressed against his broad chest. She had been standing in the orchard, drinking in the beauty of it all. He added, "Such a little thing you are, Jerusha, but so determined. With you beside me, how can I fail to make a go of things here?"

It spoiled the magic of the moment when they heard someone approaching. They parted quickly to see Bart grinning at them. Jerusha's initial misgivings about the boy had been confirmed: he leered at her and made lewd remarks if Dan was not within earshot. She said nothing of this because she could not bear the thought of upsetting Polly. She knew that she would be afraid if ever she found herself alone with him, but fortunately Dan was never far away. *He* had the measure of Bart.

As it always did, when she was happy, time seemed to pass quickly, although it surprised her one day when she realised that she had been married nearly three years. This Christmas she would reach her majority.

They were cut off from the wider world and the bustle of London seemed to Jerusha nowadays unreal, though she learned what was going on elsewhere, through the weekly bundles of the broadsheets Polly passed on from a well-to-do widow whose goods she carried. "*You* read 'em, dearie, keep up with the ways of the wicked world, eh? *Me,* I find they give a good blaze, so pass some back when you've finished with 'em!"

The Old Queen died a year after Jerusha became Mrs Applebee and the popular, corpulent Prince of Wales became King at last. There was great relief in the country when the peace treaty was signed at Pretoria in May, 1902 and the Boer War was over, but public anxiety shortly afterwards when the coronation of King Edward VII was postponed in June when the new King was operated on for acute appendicitis. However, the Coronation took place without further hitches on 9th August. Jerusha did wish then she could have been in London with Essie among the great crowd cheering the procession, but it was a busy time of year for her and Dan.

Here at The Homestead, as they had decided to rename their cottage, fancying it had a colonial look now that Dan had built-on a verandah to make the most of the evening sun in summer, their main concern was the weather and the eventual harvesting of the fruit. They grew potatoes and other root crops, peas, beans and cabbages in turn, on the land Dan cultivated with his old hand plough.

There was only one thing lacking in Jerusha's life. Polly put it into words one day when they were enjoying tea and cake in Polly's kitchen late one afternoon.

"I rather thought you'd be calling me Auntie Poll by now, Ru!"

She couldn't confide in Polly, that would be disloyal to Dan. She managed to smile and say, "One of these days, Poll. I'm not twenty-one yet you know. There's *plenty* of time."

Polly looked at her. "For you there is, but remember, dearie, our Dan is not getting any younger."

For several days Jerusha brooded on this conversation, but said nothing to her husband. She knew he was wondering why she was so quiet.

"You look tired, Jerusha," he said at last. The flames were dying down in the parlour grate. "I hope you didn't get too chilled helping me pick the last of the Bramleys." Summer was no more, it was autumn.

"It was a job that had to be done," she replied. She had spent most of the evening wrapping the fruit and filling boxes to store in the cellar. Polly would take no more apples to market for them, for the winter months at home must be catered for.

"Is something wrong?" he persisted. Dear Dan knew her so well. She suspected that he was also aware of what, until now, she had been unable to put into words.

She cleared her throat, spoke to his back as he stooped to place a final log on the fire. "You say you love me, Dan—"

He straightened up, looked at her. "Of course I do, you *know* that." He looked wary.

"I want us to have a baby, Dan, but that's impossible, isn't it, as things are? *Please*, Dan, won't you talk about it? It's *very* important to me."

She saw the distress on his face but he said only, "You go up to bed. I'll bring your cocoa up. There's a rat in the woodshed I intend to deal with tonight. I shall be some time . . ."

"I *knew* you wouldn't listen!" It was the first time she had shouted at him. She felt the tightening of her chest, realised that the wheezing was about to begin, but perversely she didn't want his sympathy, his ministrations tonight. Without another word, she went out of the room, climbed the stairs and slammed their bedroom door.

She lay on the bed, gasping, trying to calm herself. Such a stupid argument, she had gone about it entirely the wrong way. This problem should have been talked over long ago, but she had been too shy to do so in the beginning. If only she had confided in Polly while she had the chance, she might have been able to advise and help . . .

Dan rubbed at his eyes fiercely with his sleeve. He would have to brace himself to explain to Jerusha things he was not too sure of himself. He should have been prepared for this, he knew that, but until now he had been so happy with his life as it was. Then he cautiously opened the woodshed door, moved stealthily inside and prepared to wait. He had baited the trap earlier. He had already doused the lamp, hanging it from one of the nails on the beam above, close to a great, dangling, rusty chain under which he ducked. He really should tidy the place up, he thought. He kept the logs well stacked that Ernest delivered each month, but nearby, on the ground, was a heap of buckled, but still dangerously sharp plough shares, among other old iron.

He lowered himself on to a sack of wood shavings, his shotgun across his knees. He shuddered suddenly. This was a draughty, sighing place, with chinks in the rough wooden walls. Outside, the moon would soon be up. Enough pale light would then filter through, he hoped, for him to spot his darting quarry.

The gloom, the dark corners of the barn concealed the presence of another, also poised and waiting. And there was someone else out and about too, unknown to the other two, moving stealthily across the top field then pushing through the hedge into the orchard. It was too late to call at the house tonight. The barn offered shelter of a sort.

Jerusha slept at last, lying on top of the bed still fully dressed. The nightmare was all too real: the unmistakable sharp *crack!* of a gun, then a single, bloodcurdling scream woke her, *"Jerusha!"* It was an episode in her life she would never forget, one she would relive over and over again.

An agonisingly long five minutes or more later she had

regained enough breath to get downstairs and out of the kitchen door.

She ran stumbling towards the woodshed. In the light of the lamp now beaming, she saw figures bending over a motionless body on the ground. She pushed past Polly and Bart, both obviously also aroused by Dan's scream.

She fell heavily to her knees beside Dan. Even as she attempted desperately to lift him free of the thing that had impaled him, Polly pulled her roughly up, and away.

"He's beyond our help, Jerusha," Polly babbled. "A *terrible* accident . . . He must have shot at a rat, dislodged that chain, and when it struck him he fell on that iron . . . Run hard up to Ernest's, Bart, he'll know what's to be done, he should be in the lodge at his supper now—" She kept her arm firmly round Jerusha's shaking shoulders, led her back to the house. The pain in her chest prevented her from shouting out, she could only gasp incoherently: "*Dan* . . ."

Back in the kitchen she saw the awful stains on her dress, where she had rubbed her hands.

Dan was dead and she was utterly desolated.

Part Two

1904–1905

Chapter One

Apples lay in the long grass under the trees, some already soft and brown, oozing heady cider juices, others fresh fallen, busily bored by droning wasps. A few fruits still clung to the top branches, tantalisingly out of reach of questing hands.

Jerusha Applebee, despite her name, had had quite enough of apples. She had bitten into crisp Newtons in the first flush of picking when she had climbed the long, swaying ladder; she had baked giant Bramleys stuffed with dates and brown sugar until the glossy green skins burst; forked flour and fat into soft pastry, taking pleasure in crimping the edges of pies and tarts into familiar flutings. Now there was a man again in the house to feed she was not forced to throw so much to the crows. After packing the fruit for Polly to take to market, for it provided very necessary cash, she had wrapped the remaining keepers and also threaded apple rings to dry slowly in the oven in case the mice nibbled too many of the former. A pile of bruised apples, all sorts, retrieved earlier from the orchard, now awaited her attention. On the next wet day she would chop them with a will, together with unripened tomatoes and onions, to make the chutney which livened up the suppertime bread and cheese. A man appreciated that; Dan certainly had.

Now she bent over the young nut trees, feeling with pleasure the smooth, sensual curve of the burgeoning cobnuts. She had been unable to resist picking a few at the beginning of the season in August, when the husks were green and frilly and the kernels softer to the bite, but now the nuts were brown and to her taste. The wild hazel trees which marked her boundaries had pollinated these as Dan had said they would.

Those three precious years together were all she had to hold on to. His death had been tragic, the memory of it haunted her, but like the nut trees she had put down roots, determined to realise the dreams they had shared. The nut trees were flourishing. She must pick their bounty shortly, squirrel them away for Christmas, she thought. Next year there should be many more to sell.

The first chill wind of autumn licked her hair from her forehead, snatched and lifted her long alpaca skirt above her laced boots, reddened her cheeks and nipped at her ears. She looked very like her mother at the same age, although her practical, shabby clothes were those of a working woman. Her pointed chin was more accentuated than it had been when she and Kathleen gazed on their reflections, a moment in time she still vividly recalled. There was a determined tilt to her jaw, and her dark eyes were no longer shadowed as they had been in the months after she lost Dan. She had tied her long hair severely back with a frayed bootlace. She was almost twenty-three years old now and there had been no man since in her life, except for Oliver in London of course, for who could match up to Dan? She believed she had not finished mourning yet.

She sighed. Time to go in for dinner. The hired man would already be sluicing the day's grime from his face and hands at the pump outside the back door. Perhaps she had unconsciously delayed the moment when they would enter her house together. Maybe she had grown too used to her solitary life. Yet other women were fighting for independence, rights . . . If she had stayed in London, she sometimes mused, she might well have joined their cause. Essie was full of enthusiasm for it. Yet, wasn't *she* battling *here?* A woman doing what was regarded as a man's job?

As she pulled off her boots to leave in the box under the covered way, the hired man shook the water from his hands and waited respectfully for her to open the door. There were cracks now in the kitchen window but she had hung fresh checked curtains in green and white, and inside the kitchen all was clean and comfortable, with chairs drawn invitingly round the square table. She rarely used the parlour nowadays.

"Something smells good, missus," Joe Finch observed in his deep, slow voice, looking at the stove. He was hungry.

Jerusha slapped down knives and forks on the table, cut great hunks of bread on the board, replenished the butter dish, pared the rind from the cheese. She would soon need to fetch new supplies from the dairy. She sniffed the milk. It would do, if the tea were strong enough to disguise the strange sweetness which meant it would shortly go off. She did not indulge in idle chatter, but wryly acknowledged to herself that she found this man disturbing. Wasn't that *really* why she bolted her door at nights?

'*A charm of finches*', didn't they say? This one lived up to his name all right, with his smiling face, amused blue eyes, even the way he ran his fingers through his springy, brown hair when it glistened with water after his ablutions. Had she been foolish to take him on a couple of weeks ago? A traveller, he must be, she mused. He certainly did not come from hereabouts. When he asked for work she had hesitated. Ready cash was always in short supply, but she was more or less self-sufficient. However, there was the loan on the place to consider; she struggled to meet that commitment each month. He did not require much in the way of wages, it appeared, he was more interested in good food and a warm bed as winter swiftly approached. She had suspected that there was more to it than that.

Her friend and neighbour Polly Pepper had seen it too. "People'll talk, Ru. And a woman living on her own, particularly a young 'un like you, needs to take care. You get me?" After all, *she* knew the ways of wandering men only too well, with Bart to show for it.

"I get you, Poll," she said, "but after he's eaten in the evening, he takes himself off to his room, lights the lamp, and reads, no doubt—" She didn't really know.

"He ain't a *real* traveller, then," Polly said firmly.

Jerusha ladled the thick stew and dumplings generously on to his plate. "Enough for you, Joe Finch?" Her voice was husky. Did her hands betray her nervousness?

He nodded, raised his fork to his mouth. "Thanks, missus." She had felt from the start that his use of 'missus' was not subservient, maybe even a trifle mocking. He ate his way steadily through the plateful. He was not lacking in manners, she was glad of that. Early on, she had been brought up properly, like Dan. But she no longer said grace. Her faith had faltered when Dan died.

Then he said, startling her as she took the apple charlotte with its suety crust from the oven, "I wish to ask you a favour missus . . ." His gaze held hers.

Not a loan, she hoped, or she would have to refuse.

He seemed to pick his words carefully, "I have a young daughter, missus, called Marigold – Goldie to me and her mother, I got a message, see, that she's being sent to me;

relations who cared for her no longer able, so I hear. It's an – imposition – to ask, I know that, but—"

"Can she come here for a bit – is *that* what you're trying to say, Joe Finch?" Her voice was unintentionally sharp.

That slow nod again. "It is, missus."

"How old is she?"

"Old enough to work, to help here and there, missus, I'd make sure of that."

"That's not a proper answer! What age is she?"

"Eleven years old, I reckon."

"Don't you know?" Not much younger, Jerusha thought, than she had been when she went to live with the Mastersons. Still a child, but not treated so . . .

"I'll be honest with you, missus. I'm not too sure she is my daughter. When I – came back, you see, her mother—"

"Your wife?" Jerusha demanded sharply.

"Her *mother* said she was a Finch. When you see her, you can make your mind up, same as I did. She'll be arriving soon, maybe tomorrow, friends looking out for her on the way—"

"Took it upon yourself, did you, to tell that chap I saw you talking to earnestly in a corner of my orchard earlier on, that I'd agree to having her stay?"

"You're a good sort, missus," he said, and his smile disarmed her. She knew he found her attractive. Men always did, that irked her, especially when they thought her little and helpless. Even dear Dan.

She turned her face away. "I'll make the truckle bed up on the landing, only place for her. Just a few days, Joe Finch, 'til you can sort something else out – and don't expect me to work a child that age hard, she ought to be in school." No girl should go through what she had at the Mastersons.

"She can write, and read, I showed her myself," he said. He rose from the table, did not attempt to help clear it, for she had made it plain the first evening that his day's work was done when he sat down to his meal, provided he had brought in the wood for the stove. "Good night, then," and Joe Finch climbed the stairs which wound upwards from the kitchen to the sleeping quarters above. When Jerusha went to bed, later, she would leave his supper outside his door on the wooden tray Dan had made, with a steaming cup of strong cocoa. One rap on the door and another brief "Good night." He rarely responded, although the tray always vanished, for he was seemingly absorbed in his private affairs.

Polly Pepper, from her cottage, thoughtfully observed the glimmer of light showing from both windows long into each night. She always watched out for her friend. For her own sake now, not for Dan.

Jerusha trundled the little bed from her room and positioned it against the wall beyond her door. Joe had the room opposite. She tucked in a doubled sheet, added blankets, a cotton cover. There was just room for Dan's grandmother's little chest of drawers at the foot of the bed, for the girl must have somewhere to stow her things, she thought, and slid a spare chamber pot into place, remembering how bewildering it was to grope your way down unfamiliar stairs to a dark kitchen and to fearfully lift the door latch before scuttling down the path to the privy. She wasn't sure why she felt she must do all this tonight. Could it be the worry she had sensed underlying Joe's request?

Had she forgotten anything? Of course, pillows. She was forced to knock again on Joe's door. "I don't want to disturb you, Joe, but there are spare pillows in the cupboard in your room. I need them for your child's bed."

"Just a minute," he said, and closed the door, making it obvious that he did not wish her to see inside. She felt cross at that, for she was not one to pry, but he had insisted at the start that he would keep his own room clean and tidy. The door re-opened and he piled the pillows in her arms. "It is very good of you to go to such trouble. Thank you," he added, seeing the bed and chest in place.

She had forgotten the suffocating effect that feathers had on her breathing. Even as she shook the pillows into clean cotton cases she felt the tightening of her chest, the breathlessness, the gasping for air, the sweat breaking out all over her – then sheer terror as she dropped the pillows and flailed her arms desperately. She must have been making that awful rasping noise for Joe's door opened immediately and he came to her aid.

She was lying on her bed, he had pulled off her shoes, loosened the buttons at her neck, propped her up. He left her briefly to return with the steaming black kettle and a towel, filled the basin on the washstand, then went out again and returned with a handful of dried herbs which he scattered in the water. "Here, Jerusha," he said, using her Christian name for the first time, "breathe deeply, the herbs and steam will ease you, let me cover your head with the towel, support you, don't fight it." His deep voice was soothing.

His arm round her shoulders was strong, comforting. She inhaled obediently. It was a while before her airways relaxed and her sigh of relief was echoed by one from him. He carefully removed the bowl, lifted the towel, let her slip down gratefully on to her bed. Her face was deep pink from the heat, her lips were still parted. The wariness returned to her eyes. *Please don't take advantage*, she silently implored.

Instantly he stepped back. "Leave your door unlocked," he stated evenly. "If you need me again, don't be afraid to call." The word 'afraid' was slightly emphasised.

"Joe . . ." He must have read her thoughts; she was sorry.

"Yes?" He turned at the door. His smile reassured her.

"Thank you . . . What was it you put in the water?"

"A mixture of herbs; only Goldie's mother could tell you what they are, she always insisted I take a bagful on my travels—" he paused.

"Joe – is she—?"

"Yes, she is dead," he said quietly. "I am also alone, like you, missus." Was that a mild reproof?

She disrobed dreamily, let her clothes fall into an uncharacteristic heap on the floor, pulled the bedclothes up to her chin. If Joe Finch should look in on her, all he would see would be her dark hair spread on the pillow.

Tomorrow he would no longer be on his own. He had something precious, a child, who might or might not be a Finch by blood but whom he thought of as his daughter. She was not so blessed. The thought still pained her.

She had doused the lamp, but sleep was a long time in coming. However, she did not fear the nightmare would disturb her tonight. Deliberately, she dwelt on happier times here.

In his room, Joe Finch turned up the wick to shed more light on the table Jerusha had provided at his request. He did not pore over books spread out but gazed reflectively at a half-finished painting. Brushes soaked in a jar of water, colours were mixed, he dried a fine paintbrush and stroked the tip, dipped it in yellow. A goldfinch, that was what was missing, fluttering by one of Jerusha's nut trees . . .

Chapter Two

Goldie Finch had been walking since dawn. "He's gone to find work in other orchards," friends advised. One, knowing more went ahead, returned to impart positive directions. She was unafraid to travel alone in the day, whilst minding the advice to be wary of strangers. She had eaten the last of her food earlier, but she had remembered to fill her water bottle whenever she came across running water in a stream.

She lived up to her name with her tangle of fine yellow curls; her colouring was inherited from her mother, Margaret. Jerusha was mistaken, Goldie was not a traveller's child, but the gypsies who came every year to Kent for the hopping, picking of fruit in season – strawberries, raspberries, currants and now apples and pears – did indeed look out for her as if she was one of their own. Margaret was the only daughter of elderly sheep and hop farmers, had carried on alone when they were gone, apart from the travelling folk's help in the busy times. 'The herb lady' they called her and she was generous with her remedies. They mourned her when she died, unable to cure herself.

Goldie wanted to believe that Joe Finch was her natural father. She was sure that her mother had loved him deeply but he never seemed to stay long enough for her to feel he really was part of their lives. The farm had to be sold up during her mother's fight for survival; cousins had taken her in. When the money was gone, they turned her loose. "Go to your good-for-nothing father," she was told. She couldn't blame them; they had done their duty, as they saw it, for the child of a strange woman who had cared more for her intinerant friends than her decent, God-fearing relatives. Anyway, she hadn't been happy with them, she had upset them by what *they* saw as wilfulness.

At nightfall she stayed out in the open. She might sleep too heavily, be discovered, if she took refuge in a barn, she thought. She curled up under a hedge, her mother's fine soft shawl opened out and spread over her chilly limbs, her head rested on her rolled-up canvas bag. As protection against the elements she rubbed a little of Margaret's precious liniment, which she had brought from her old home in its ribbed, corked bottle, on her forehead and neck. The pungent, familiar odour was a comfort to her senses. She rinsed her fingers, wiped them on the grass. She did not feel alone, for in the field beyond she glimpsed gypsies encamped. If they were so inclined they would approach her. The sound of their voices, the crackling of their fire, soothed her to sleep. She was exhausted from all the walking.

She felt a touch on her arm, sat up abruptly, her heart pounding. The moon was now high and its silvery beam seemed to render everything colourless: the boy who stood there was a study in shadowy grey, but she knew he was dark, a gypsy boy. She felt herself shivering, it was cold as charity.

"You all right?" he asked. She nodded silently.

"Hungry?" She nodded again. Then she focused on what he was holding out to her. It was a wooden bowl, hand-hewn, filled with thick, hot, rabbit stew, still bubbling.

"Dada saw you, said you'd need of it. Here you are." He handed the food to her and was gone. There was no spoon but she blew on it to cool it and scooped it up with her fingers. She spat out a bone or two, but not before she had torn off every shred of meat with her strong teeth.

She said aloud, "That was the *best* rabbit stew I've ever tasted!" Then she put the bowl down, slid back into her hollow and slept. She was unaware that the boy had returned with several thick horse-blankets in which he swiftly cocooned her against the night chills. One he draped over the hedge like a tent as added protection, then he walked away.

The strong whiff from the coarse blankets was the first thing to assail her nostrils when she awoke again at first light. Being her mother's daughter she was not afraid. Her new friends had provided her with shelter. She was grateful.

The supper dish had disappeared and the gypsies were already busy, cooking breakfast on the rekindled fire, they were breaking camp, the men rounding up the ungainly, piebald ponies in readiness. Dogs barked, children shouted in play.

Her new friend approached, bare-footed in the dew-damp grass, a lurcher dog slinking along at his heels. He had brought more food, a bowl of cooked oats, unsugared. She thanked him shyly and he waited this time, rubbing the back of his leg where the nettles had stung him. The bowl was removed and a mug of tan-coloured tea brought in its place.

"Dada says—" the boy hesitated, "would you like to ride with us? We are going your way." He was a tall lad, good-looking in a smiling way, reminding her of her father. He was probably three or four years older than herself. "I am Robey," he added.

"But *how*—" How did they know which way she was going, she wondered? "Thanks, I should be glad to," she said. He turned away, while she tidied herself as best she could. She had a change of clothes in her bag but she would not take off the rumpled ones she wore in his presence because she was not a little girl anymore, her mother had told her so. Her wide eyes, which her father had decreed were duck-egg blue, although Margaret had smiled and told him he mustn't encourage her to be vain, or where would that lead to? regarded the nape of the boy's neck, where his dark hair clung, almost in ringlets. He was nice, she thought, kind.

It was a lovely fresh morning as the gaily-decorated gypsy caravans, called the vardos, were pushed out on to the road and the ponies put between the shafts. The children were rounded up, the fire put out, covered with earth, the turf replaced, the dogs were tied behind the vans to follow at a brisk trot.

To Goldie's delight she found herself sitting up front on the leading vardo, between Robey, handling the reins with practised ease, and his mother, with her hair dangling in a long, oiled plait over one shoulder, a snowy apron over her dark dress and a baby cuddled to her breast, wound like an Egyptian mummy in her shawl. Her companions didn't talk, but it was a friendly silence. Her spirits began to lift. "I will be with you soon, Joe," she said to herself as they trundled in convoy along the winding country lanes with not a soul in sight. Her mother would have been glad.

Polly Pepper flipped the eggs over in the sizzling fat in the big pockmarked pan on the range. It had been a long while before the light faded in the traveller's room last night, but Jerusha's window had darkened early for once. She had not slept well since Dan went.

She thought how happy she had been for Dan when he married young Jerusha. "I miss you, dear Dan," she sighed, as she placed dry bread in the remaining fat to fry to a crispy brown just as Bart liked it. "You were a good influence on my boy. And your young widow and I are firm friends, just as we were . . ."

Bart was not yet back from his night out. She had given up asking where he went. Poaching obviously, from time to time, which was a worry with the game birds in the nearby woods and the vigilant keeper, Ernest Apps, with his gun. Maybe he turned a bit of a blind eye to Bart because he'd had a soft spot for her before she met – She shook her head. Don't think about that rascal, Poll, she reproved herself. No doubt he got his come-uppance.

She put Bart's plate in the warming oven, took her own to the table. She had to be at her first job before eight o'clock. She ate heartily, two eggs, thick slices of bacon, mushrooms with tender pink undersides plucked from the field at the back less than an hour ago, fried potato and the fat-soaked bread together with three slices of thickly-buttered homemade loaf. The last of these she spread with her tart, coarse marmalade and washed the lot down with two big cups of strong tea. She needed to keep her strength up, she always told herself, with such a physical job, but the good food was also a comfort, boosted her when Bart was particularly troublesome. Anyway, she didn't seem to put on excess weight and even if she did, like her mother when she turned fifty, she told herself, she had the height to carry it off.

Bart was strolling towards the gate when she opened the door to go out. There was a suspicious bulge under his jacket. He opened the gate too wide as he always did, damaging her favourite rose bush and treading carelessly on the last of the summer flowers which strayed across the flagged path.

"You can get the horse harnessed before you go in for breakfast," she told him, hands on hips, "and you needn't think you are going to slouch about here all day – you can get on your bike and pedal over to Hogbins as soon as ever, and help me load up the rest of them apples."

He smiled at her and her expression softened. Looked like her dad, he did; pity he hadn't got the old man's strength of character.

"Got a present for you, Ma," he told her, not letting on whether it was a bird or a rabbit, "and guess what I just saw while you were feeding your face, no doubt? The gypsies have been along our lane and they dropped off a visitor for the young widow Jerusha—"

"Mrs Applebee to you," Polly flashed. "And get shot of that lot in the shed—"

"And that chap she's got working there came rushing out and picked her up and hugged her—"

"Who?"

"A *girl*, Ma. Pretty as a picture with bright gold hair."

Polly shivered: *Someone's walking over my grave . . .*

Chapter Three

Jerusha had just come downstairs wearing her old flannel wrapper with her long hair still uncombed and loose to her waist. She had slept as she had not since Dan died and she felt unaccountably guilty that she had not risen as usual at six to stir up the fire in the stove, make the first cup of tea of the day and start breakfast for the two of them. She found the table laid, plates warming and tea brewing. Eggs were coming to the boil and Joe had cut bread to toast. There was no sign of him, but the back door blew open in the wind even as she wondered about the three mugs, the three egg-cups on the dresser.

She had no chance to retreat, to tidy herself, for what might Joe's daughter read into her dishevelled state? when they came in, laughing, hand-in-hand.

"I *knew* she'd be here for breakfast! This is my employer, Goldie." He looked, well, *joyful,* she thought.

"Jerusha," she said impulsively. It had been nice last night to hear her given name, 'Missus' made her feel old and frumpy, she realised. Joe was a friend now.

"I *like* that," the girl said, "but I ought to say I've eaten already with the people who gave me a ride the last leg of the way." Dimples flashed in and out of her rounded cheeks. Jerusha warmed to her immediately.

"Oh, you can manage a second breakfast, I'm sure. Joe, how could you let me sleep on like that?" she reproached.

"You looked so peaceful," he told her, wickedly aware of the interpretation Goldie might put on this. He turned to the girl. "Jerusha suffers from bronchial trouble – feathers set it off eh? I infused some of Margaret's herbs for her, they help with sleeping, too. Sit down, both of you, I'll pour the tea before it spoils and make the toast."

The young woman and the girl eyed each other covertly as they spooned the yolk from their boiled eggs.

She's a lovely child, seems sweet-natured, quite grown-up, Jerusha thought. I imagine she has a romantic view of her father, thinks they will be together from now on. I hope she isn't going to be disappointed, hurt. He's not the steady sort, like my Dan. Yet I can tell he is genuinely fond of her. *Is* she a Finch? She must look more like her mother – and she must still miss her terribly; I know how that feels . . .

"We both badly need to comb through our hair, Goldie," she said smilingly, at last. "Come with me, you can freshen up in my room and I'll show you where you are going to sleep. Let's pile the dishes in the sink, we can see to them later."

Joe drained his tea, pushed his chair back. "I'll get on then."

"You know what needs doing?"

"I always do," he said cheerfully, making her blush.

Goldie sat obediently on the side of Jerusha's bed while she teased out the tangles. "Anyone would think you'd slept in a haystack, Goldie." Her hair was like spun silk.

"Under a hedge!" Goldie said ruefully.

Jerusha provided her with a clean flannel and towel, a cake of soap. "Have you got a clean petticoat, drawers?"

"Came as I was, except for another dress and Mother's shawl," the girl confessed. She had been in a hurry to leave.

"Never mind, I've got plenty. I'll find you some." Dan was a generous provider, she thought, he wanted me to have it all. But he couldn't give me what I *really* longed for . . .

The petticoat fitted. "I'm as tall as you!" Goldie exclaimed. "You're what Mother called a little dot—" she bent over the bowl on the washstand.

"She sounds nice, your mother," Jerusha said gently. "Would you like to tell me about her?" She guessed that Goldie was drying tears as well as water from her face.

"She wasn't small like you, or young, Jerusha, for she was forty-two when I was born—" a tremulous voice.

Jerusha hoped she had concealed her surprise for if Margaret had lived she would have been fifty-three now, if Goldie was eleven years old, as Joe had suggested, whereas she supposed him to be around thirty-five or so. Still, look at the difference between her and Dan.

"I was her last chance to have a baby, she said, but it was too much to expect him to marry her—"

"Joe?" Was she being too curious?

"Yes. But he went away before I was born, didn't come back until I was three, he taught me to read and write then, my mother was *so* proud of me! He stayed with us for a while then he went away and I never saw him again until I was quite big and Mother was already ill. She did love him so, Jerusha – it's *very* easy to love Joe . . ."

A charm of Finches – yes, Jerusha thought.

"Do you think he'll keep me? Do you think he'll go off again?" The blue eyes were beseeching.

"If he does," Jerusha said, "you are welcome to stay with me." She surprised herself, but she realised she meant it. "I should be glad of the company," she added.

"Nice child," Polly Pepper said when she popped over after her day's work. Joe was chopping wood in the shed. "But at that age, with those striking looks, she'll grow up before you know it, and then she could be a liability. Think what you might be taking on."

"I know what life was like for me at that age, Poll, in that foster home. I wasn't told what to expect. If I hadn't had Essie championing my cause, things could have ended badly. Then, I was so fortunate to meet Dan, but sometimes I wonder if I was fair to you, marrying him and coming here—"

"I only loved one man in that way, Jerusha, and sadly, he wasn't worth it. No, Dan, you could say, was a true friend and that's what you are to me now he's gone."

Jerusha squeezed her hand briefly, then gave a "shush!" for the girl was opening the door for her father who was carrying a sack full of split wood. Behind him was Bart, with his mocking grin, and his hands in his pockets.

"Wondered where you'd got to, Ma. So this is the package the gipsies left behind, eh?"

Jerusha still didn't trust Bart. She wanted to like him for Polly's sake, but he was too devious. Dan had had the measure of him, he had helped Polly control her son, but anyway, he was a grown man now. A rogue like his father.

"I'm not a package," Goldie sounded indignant, "I'm Joe's daughter."

"Don't see the resemblance, but then Ma says I don't take after my pa for looks – not that I'd know, eh, Ma?"

"Before you say too much, Bart, we'll get off home and have our supper – it's been a long day," Polly said tartly.

As she propelled him over the road with a firm hand on his back she hissed, "And don't you go getting any ideas about *her* – you could get into big trouble!"

"Ah, Ma, I meant she'd be a little beauty when she was grown a bit, but she's at least four or five years too young for me – I like a woman with experience, maybe a bit older. Now, your dear friend Jerusha, the widow, would do . . ." He enjoyed baiting his mother.

"You keep away from *her*! I promised her husband—"

"That don't worry me. And who are you to be a guardian of morals? Didn't you roll in the hay with my pa, despite being old enough to know better?"

"Don't be coarse, Bart! I told you—" He had really upset her now. That was the reproach her mother had made.

"Yes, you told me *your* side of it. It was harvest and he plied you with cider and was gone before you knew it. Maybe I'm my father's son – can you blame me for that?"

She opened the door, tears in her eyes. "I blame myself, Bart, I guess I always will." Yet she loved Bart dearly, could forgive him almost anything.

"Oh, I like my little bed, it's really cosy!" Goldie exclaimed. She smiled up at Jerusha as she tucked her in.

"Sleep tight," Jerusha told her, turning the nightlight low. Joe had stayed downstairs this evening, she wondered if he wanted to talk things over. "Look under the bed if you want to 'go' in the night," she added. "Good night."

"Jerusha—"

She turned on the top stair. "Yes?"

"I do like being here. I'll help you all I can, I promise!"

"I'm sure you will, but you'll help yourself more if you start school directly. We'll walk down and see the headmistress tomorrow, I think."

Joe was sitting at the table. He looked at her quizzically as she came into the kitchen. "Settled?"

"I think so." She crossed over to the sink where their cocoa mugs were soaking, and put her hands in the hot, soda-laced water. 'Settled' did not describe her own feelings.

When his arms went round her from behind, his hands clasped just below her breasts, over her racing heart, it was so unexpected, she gasped. He rested his chin on her glossy hair. For a long moment she stood very still. She said nothing. She couldn't. It would break the spell.

"You are a sweet person," he said quietly. "Let me tell you about Margaret and me—"

"You don't have to," she managed. She did not turn, pull away as she knew she ought to. His breath tickled her neck as he spoke almost in a whisper.

"I've never looked to be tied down, she knew that. There was no passion on my side, I was just one of Margaret's lame ducks whom she fussed over and fed well when I turned up looking for work and shelter from time to time, just as I did here . . . I was very fond of her, as we all were. Only once did I share her bed, at her invitation. I guessed that she was lonely and needed to be shown she was loved for herself, not just for what she could provide. I went off next day, as I had planned, and didn't come back for over three years. How do you think I felt when I returned to the farm to see Margaret with a child, a daughter she said was a Finch? I stayed on then despite myself and tried to act the husband and father. It was Margaret who saw I needed to feel free again; she let me go. That's the kind of wise woman she was. I'm sad she died, but I'm glad Goldie wanted to come to me, because I had no right to expect that."

"I'm glad too," and now she turned involuntarily.

When they had kissed, she let her hands slip down from his shoulders and she gently but firmly pushed him away.

"I am going up now, Joe Finch, and I want us both to forget that happened – *please.*" she insisted.

"I think it's fortunate," he said wryly, "that you have a guardian sleeping just outside your door! Good night, Jerusha – Goldie and I fell into good luck when we met you . . . I shall behave most properly in future, I promise."

He didn't say he was sorry, she thought, as she undressed. And remembering the pleasure and breathlessness of their kissing, she had to admit to herself that she was not sorry either.

The gypsies had come to their winter quarters some miles distant, beyond the village where Jerusha lived on the outskirts. They were camped in the big meadow near to the river, out of sight of the road behind high thorn hedges and under a canopy of old trees. To the right of the track which meandered to the meadow there was a crudely-fashioned stile, which in turn led to the bridge, and almost on the edge of the water stood the Stilebridge Inn. The gypsies were welcome there – most of the time – unless fights broke out with disgruntled local men who feared they would take their work and wages even though the farmers depended on the summer workforce to garner the crops when the weather was right and everything came to fruition in a rush.

Robey's extended family were a peaceable crowd, not seeking or wanting trouble. They knew they had their place in the farming economy. They would set to woodcutting and other seasonable jobs. They liked it here.

He sat with the men in the evenings now, not racing around and tussling with the other lads. Growing up was a serious business. As he watched the smoke from his father's pipe he knew that soon he would be expected to find a girl, in two or three years to marry and continue the line, the way of life as it had been for generations. So why should he recall a smiling, dimpled face, a fuzz of yellow curls, a girl who would surely mature into a beauty? Goldie Finch – he'd watch out for her he thought, over the next few years . . .

And Bart was out and about too, with Dan's old shotgun, which Polly had taken for Jerusha's sake and thought safely hidden away, and also his poacher's pocket. He was getting bolder with each foray.

Chapter Four

Jerusha lay in bed, refreshed after another good night, bemused, brushing her mouth with her fingers. One day she had been sure that no man would ever step into Dan's shoes, the next she had succumbed to an embrace from one who had already shown that he could not commit himself wholeheartedly to a woman and a child and who had, indeed, walked away from responsibility. But Joe, she had discovered, had the power to stir her, excite her as dear Dan never had. He had been a good husband, she had felt secure and loved but she realised now that he had perhaps replaced the father she had not had the chance to know. Was she being disloyal to Dan's memory? If he had not died, would she be feeling so restless? There was no satisfactory conclusion to be drawn.

Goldie tapped on her door. "May I come in to wash, Jerusha? Joe's gone down to make the tea."

Surely she hadn't slept in again? She sat up in bed biting her lip. "Yes, of course, come in, Goldie!" she called.

Goldie didn't wince at the cold water but she washed swiftly and was soon dressed. She sat down on the edge of Jerusha's bed to lace her boots.

"Aren't your feet sore after all that walking?" Jerusha asked, concerned.

The dimples appeared. "Oh no, Jerusha, I rubbed them well with Mother's liniment to harden them – I didn't get a single blister!"

"It must be – sad for you, Goldie without your mother—"

"Yes, but you know, I don't feel she's far away. Sometimes – can I tell you a secret? – I can sort of hear her talking to me, in my head; it's a very comforting thing."

"I'm sure it is," Jerusha said, as the door opened and Joe appeared with a tray.

"Will you take this, Goldie?" But he looked beyond his daughter to Jerusha in her decent flannel nightgown, for which she was thankful, at her flushed face, her wary eyes. He knows, she thought, exactly how I feel about last night.

"Thank you, Joe," she said primly. "That was good of you, but you had no need. Making the tea is my job. I will be down as soon as ever, but I need you both to leave me now, please, to wash and dress."

The rebuke seemed to amuse him. "Come on, Goldie, we must obey the missus!"

They walked together along the lane in the direction of the school, which was in the village proper. Goldie looked with interest at the groups of farm cottages and occasional bigger detached houses almost concealed by high hedges and stout double gates. The cottages were weatherboarded like The Homestead, with tacked-on porches to protect against the winds of winter; most were well-kept, with neat gardens and washing blowing on lines looped round tall trees.

Dogs rushed to bark at the gates as they passed, and children not yet of school age made mud pies in the dirt where the water splashed from the pump. The cottage gardens were small but crowded with winter cabbages and michaelmas daisies: the farmers hereabouts were loath to part with much land. The tenants did not mind, because there were perks in the way of produce from the farms they worked so diligently and uncomplainingly. These were vital to their survival when wages were so low.

Jerusha wore the smart outfit Dan had bought her for their wedding. She really didn't know why, for she wasn't going anywhere special, after all. She told herself that it was a pity not to wear it now and then, for hadn't Dan spent far more than he could afford? She had studiedly ignored the appreciative look from Joe when she called him back from the orchard to tell him that they were going to the school.

"Green is your colour," he told her. The compliment made her glow.

Goldie was also self-conscious in a warm jumper of soft pale blue which complemented her colouring. She swung her lunch box from its strap with studied nonchalance. Jerusha had knitted the woolly for herself during the long, lonely evenings in the kitchen. Joe commented yet again on her thoughtfulness, "Shall I start picking the nuts while you are out?" he added.

"No!" she exclaimed impulsively, then seeing his surprise,

added lamely, "I always pick the first tree myself." That was Dan's idea: 'Your trees, Jerusha.'

"Ah, you cannot ignore tradition," he replied, and went whistling away.

The shops curved round one side of the village green, the church was at the far corner, the school and the busy blacksmiths forge were on the other side.

They crossed the grass, skirting the tethered goats.

"Are you nervous of animals, Jerusha?" Goldie asked curiously. There were none on the smallholding.

"I have to admit I am. Dan – my late husband – would have liked to keep sheep in the field at the back of the orchard, and maybe a house cow so we could provide ourselves with milk, cheese and butter, but, well, I wasn't brought up as a country girl like *you* were, Goldie. I didn't even like the thought of a dog or cat around the house, but that was because I was afraid the fur would set me wheezing, like feathers do." Her hand went up to her throat.

"Mother said a woman on her own needs a dog for protection." Goldie told her candidly. "I would look after one for you, if you would let me. It could have a kennel outside—" Her blue eyes sparkled.

"You had a dog of your own at home, Goldie, eh?"

She nodded, her lip trembled. "Cousin Florrie had him put down when I went to stay with her. She said dogs have fleas and are always scratching and chewing at the furniture."

"Here we are, this is the school. Goldie, I'll think about a dog – I can't promise, mind—"

Goldie's arms went round her in an impulsive hug. "Jerusha – like Joe said – you're so kind to us!"

After a few simple tests in reading and arithmetic, which she passed with flying colours, Goldie was made welcome in the top form at the school and allotted a scarred desk. She was soon provided with a scratchy nibbed pen, sharpened pencils, exercise book and pink blotting paper. "We never rub out," she was told solemnly by the girl appointed to help her settle in. "We have to cross out any mistakes neatly and write the corrections above. Watch out for bunged-up inkwells, the boys like filling 'em up with bits of blotter. You can make big splats on your copywork if you ain't careful!"

Someone poked her in the back. "Where you from?" a voice hissed. Goldie knew better than to turn round or to pass a note. "Tell you later," she murmured in return. She wouldn't tell her new schoolmates though that she had unofficially left school months ago when her mother became so ill or that she had played truant from the school her relatives sent her to later. She had slipped back to the farm, where she felt somehow closer to her mother, keeping out of sight of the new owners, of course. But if Joe, and Jerusha, wanted her to continue her education, well then, she would to please them, because she did so want to stay on here, with Jerusha and Joe.

Jerusha hurried home for there was work to do. Joe was right, those nuts should be picked. The weather looked grey. Should there be a week or two of rain, the best time would be past. Would Joe heed her request to forget that foolish embrace, she wondered?

She needn't have worried. When she joined him after changing into her working clothes he merely said: "Ready, missus?" and she regretted not being called Jerusha today. He handed her a basket. "Pick the first tree, as you said."

"Joe," she said impulsively, "we'll pick it together – and I like you calling me by my first name."

His wide smile seemed to warm her through, making her glow. "And I know you meant what you said last night—"

"Leave it be, Joe," she interrupted. Then, "Goldie would like a dog around the place – what do you think?"

"Well, it's not really for me to say, is it, but, yes, a dog would have its uses, a working dog, mind, you shouldn't let the girl make a fool of it. A smooth-coated dog, eh, with your bronchials in mind. Why not ask Mrs Pepper's advice?" It was nice he called Polly 'Mrs'.

"I will," she said, and she cracked a nut with her strong white teeth and pronounced it: "Just right!"

They carried four full baskets back to the house for Jerusha to sort ready for storing. "I keep them in the cellar, it's dark and cool there, and sprinkle them with a little salt, but we'll have a basket in the kitchen to enjoy eating now. See that little hole in this one? That might well have been made by a goldfinch! They love cobnuts! Such pretty birds, I don't grudge them their tasting. I'll make the tea now, shall I, Joe? Then will you fetch me a sack of potatoes from the shed? I'm just about out." She didn't usually chatter like this, she thought. But she felt quite young and carefree again today. She had been weighed down with such responsibilities since she lost Dan, she realised, being so determined to carry on here despite her grieving.

"There's the winter greens to cut in the field, Jerusha. You'd like me to start on those this afternoon?"

"Please, Joe." He really was aware of what needed doing next, she thought. Polly could take a load to market at the end of the week. She would tell her friend how useful he was, how she hoped he would stay for a time, but she knew Poll would guess at the truth . . .

Polly had not yet set off this morning. She had been preparing the monthly bills for customers she was due to call on this week. Like Jerusha, she made tea, took scones from the oven, split and buttered them. "Bart!" she called. "Get up you lazy devil. Whatever time did you get back last night?" It was after ten-thirty now.

"Just what *I* was wondering, Poll," said a man's voice from the open doorway. She looked startled, became immediately wary.

"Oh, it's *you*, Ernest. Come in. Cup of tea? I'm just about to pour out." She guessed it was not a social call.

He sat down at her invitation, but his expression was serious. "Someone's taking my game birds," he stated. "Chap's got a gun. The guv'nor gave me a bit of plain speaking when I reported we'd got a slippery poacher on our patch. He said I was to deal with it and not pussy-foot around. Can I have a word with your boy?"

"I won't pussy-foot either," she said unhappily. "Bart, come here at once, Mr Apps wants to—"

Bart appeared at last, yawning widely, still in his nightshirt. "What's all the commotion, Ma?" He ignored the gamekeeper.

Ernest stood up. He was short and powerfully built, light on his feet, quietly determined. "Mind if I take a look in your outhouses, Poll?" he asked.

"Do what you have to," she sighed. Bart lounged there grinning and she was sorely tempted to hit him. But she never had yet.

"Don't worry, Ma, there's nothing here," he told her, as they watched, through the kitchen window, Ernest cross the back yard. Bart lifted his nightshirt and impudently revealed his rolled-up britches. "Nipped in and out through the bedroom winder, didn't I, when I heard old Ernest's voice."

"Get dressed properly, do you hear me?" Polly raged. She rested her head in her hands. Sooner or later Ernest would catch him at his larks and then the law would become involved. Where on earth had he hidden the spoils this time, she wondered?

Joe went into the woodshed to fetch the logs, his late afternoon task. Goldie was already back from school and bursting to tell Jerusha all about her day, while Jerusha was making one of her wonderful apple tarts on the kitchen table. Quite a family picture, he thought wryly. She was so good with the girl.

The sack was tucked away behind a pile of ash logs which Jerusha reckoned gave the best heat of all. Joe pulled it free, untied the top, already guessing at the contents. There was more than a brace of pheasants, that was obvious. He retied the string, replaced the sack in its hiding place. There was no mystery, he thought, as to *who* had put it there, but tonight, he determined, he would watch and wait, after dark. As he had, although Jerusha did not, must not, know, two years ago in this very same place. The night he had washed blood from his hands in the stream beyond the orchard. Then, dazed and shocked, he had walked away . . .

Chapter Five

"Shall we light the fire in the parlour this evening?" Jerusha suggested, determined that Joe, too, should hear about Goldie's day before he could rise from the table and go as usual to his room to shut himself away.

He looked at her in surprise. He had not been invited into the other room before. He had somehow fancied it to be a sort of shrine to the late Dan.

Jerusha opened the door quickly and ushered them in. "It seems a shame not to use the space, the comfortable chairs. Dan and I always came in here when the nights drew in. I didn't want to be in here on my own, I suppose," she added, as Goldie crossed immediately to the bookcase and began to examine the contents, just as Jerusha had done the day she arrived here. She added for Joe's ears only, while Goldie was preoccupied, "You should make time to talk to your daughter, Joe, after all she's been through."

"Don't you think I know that?" he replied honestly.

She put a match to the fire, already laid, and the sudden blaze lit up the room. The resulting warmth soon dispelled the mustiness, particularly when the heavy curtains were closed. The chairs were high-backed, tapestry-covered, old, but, just as Jerusha had promised, comfortable. She and Joe sat opposite one another, seemingly absorbed in the books they had chosen to read. Goldie sprawled between them on her stomach on the hooked rug, propping her chin with her hands, leaning on her elbows, while she turned the pages of a big, dog-eared atlas which had belonged to Dan in his schooldays. "I like to explore in my imagination . . ." she murmured. She glanced up fleetingly at Joe. "One day, Joe, I'll *really* travel abroad, like you."

Jerusha tried to conceal her surprise. A traveller, yes, she had supposed him to be just that, but in the sense of most wandering workers. As with the gypsies, the real nomads, there was a pattern, a rhythm to this constant moving-on, strongly connected to the seasons and the land. There was also a restless band who seemingly could not settle and only worked when they were hungry or the winters hard and the workhouse loomed ever nearer. She shivered.

She suddenly realised that Joe was the first man to sit in that chair since Dan died. She hoped fervently that he had died instantly that terrible night they had had that stupid argument over the one thing that was lacking in their marriage. She bitterly regretted that. In her recurring nightmares since she always heard the scream, *Jerusha*! and was powerless to help. She still could not accept that it had been an accident, but that had been the verdict at the inquest.

A tear dropped on to the page she was supposedly reading. Then she became aware that Joe was trying to tell her something.

"I suspect there's a rat in the woodshed, Jerusha. When you and Goldie go up to bed, I'll go outside and wait for it to show itself. Then I'll deal with it."

"I hate rats!" Goldie exclaimed.

"Oh, so do I!" Jerusha shuddered. After all, Dan had gone out to shoot rats that night, no doubt to relieve his feelings. Rats got into the sheds each autumn, inevitably.

"Joe," Jerusha said, as she tipped the kettle and stirred the boiling water into the cocoa mixture in the jug, "*What—*" she glanced at Goldie, waiting to take her mug upstairs. "What will you use? You see, I got rid of Dan's shotgun,"

"It's best you don't think about it." Joe took his jacket from its peg, accepted his steaming mug and went out.

"May I take the atlas with me?" Goldie asked.

"Of course you may, but mind you don't spill cocoa on it. Goldie?"

"Yes?"

"Where did Joe go, d'you know, on his travels?"

"When he went away last time, when he was gone three years, Mother said he was in Europe, Italy, she thought. But he doesn't talk about it, unless I ask."

"Didn't he write to your mother? Well, surely he *must* have done!"

"There wasn't much point you see, Jerusha, because Mother couldn't read or write."

"Oh!" Jerusha couldn't imagine what that must be like. Reading, to her, had always been a delight, often an escape from unkind reality.

"Joe says she was *still* the wisest woman he ever met."

"I'm sure she was." She cleared her throat. "Don't read too long. I'll be up shortly."

Did she sound like a mother-hen? Her words were an echo of those often repeated by Essie, when she lived with her as a girl.

She crossed to the window, shifted the curtain slightly and peered out. She just caught the glow of Joe's lantern, then even that disappeared from view. It was moonlight, just as it had been two years ago. She let the curtain drop into place, turned and went up to bed. Why was she shivering so?

Joe settled down on the bale of straw he had moved into position earlier. He prepared himself for a long wait, folding his arms across his chest against the cold. He recalled the sadness on Jerusha's face earlier. He knew the reason why. Unclasping his arms, he felt for the heavy stick lying beside him. His hands were shaking. Could he corner the rat, scare it off? Violence was alien to him. It sickened him, and he hated the sight of blood.

Robey was waiting by the stile for his father to come out from the Stilebridge Inn. The lurcher was sniffing about on the river bank, digging energetically here and there. The sudden excited yelping meant that she had found something interesting to her, if not to Robey. However, having nothing better to do, he went to investigate. He shone the lamp on a heaving sack. Rats perhaps: folks disposed of 'em sometimes in the water if they had trapped them but hadn't the stomach to dispatch them. More likely an unwanted litter of newborn kittens – he'd make sure in case it was the latter. He was soft about animals, as his father often said sharply. But he'd open the sack with caution, of course.

The terrier pup was too dazed and terrified to bolt or bite when Robey eased it free from the mealy sack. "Hello," he exclaimed, tucking the puppy inside his matted jersey to warm it up and give it comfort. "Wonder you *weren't* a drowned rat! Dada'll say I can't keep you, I know that, but I reckon you'll make a good excuse for me to call on Goldie, and a nice gift for her, if she'll take you." He smiled to himself.

* * *

Bart moved stealthily, unaware that he was being watched. Joe's grasp tightened on the stick. When Bart emerged from the woodshed with the sack slung over his shoulder and the lantern wick turned low, Joe spoke up gruffly: "I've been waiting for you." Sweat dripped from his forehead, his hands felt slippery on the stick.

Bart was full of bravado. "Have you? What d'you intend to do – hit me? Want me to tell the young widow what I know, what I saw two years ago? Got your girl to think of now, haven't you? Wouldn't want anything to happen to *her,* eh?"

Joe put the stick down. "You'll come to a sticky end without me thumping you, I reckon. Get off home and don't you dare use this as a hiding place for your thieving again – and keep away from my daughter!"

"And you really ought to keep your distance from Jerusha!" the youth mocked him. "And we *both* know why. Still, go back to your bed and make the most of *your* comforts while you can!" Joe should have hit him then.

Jerusha was drifting off to sleep when she heard the creaking of the pump handle outside. Whatever was Joe up to? Had he caught that rat? She shivered uncontrollably once more.

Joe was washing his hands under the gushing icy water, as if he would never get them clean. Memories flowed, too. He had hauled the heavy chain from Dan's neck that terrible night and realised instantly that he was too late. As he stood there with it in his hands, Bart emerged from the shadows and confronted him. He let the chain drop, turned and fled. It all happened in the space of a couple of minutes. Even as he pushed through the hedge he heard cries from the others who had arrived on the scene.

Now he wondered again why he had returned here. It could only mean more heartache for Jerusha. He didn't want that. Margaret always said he turned up because of his nagging conscience, when he felt guilty at deserting those who needed him most. Well, he had felt the need this time to see just how Jerusha was coping on her own. He had certainly not forseen the vibrant attraction which would radiate between them. He couldn't stay here, that wouldn't be fair to Jerusha or to Goldie – but how could he go?

Chapter Six

"Haven't seen much of you since you've had a houseful," Polly said candidly, inviting her friend in from the cold. The nights drew in swiftly now November was here. She tipped the nuts into a wooden bowl on the kitchen table. "Lovely, Jerusha, thank you! I'll shell 'em after supper then roast 'em! Then it's out with the chopping board and my sharp knife, eh? I much prefer your nuts in my Christmas cake and puds to almonds. Anyway, your nuts, for which I am grateful, are free! Time for a cup of tea and a chat?"

Jerusha sat down, wondering what was coming next. "Mustn't be too long, Polly, or the pie will be overcooked, and Goldie gets lost in her books while Joe knows better now than to interfere."

"Staying on, are they, both of them?" Polly stirred three teaspoonfuls of sugar into her tea. Everyone knew that sugar gave you energy and she needed that to keep up with Bart. "How will you manage to keep them through the winter, have you thought of that?"

"I have. Polly, can I tell you something in confidence?"

"You know you can. I don't tittle-tattle, well, not about things that really matter, my dear, And Bart wouldn't be interested in women's talk, of course."

Jerusha thought pityingly that Polly was far too naïve regarding Bart. She hoped he wasn't listening in from his downstairs room.

"He's out, as usual," Polly added, innocently answering her unspoken question. "Can't keep track of him. Well, Ru?"

"I really *do* want Joe to stay – *and* Goldie," Jerusha said.

"You mean—?" Polly's forehead wrinkled with anxiety.

"No, Poll, I don't! I'm very drawn to him, I can't help myself, that's all. And I've been so lonely, desperate sometimes despite all your kindness and help in running the smallholding, and Poll, I'm almost sure he feels the same way about me . . ." There, she'd admitted it.

"Don't rush into anything, that's all I'm going to say. I know you soon fixed things up with Dan but don't forget he married you – he wouldn't have expected you to settle for less."

"I know that. The same would have to apply to any other man."

"You've got my blessing then, Ru. Are you going off to London as planned tomorrow?"

"I am. Nothing will alter that. I promised, didn't I? and Dan encouraged me to keep it up after we married."

"Shall I look in on them, casual-like, when I get home in the afternoon? You'll be back on the last train as always, won't you? I'll meet you, of course."

"I'll be glad of that, but no, Poll, to your looking-in. I trust Joe to work all day without me breathing down his neck now and Goldie helps out when she gets home from school. There's plenty in the larder, they won't starve. Better get back."

"Would you bring up the hip bath, please, Joe?" she asked after supper. "I think it's high time we all had a good old soak. It's hanging on the cellar wall."

"I wondered why you lit the copper," he replied, adding, "I hoped my daily wash at the pump was enough to keep you from twitching your nose! I must admit my clothes could do with a wash too, and I was about to ask you if I might boil the copper for that very purpose—"

"Oh, Joe!" She interrupted, embarrassed. "It's my fault, I've got so used to being on my own, not having to think that others need a change of clothing too – you must change your bed linen at the same time. I'm so sorry, but you see, I've not had to provide for a live-in worker before, I usually just employ lads from the village when necessary, or Bart helps out from time to time. The fact is, I'm going out tomorrow and have a real need to freshen-up. There'll be plenty of water for the three of us. Mind," she smiled, "*you'll* be last, Joe, so when you've filled the bath for us, make yourself scarce!"

"I had a bath every week at home," Goldie said frankly. "I didn't like to remind you. I'll fetch some of my herbs to soften and sweeten the water, shall I? Then, we'll *all* smell nice and also sleep like a top tonight!"

Jerusha and Goldie washed each other's hair in turn at the sink, laughing and chatting as they soaped, rubbed and rinsed. Goldie insisted on infusing pounded rosemary leaves in boiling water then adding to the final rinse. "Rub well into my scalp, Ru," she joked, "they say it increases brain power! I do wish my hair would grow really long like yours." She squeezed the surplus water from Jerusha's hair and wound it round with a towel.

"Curly hair needs pulling straight to reveal the real length, I think. D'you mind if I get in the bath first? It's rather an important day for me tomorrow. I'll top it up afterwards for you, of course."

"Want me to scrub your back? Mother always did."

Jerusha tried to conceal a shudder at the word 'scrub'. "That's all right, Goldie, I can manage, thank you." She hadn't even revealed her scarred back to Polly.

She arranged the clothes horse as a screen with the big towels spread out to warm. "Why not ask Joe to dry your hair properly, eh?" She wanted to say, "It's not that I'm prudish, I don't want to have to explain how it happened . . ."

It was cosy in the kitchen, reclining in the blissful warmth of the water, roasting rather on the side nearest the stove; with the curtains drawn tightly and the back door locked in case a stranger was lurking in the shadows outside.

The herbs were indeed aromatic, even if they did float like tea-leaves in the water. She felt dreamy and contented. Tomorrow was another day . . .

At last she stood up reluctantly, stepped out on to the folded old towel which served as a bath mat, reached for the warmed towel and draped it round her. "Goldie," she called, "your turn!"

In her room, she took clean nightgowns from the press, one for herself, one for Goldie. She hesitated a moment then rummaged at the bottom of the chest. She withdrew a large brown paper parcel, which she laid on the bed. She hadn't been able to part with Dan's clothes.

She didn't usually give herself more than a cursory glance in the long mirror. This evening, she stood still, regarding her slight figure gravely. She was glad that the disfigurement was on her back rather than her front. She sighed deeply, pulled the long cambric gown over her head, buttoned it to her throat, flicked her damp hair back over her shoulders. She tied her wrapper firmly round her waist, put on the old felt slippers which Dan had sewed so patiently by hand their first winter together, and went slowly downstairs, carrying an item from the parcel.

Goldie was splashing and singing happily in the bath. Jerusha paused, draped the nightgown for Goldie on the clothes horse together with the nightshirt she had selected for Joe. "Don't forget to call your father when you've finished with the water, Goldie, and try not to get your hair all wet again, won't you?"

"I pinned it on top of my head, don't worry," Goldie said cheerfully.

Jerusha went through to the parlour. Joe was sitting in Dan's chair, feet stretched towards the glowing fire, face shadowed as he bent over his book. He cleared his throat, acknowledging her presence.

She sat down quietly opposite, leaning towards the heat to dry her hair. In her lap was the mother-of-pearl-backed brush which her mother had given her, an *I'm-leaving-you* present, she thought, still saddened by the memory.

He rose. Disappointed, she thought he must be going upstairs. He paused by her chair. "Shall I brush your hair for you, Jerusha?" he asked softly.

Nodding, she handed him the brush. This was madness, she knew, this encouraging of intimacy. But as the brush stroked steadily, rhythmically through the dark, straight length of her hair, she closed her eyes and dreamed. The sweeps of the pure, soft bristles were soporific. She was *charmed*, bewitched by her resident Finches . . .

Chapter Seven

Jerusha was waiting for the London train. She thought she was fortunate that the station was only a half-mile away from her home, being also on the bounds of the village. The station buildings were attractive, built in cottage-style, with colourful creepers growing up the side walls and always tubs of bright flowers outside on the well-washed platform. From October onwards a coal fire kept the waiting room at a pleasant temperature, even if the wooden benches were hard. Staff bustled about, greeting friends; tickets were clipped, advice readily given. Bicycles awaited the home-coming travellers and in the yard there were carts drawn by sturdy ponies enjoying a nosebag, while their drivers equally enjoyed a smoke. They were there to collect goods sent by rail. Jerusha always considered it an interesting place to be.

Because it was mid-morning, a weekday, there were not many fellow travellers, just one or two farmers' wives snatching the chance of a shopping trip to Maidstone without young children tagging along, for trains were more frequent than the carters' wagons.

A solitary man, standing aloof, obviously had business to attend to in town like Jerusha. Yet he spared her an appreciative, sidelong glance.

Joe, she mused, would be busy right now cutting the last of the cabbages for market, for shortly the plough must work the soil. Polly would send Bart over to help then. Dan always said it was not a woman's work, particularly with the ancient hand plough. One day, he had promised, they would exchange that for a modern version and hire a team of horses. That seemed an unlikely dream now.

Jerusha gave a start, back to the present with the arrival of the train, belching acrid clouds of steam. Doors clanged, feet pounded – there were always those passengers who left it to the last minute. She gathered up her things quickly and went out on to the platform. The lone male passenger held the carriage door wide and assisted her up.

She sat with her back to the engine and placed her bag firmly on the vacant seat next to her to preclude her companion from sitting there and opened her paper. There would be enough talking done later in the day without strangers engaging her in conversation now.

She was content with her country existence, of course, but if only she was still sharing it with Dan . . . Yet surely he would have been the first to tell her gently, 'Life must go on, Jerusha.'

As always, it gave her pleasure to see the great buildings, the busy River Thames, the crowded streets, bustling stores. She was a different person here. Her smart attire, the extravagant hat, the dainty boots were not conspicious now. Today, Jerusha was again a Londoner, born and bred.

After leaving the station she boarded an electric tram to the East End, for she always saw Essie before meeting Oliver for lunch. It was all as dirty and depressing as it had been ten years ago when she first went to Essie's home. Yet hadn't she found security and even love here?

Down the familiar alley, the children still played. One or two, too young for, or maybe dodging school, called out to her cheekily, "Wotcher, lidy, wotcher doin' dahn 'ere?"

"Visiting a friend," she replied with a smile.

Jerusha was expected, for Essie leaned on the gate, watching her progress. She looked just the same, no older, Jerusha thought happily, as she waved a hand in greeting. And she soon discovered, as she was crushed to Essie's bosom, that her friend was just as liberal as always with her use of scent, scorning the cheap and nasty and squirting herself several times a day with powerful perfumes from the cut-glass bottles presented to her by her gentlemen friends.

"Come in, darlin', how are you? Let me look at you. Something's diff'rent, eh? Guess you've got a secret or two to whisper to an old friend?" Essie made an impudent gesture at her next-door neighbour, gawping at her posh visitor. "Don't you recognise little Jerusha? That's right, go inside, Mrs Nosy! Here we are then, Jerusha, my dear not-so-merry widow, look, sweet cakes from the Polish bakers, I know you like those, and d'you fancy a little somethin' in your tea? *Get off*!" she scolded the cat, curled up warily on the cushion in the rocking chair kept for special visitors. "Jerusha don't want to start wheezin' . . ." She replaced the cushion with another.

The poky room was swept clean as always, the table was covered with an embroidered cloth. Jerusha was indeed thirsty after her travelling and gratefully accepted the bone china cup full of the green tea which Essie still drank, but she smilingly declined the dash of gin.

There was a sudden flapping of wings and the parrot which had been watching them from its familiar perch on the curtain pole landed on Jerusha's hat, which she had placed on the table, and eyed the artificial cherries speculatively.

"*Get off*!" Essie cried again, "and keep your distance, Perry my lad!"

"It's *lovely* to see you again," Jerusha said softly. Nothing had changed, especially Essie. "Brought you some nuts from my trees, they're specially nice roasted, and a few big Bramley apples to bake. I wish I could have carried more, but they weighed me down, you see."

"Still determined to stick it out, work the land, darlin'? You know there's always a place for you here!"

"I know, Essie, and I'm grateful, I always will be—"

The opening of the inner door startled her. A young man stood there, swarthy, unsmiling, jacketless, with shirt sleeves rolled up baring his hairy forearms. His hair flopped lankly over his forehead and when he shook it back Jerusha saw that he had deepset eyes under bushy brows. "Who is this?" he demanded rudely. He was obviously not English. Jerusha observed a flicker of fear on Essie's face, instantly belied, so that she wondered if she had misread her friend's reaction, by Essie's reply: "This is Jerusha, she's like a little sister to me, called in to see me on her way to an appointment. Come in, Sergei, and be properly introduced."

"Jer-roosha, that is a strange name," he came over to her and held out his hand, smiling now which transformed his face, yet she felt instinctively that he was not to be trusted.

"I was named for my grandmother. It was quite a common name fifty or sixty years ago," she managed nervously.

"I also, named for a grandparent – in Belorussia," he stated proudly. "I am forced to flee there from persecution, you know, but it is still my country." His use of English was fluent, he was obviously an educated man.

Jerusha recalled that Essie's men friends were usually middle-aged and full of bonhomie. This man was very different. Not Essie's type at all.

Essie obviously felt that an explanation of his presence in her house would not go amiss. "Sergei was homeless, darlin', he needed a room where he could work, be undisturbed. A friend suggested he come here. My front room suits, it seems, as it did you. He goes out for most of his meals, don't you, darlin'? But I willingly make him the odd cup of tea. There's some in the pot, would you care for one now?" she asked him.

He shook his head. "I am busy. I leave you to your talking. Goodbye, Jerusha." He retreated, closing the door firmly behind him.

Why, Jerusha wondered, did she feel so uneasy about Essie's lodger? After all, she had herself once worked in Essie's front parlour.

Essie refilled Jerusha's cup instead. "Now, what news?"

Jerusha found herself telling Essie about her own lodgers. Because of the feeling that Sergei might be eavesdropping, she did not confide everything. Anyway, what was there really to tell?

Essie looked at her keenly. "This is the first time I've seen you look so, well, light-hearted, since poor Dan went."

"I can't hide anything from *you*, Essie! *Or* from dear Polly Pepper, you both read me like a book! But I reckon that, like Poll, you'd urge me to be cautious, if you met Joe. After all, you approved Dan for me, didn't you?"

"Dear chap was a real country innocent, Jerusha, coming to London to find a wife! Such a pity it all ended the way it did – but you *were* happy, you two, while it lasted, weren't you?"

"I was happy, so was he, Essie, but – I never told you – *anyone!* – this before—" she paused, flushing.

"You don't have to put it in words, darlin', old Essie guessed. Given time, which was not to be, maybe things would have changed." She patted Jerusha's hand.

"I loved him anyway, Essie, he was a good and generous man." It was a relief to have confided in Essie at last.

"Then, *no regrets*, darlin'. But Polly Pepper's right, we do seem to have the same view on things, don't fall headlong for the first man to promise more. You'll be leaving me shortly to see Oliver? Going from East to West, sort of—"

"Oh, he'll be wondering where I am—" Jerusha suddenly realised the time.

"Better not keep him waiting, darlin', then," Essie said. It was almost as if she was relieved Jerusha had to go, and Jerusha was sure that the man behind the closed door had something to do with that. She hoped fervently that he was not one of those social democrats or, much more sinister! an anarchist, who had got round the Alien's Act, passed in 1905 during the last months of the Conservative Government, which attempted to control the numbers of immigrants. Vessels not previously regarded as immigrant ships, carrying less than twenty aliens as steerage passengers, were now routinely boarded and the occupants interrogated. However, there were other ways of slipping ashore unchallenged. These illegal immigrants merged swiftly, silently among the London masses, the mixture of races.

Jerusha knew all this because of her avid reading of the London papers, courtesy of Polly.

Chapter Eight

Another journey by tram, a return to a more salubrious area near the oasis of Regent's Park. Not quite east London to west, more central, Jerusha mused.

She took a deep breath or two before pushing open the double doors of the hotel and entering the foyer. She approached the reception desk. A bald man with a high wing collar looked at her enquiringly. "Mrs Applebee – Mr Oliver Smith is expecting me."

"Just so, madam." He pressed a bell and almost immediately a boy in uniform appeared beside her. "Bertie, will you escort Mrs Applebee to the dining hall, please? Mr Oliver is waiting there for you, madam. He has already ordered luncheon for you both. You are a little later than expected," he reproved her mildly.

I could have bypassed you, Jerusha thought, for you must have recognised me, but there are rules to be followed here, too. She meekly followed Bertie.

She still found it quite daunting to cross over to where Oliver sat in a discreet corner at the table for two. A party of people occupied a long line of tables down the centre of the hall; she heard laughter and animated talking – the wine was obviously flowing.

Oliver put down his glass, pushed back his chair, rose to greet her. Meeting Oliver on her mother's birthday was a tradition she never thought of breaking, for it was a tenuous link with Kathleen.

"Well, Jerusha," he said now, settling her opposite his seat, "is all well with you?" He had already gravely kissed her hand. "You smell very fragrant," he added. "Frangipani? Instantly recalls for me the red jasmine of the West Indies, despite the years between." So he had travelled too, no doubt to see her mother.

"The most lasting of all perfumes," she agreed ruefully. "Lovely

– but passed on to me second-hand when Essie hugged me, Oliver!"

The heady scent suddenly made her recall the flowers he had given her on the day of Dan's funeral. He had come, so unexpectedly, because she had not presumed to send for him, although she had telegraphed both him and Essie to tell them of her bereavement, for weren't these two her 'family'? She wrote to Valentine later; her cousin was herself now in indifferent health, following the loss of her friend.

The country folk, Dan's old friends, had concealed their curiousity at the appearance of a man so stylishly dressed, so urbane. He had discreetly pressed into her hand, on leaving, immediately after the service, an envelope containing a cheque, more than enough to cover the funeral expenses. She had told Polly Pepper what she knew about Oliver then. It was surprisingly little.

"Quite well, thank you, Oliver, and you?" she replied now.

"Quite well," he repeated. Then, "There's something on your hat, Jerusha—" he looked faintly amused.

She unpinned it immediately and saw the tell-tale splodge on the crown. "Oh, Essie's parrot, Perry! He's always leaving his calling card in inconvenient places!"

"Here," he proferred his table napkin. "How is Essie? It's a while since she came to see me." He gave nothing away with this polite question.

"Quite well," she said again. It was puzzling, the feeling she always had that he and Essie knew each other well, apart from the connection with herself. Dan had advised her not to pry: 'You never know *what* you might stir up, Jerusha . . .'

"I brought you some of my cobnuts," she fished once more in her capacious bag. They usually exchanged gifts.

"And here is something for you. Open it when we have toasted Kathleen on her birthday—" he passed a small box over the table. "Ah, here comes the soup – consommé – your usual choice, eh?"

They spoke little while they ate. It was never a heavy meal as they always walked afterwards. Jerusha appreciated the delicate flavour of the lightly grilled plaice, for now she was not averse to eating fish; the tiny potatoes drenched with butter, the slice of lemon to squeeze. Oliver drank white wine, she sipped at her iced water.

While she dipped her spoon with undisguised pleasure into chocolate ice-cream, Oliver spread butter on his biscuits with finicky little strokes and added mottled cheese. She couldn't help thinking that his beautifully manicured nails were filbert in shape like the cobnuts. Joe had nice hands too, he cared for them by rubbing in a little lard after a hard day's work. She bit her lip, remembering Dan's careworn hands.

They toasted her absent mother in champagne; the bubbles as always made Jerusha want to sneeze. She didn't really like the taste, but would never have told Oliver. "To Kathleen . . . Many happy returns . . ." Then Oliver added, "I know she would be here if it were possible, Jerusha. Anyway, she sends her love. I shall let her know that you are obviously enjoying life once more and becoming quite the lady farmer and the grower of splendid Kentish cobnuts—"

"Nothing very ladylike about my life and work!" she put in wistfully. "*Why* can't I contact her myself, Oliver?" There, she'd said it at last.

He drained his glass before answering. Unsmiling he told her: "I made your mother a promise that I would always keep in touch with her, regarding yourself. That is all that is permitted. I am sorry, but there it is. Shall we go to the park now? I wondered if you might care to visit the Zoological Gardens for a change?"

She nodded silently. At least she knew that her mother was still alive. She had no interest in her father's welfare. None at all.

Jerusha opened her gift at last. It was the solid silver snake bracelet with glowing red eyes. She forced herself to slip it on her wrist, to say thank you. How could she tell Oliver that the bracelet made her shudder? She hoped fervently that they would not visit the Reptile House at the zoo.

"It was your mother's," Oliver told her. "She intended you to have it one day, when you were old enough to appreciate it, and it seemed to me this might be that day. I gave it to her on a birthday long ago. It was all she had left to send to you, she said. She gave it into my keeping when last I saw her."

Had Kathleen forgotten her dislike of the bracelet as a child? Jerusha wondered. She touched the fine silver chain round her neck. The little hands were sadly long lost. It must have cost much less than the bracelet, but she never took it off.

"You don't like the bracelet," he said perceptively. "It was

Kathleen's choice. It is quite old, possibly valuable. If you need money at any time, you should sell it."

As usual, no bill was presented to Oliver for the meal they had partaken of. He waited for her discreetly in the foyer while Jerusha visited the ladies' powder room, tidied her hair, washed her face and hands and put on her hat. For once she was impatient with the ritual of it all; she wanted the time to pass quickly so that she could return to Kent, to the Finches.

They did not stroll in a leisurely fashion round the enclosures, for the exhibits of the Zoological Gardens were of secondary importance. It was as if, Jerusha thought, Oliver wished to be somewhere so vast, so alien in its way, that they would become anonymous, able to converse more intimately than they could at that hotel table.

She disliked the hard-standing of the great cages, the powerful odours from creatures she considered should have been left in their own environment, however endangered by hunters, whether local or otherwise. She was not sure she could agree with Oliver when he said the gun had lowered their chances of survival in the wild. A pride of lions . . . These creatures, with their rather moth-eaten coats, despite the attempt to simulate their home terrain, were hardly that.

The exotic birds seemed to have adapted, preening plumage which would surely have otherwise adorned ladies' fashionable hats. She was reminded of Perry and the splodge on her own hat: "Essie has a strange lodger," she said suddenly to Oliver.

"I understand that she has many such, who come and go," he remarked. "That leopard, such a magnificent pelt, Jerusha! Would you not like a coat from that?"

"I would *not*!" she said instantly. "I would rather see it alive, even if it is caged!"

"How like Kathleen you are! Well, have you seen enough? Are you anxious to return to the depths of Kent? To the animals who run wild there, eh?"

"Don't mock, Oliver. There are beautiful game birds, working horses, small creatures untamed and free, like the fox, badger and otter."

"But they shoot them there, too, don't they?"

"We may have a dog soon—" There, she had let her secret out with that use of 'we'.

"*We*, Jerusha? I thought you were, sadly, alone since you lost your husband—"

"I have a man to help out on the smallholding," she floundered. "I allowed him to have his daughter to stay too – her mother died recently, you see."

"You are glad of the company, I'm sure," he said smoothly as he stood back to allow her to go first through the exit. "Take care of the bracelet, Jerusha. Well, I shall escort you to a cab, to take you to the station, then I must return to my business. As always, I have enjoyed our time together. The year between soon goes."

A lot can happen in a year, she thought, and I do so hope it does! She couldn't help blushing at her wayward thoughts.

"Frangipani," he said appreciatively again, as he planted a decorous kiss on her flushed face. "How it makes me want to be back there, in a warmer clime. Especially from November until March. Take care of yourself, my dear. You know how to get in touch if you should ever need me. Goodbye."

"Goodbye, Oliver, and thank you for the nice meal." She allowed him to assist her into the cab.

He curled her fingers round an envelope. "Will you buy yourself something from me, for your birthday and for Christmas? Think of it as coming from Kathleen, too."

"I will," she promised, as she always did. She put it in her bag. She guessed that it would be the usual cheque for £50.

Oliver wondered unhappily why he had failed yet again to tell Jerusha the truth. That he had heard nothing from Kathleen since she wrote to them both just before Jerusha's marriage to Dan, nearly five years ago. He tried to convince himself that no news was good news; the enquiries he had made on the island, through a business contact, seemed to indicate that the Careys had moved on. One step ahead of retribution, as usual.

The picture of Kathleen he had always been able to conjure up at will, in his mind, seemed to have merged with the vivid image of Jerusha as she looked today. Now that she was at last recovering from Dan's death, she had lost that wan, haunted look. It had come as something of a shock to realise that he found her so attractive, disturbing, in fact. It was his loss, he thought, because he had persisted in treating her in an avuncular fashion, even though she had grown up long ago. It was too late for a change on his part now that Jerusha had, whether she realised it or not yet, found someone else to fill the void in her life.

It was raining when Jerusha alighted at her station. The place was almost deserted, the platform darkly wet but illuminated by the lamps. No one else from the village was on the last train. It was with relief that she saw Polly hurrying towards her with a sack slung round her shoulders to keep her dry.

"Hurry up, Ru, you can cover up under the tilt in the back, eh? Had a good day?"

"I had a good day, thank you, Poll," she sighed.

The tilt, of greasy tarpaulin, was better than nothing, she supposed. She would have to sponge and steam her hat anyway. They journeyed at a fair trot along the homeward lane until they saw the welcome lights of their properties. It was nice to think that tonight she would enter a warm kitchen and have someone to greet her.

"Won't stop to chat now – I'm ready to fall into my own bed – had a really hard day," Polly said candidly. After Jerusha stepped down and gave a little wave of thanks at her gate, the pony turned of her own accord and trundled into the Peppers' yard.

It was raining really hard now. Jerusha scurried up the path and ran full pelt into a figure coming towards her. "*Whoa!*" Joe exclaimed, and his arms went round her, steadying her as she stumbled. "You're all wet," he said softly. "Come in quickly and dry off. Goldie insisted on staying up, and she's making the tea at this very moment."

He kept his arm round her shoulders as they approached the back door. She did not demur for it felt good and right to be so greeted after a long day out. The Finches were like family now, she was sure of that, and besides, she must admit to herself that she had fallen in love with Joe, however foolish it might seem to anyone else.

Chapter Nine

Goldie rushed to the door. She had seen who was knocking, through the kitchen window. "Robey! I thought you'd forgotten me!" she said breathlessly.

He grinned engagingly. "'Course not. Got somethin' for you, Goldie, comin' out here to see?"

"Why don't you come in?" she invited. Jerusha and Joe were working up on the top field and she had only just arrived home from school. Her first task was always to shift the kettle on to the hot plate to come to the boil and then call the others in for tea and a welcome break.

"Better see what I've got first. You might not be allowed it. I had to keep him a week or two after I found him 'til I was sure he was weaned proper, like . . ."

"Oh, it's a *pup*!" she exclaimed, as the foxy little head with half-perked ears emerged all of a sudden from inside Robey's shabby jacket, then disappeared again as the puppy wriggled vigorously in an effort to be free.

Robey unbuttoned his coat, held the warm little bundle out to her. "Watch out, he piddles when he's excited!"

"So I see," she said ruefully, as the puppy squirmed in her arms and ecstatically licked her face, "I'll have to wash my hands now!" But she did not put him down, letting him climb to her shoulder and put his paws on her neck while he nibbled her curls. "Is he *really* for me, Robey?"

"Yes, is he?" echoed Joe's voice. He and Jerusha had come upon them unnoticed. "Tea ready, Goldie, for the workers? Let's all go in, but I'm making no promises. It'll be up to the Missus, of course, and whether his fur sets her wheezing or not."

"I've thought of a good name for him already," Goldie told Jerusha hopefully.

"Well, we'll see, shall we?" Jerusha smiled. "Better get another cup, Goldie, and fetch the scones from the larder. Your friend's had a long walk here."

Robey sat down awkwardly at the kitchen table. He rarely set foot in a house. But it was worth it today to slyly observe Goldie's face as she cuddled the pup and crooned to him.

"Nibbles, that's his name, 'cause that's what he obviously likes doing best of all! I bet my hair's an inch or two shorter this side, eh? Oh, Ru, please don't say he makes you feel all wheezy? Look, his coat is smooth and he's only *little*!"

"He'll grow," Robey had to tell her. "Just look at the size of them *feet* . . ."

"*Puddy paws*!" Goldie cried. "And Joe can make him a kennel outside—"

"He's too small for that," Jerusha decided. "He can have a box by the stove. That's the best place for him."

"He can stay, then?" Goldie asked in delight.

"I don't see why not. I don't feel breathless at all. Maybe your mother's herbs have cured me," Jerusha joked, fervently hoping it was true. I'm contented now, she thought, for stress definitely contributed to the attacks. However, she demurred when Goldie held the pup out to her.

"One step at a time, Goldie! Robey, you'd better advise her on his feeding. We must get on, Joe." She drained the tea from her cup.

As they walked back to the top field Joe said, "Thank you, Jerusha. You've made a young girl very happy." And the smile he directed at her made her glow, even though a cruel wind blew.

"Not exactly a good-lookin' pup – unlike his new missus," Robey dared to say, as he picked up his cap from the table and stuck it jauntily on his head.

Goldie blushed fierily, but the dimples deepened in her cheeks.

"Got a long walk back before dark, dodged out when Dada weren't lookin'. He said I'd got to split a lot of logs before nightfall . . . Still likes milk, the little blighter, a saucer mornin' and night. Scrape the porridge pot out for his breakfast. He'll wolf down all the scraps you can spare; dry bread in gravy, he loves that. But he's too small for bones, mind." He tickled the pup's pink bare tummy.

"I've had a dog before, Robey," Goldie said demurely.

"I'll look in now and again, shall I, to make sure you're getting on together?" he asked casually.

"That'd be nice," she agreed.

He tweaked her curls as he went out of the door, rubbed the pup's head. He whispered something in her ear, then quickly went whistling down the path.

Did Goldie imagine what he said? Was it really, "You'll be my girl one day, you can count on that."?

Then he turned at the gate and called boldly; "Gotta while to wait for that, I know. Cheerio!"

Bart, lurking under his porch, furtively smoking, a habit his mother frowned upon since he had set his bed smouldering one night, grinned to himself, guessing exactly what the boy meant. "That little peach ain't going to fall into your hands when it's ripe. *Oh no,* gypsy boy," he mouthed as he waved away the telltale smoke. Meanwhile, there was the postman's youngest daughter, not too bright, but delightfully obliging, welcoming him to her bed after her widowed father departed on his rounds early in the morning. And he hadn't given up lusting after Jerusha just yet. It only added to his desire when his prey was reluctant.

"Want some milk, Nibbles?" Goldie asked. She put the pup down and fetched a saucer. *Boys*! She wasn't interested in all that yet. It was enough for her right now to be settling down in a real home again at last. Margaret had shown her it was possible to survive as a woman on her own, just as Jerusha had been doing until they joined her. But she hoped that Jerusha would be able to persuade Joe to stay on. Still, she certainly looked forward to seeing Robey again, he was nice!

Joe excused himself that evening from the now familiar relaxing in the parlour. He had work to finish of his own, but he did not talk about it, any more than Jerusha had confided in them where she went on her long day out.

He examined the finished paintings, leafed through the sketches. He had neglected them too long, he thought. His art was usually inspired by his travelling; when his elderly patron paid for this latest commission, *The Orchards of Kent*, he would be free to pack up, perhaps journey at last to Canada, or maybe Montana, for the thought of experiencing, capturing in paint, such wild winter scenes excited him. He kept quiet, as was expected of him, about his talents and expectations. To those like Jerusha who provided his bread and butter, a roof over his head in the times-between, he appeared to be a traveller, in a different sense of course.

The problem now was, having come back to see how Jerusha was coping with her loss, like Bart's poor creatures, he thought ruefully, he had become ensnared. Yet, wasn't he in a most tender trap? With regard to Goldie, he had shut his eyes to the fact that she was unhappy in that place where she had been taken after Margaret's death. It was difficult for him to imagine shouldering responsibilities, Margaret had made no such demands. He wasn't greedy, but he admitted to himself that he was selfish, a loner by inclination.

He heard the rattle of the supper tray outside his door, but it was Goldie's voice that told him: "Don't let your cocoa get cold, Joe. Goodnight. I'm just off to bed."

"Goodnight," he answered, without opening the door. He would ask Jerusha for an hour off tomorrow and post off the paintings he had ready. Like Margaret, she did not ask questions. But this time he was forced to admit to himself that he was, despite his resistance, in the process of falling in love.

The pup was whining in his box. He had puddled the paper and now he was missing Robey, for he had curled up each night with the boy in his bunk. It was dark in the kitchen and the heat was diminishing from the stove.

A candle flickered. Goldie bent over the box, scooped him up with her free hand. She made soothing noises. "Come on then, you bad little boy," she murmured. "You can curl up on the end of my bed. Where's that woolly Ru found you?"

Both Jerusha and Joe were still awake, lying in their beds, thinking. They knew just what was going on with the pup and smiled to themselves.

In the morning, Jerusha, treading quietly past the truckle bed, observed the girl and pup slumbering peacefully. Nibbles had determinedly wriggled his way up from the foot of the bed to the warmth of Goldie's arms.

Chapter Ten

Jerusha and Goldie were stirring the Christmas puddings. The recipe was a well-tried one, given to Jerusha by Polly, who had inherited it from her grandmother.

Polly popped over to see how they were doing. "Done much cooking before, Goldie?"

Goldie was crushing the roasted nuts on a tray with the rolling pin. "I always helped my mother – she used her own herbs in everything, and homemade wine. Are these nuts all right, Jerusha?"

Jerusha was turning the handle of the heavy mincing machine. The mixed dried fruit dropped in dark dribbles into the strategically placed dish. "They look fine to me, Goldie. I suppose your puds are already tied up in their turbans like eastern potentates and sitting ready on the shelf, Poll, eh?"

Polly nodded. Wishing to help, she weighed out the grated suet and breadcrumbs. "Don't forget the carrot, Ru—"

"Or the marrow brandy! I won't," Jerusha told her.

Goldie added the spices, beat the eggs with a potent brandy which over many weeks had dripped into the bottle from a marrow fed with demerara sugar. Another of Polly's specialities.

"Smells like Christmas already," Joe remarked appreciatively, coming into the kitchen, ruddy-faced from the cold, carrying an armful of logs for the fire.

"You can have a stir, Joe, and mind you wish – *I* have," Goldie told him.

"He'd better wash his hands well first," Jerusha advised. *She* had wished fervently too as she stirred. *Please let Joe stay this time . . .*

Last Christmas, Jerusha thought, she had gone over to Polly's. This Christmas she could invite her here. The only drawback was Bart, of course, but she couldn't ask one without the other.

But Polly, thinking that Jerusha would have company for once, had already asked Ernest Apps to join them for Christmas day. "Didn't like to think of him on his own, since his wife died last spring, and his daughter married and gone to Birmingham. Thank you all the same, Ru."

Bart will really appreciate Ernest's company, Jerusha mused wryly to herself, and the gamekeeper will know just where he is . . .

Goldie, watched by the two women, packed the pudding mix firmly and expertly into the greased bowls.

"Six o'clock now – let me see, four hours after it's put to simmer – by ten o'clock, bedtime, the first boiling-up will be done. Help me clear the table now, Goldie, there's a good girl, and you can wash up while I dish up the supper. Care to stay, Poll?"

Polly helped carry the dirty dishes to the sink. "I'd like to, but we've got boiled beef and carrots to finish up tonight. Well, now you know how to make my old Granny's pud, Goldie. The secret's in the mincing, makes the pudding really dark, no need for gravy browning. See you tomorrow, I don't doubt."

"What did you wish for, Ru? Joe?" Goldie asked artlessly as she let the syrup trickle over her share of the roly-poly.

"We mustn't say or it won't come true!" Jerusha said quickly. She glanced at Joe. Had they wished the same thing? She dared to hope so. She told them, "It's my birthday on Christmas Day, too." He must be here for that.

"Then we'll have a double celebration," Joe put in, moving his plate forward slightly to indicate that he would be pleased to receive a second helping. A familiar gesture to Jerusha, for hadn't Dan always done the same?

"When's your birthday, Goldie?" Jerusha scraped the rest of the pudding onto Joe's dish, and passed him the syrup. Not much wasted nowadays, she thought, with Joe and the pup!

"February 5th. I'll be twelve then – and how old will you be, Jerusha?"

"Twenty-three," she said with a mock sigh.

"Babes compared to me," Joe grinned, "we almost share a birthday, Goldie, I was twenty, two days after you were born—"

"That makes you thirty-one now, and thirty-two soon!" Goldie said. "Old enough to settle down for good," she added hopefully.

There was a long silence. Then Joe rose abruptly and remarked, "I'll make the fires up and then, if you'll excuse me—"

"What did I say wrong?" Goldie worried, when he had gone.

"Nothing, Goldie, nothing at all." But Jerusha could guess.

She sat alone in the parlour after Goldie had gone to bed, watching the dying fire with the lamp turned low. She hardly realised that she was silently crying, trying to face up to the fact that when he became too restless Joe would undoubtedly go. She heard footsteps coming down the stairs, the back door opening. She sat very still; perhaps he would think she, too, was asleep upstairs.

After some time, the door opened and he looked in at her. "The pup needed to go outside. He was scratching at my door and Goldie was wide to the world. Your puddings were just about to boil dry so I spread some newspaper on the table, stood them there – I hope I did right . . . Had you dozed off?"

She cleared her throat. "No. Thank you for saving the puddings, Joe—" Her voice sounded thick, strained.

He came into the room, closed the door behind him. "Is anything wrong, Jerusha? Have I upset you in some way?"

The foolish tears gave her away, although she repeated, "No." She rose from her chair, patting the cushions into place so that he would not see her face. As she had the night of her return from London, she walked blindly into his arms.

He held her close, sensing her need. It was most comforting. "Tell me, Jerusha, please . . ." he coaxed.

Her voice was muffled against his chest. "You're going away, aren't you, Joe?"

"You don't want that?" he asked. He pulled back, cupped her face with his warm hands, looked down into her brimming eyes. His own gaze seemed luminous.

"I want you to stay, Joe – you *and* Goldie – you've made me feel, well, *whole* again after all the lonely, crying times—"

"You're crying *now*," he observed tenderly.

She allowed him to lead her back to Dan's old chair, watched as he gingered-up the fire, set another log in place. He sat, as Goldie usually did, on the rug at her feet, looking quizzically up at her, waiting . . .

She lowered herself slowly beside him, slipped into his embrace, allowed him to caress her hair. No more than that. The firelight flickered, the glow was relaxing.

"*I love you*, Joe Finch . . ." she said painfully at last.

"Are you asking me to *marry* you?" he sounded almost teasing. He fingered a stray tendril of hair behind her ear, a tender, intimate gesture.

She clutched at him. "I suppose so – *yes, I am*! But I *know* what your answer will be!" she sobbed afresh.

"You don't know anything at all, little Jerusha Applebee," he said softly. "Because I *will.* Marry you, I mean. But you have to understand that you can't change me. Margaret knew that, suffered because of it. I need to be free when the desire takes me – I don't want responsibilities, possessions. This place is yours, it will never be mine. It's in my nature, I'm afraid, to keep secrets. Despite what you may imagine, I've not flitted from woman to woman – in fact, I've led a mostly solitary life – but I can't deny it, I *want* you, Jerusha . . ."

She willed him to say he loved her but instead he kissed her briefly again before he lifted her gently to her feet and told her ruefully, "Time to tiptoe past Goldie. And before you start worrying about me keeping my word – we'll get hitched just as soon as you like!"

She lay in bed in a deliciously dreamy state for some time before she fell asleep with a smile on her face. It was almost dawn when she woke again with a start. What she felt now was guilt – oh, not for loving Joe, that was a joy she hugged to herself – but because she knew that, unlike Goldie's mother, she could not, *would not* let him go.

Chapter Eleven

"I think it's wonderful news!" Goldie dropped a bacon rind to Nibbles, hovering under the table. She judged rightly that she wouldn't be reprimanded this morning. Joe had told her himself and her reaction seemed to amuse him.

Jerusha didn't want her to get the wrong impression, well, as far as Joe was concerned . . . "It's not a great romance, Goldie, you know," she said lightly. "We just seem to make a nice family between us—"

"Well, *I* think it's romantic!" Goldie insisted. "When will the wedding be?"

"We must allow time for the banns in church, of course. Let me see . . . I've heard of a wedding on Boxing Day before; we'll ask the parson if he's available then. We'll be taking a week off at Christmas anyway, that's usual, when you've not got stock to feed. Joe, you'll come with me to see the parson this morning, won't you, and then we'll need to go to Maidstone to tell the bank . . ."

Joe spread marmalade on his toast. He had gone quiet again, Jerusha thought, no doubt realising just what he had committed himself to. She must strike while the iron was hot.

"No fuss, Goldie, no party afterwards, there'll be plenty of good cheer left over from Christmas Day, after all—"

"And your birthday," Goldie pointed out with a sigh.

"We must tell Polly, of course, and ask her to come—"

"Not Bart, though?" Goldie pleaded. "I don't like him one bit, Jerusha!"

"We-ell . . ." Jerusha had seen the way Bart looked at Goldie and it worried her rather, but then he had always eyed *her* boldly too, without actually doing anything, she thought. Goldie, young though she was, was fortunately already wary of Bart's sort. Margaret had raised her child wisely.

Joe rose suddenly. "I'll pump up the water," he said, taking the empty pails from under the sink.

* * *

Essie put on her coat, pinned her hat to her hair. She poked the letter into her pocket, picked up her bag. She was just about to open the back door when the inner one was flung wide. Sergei stood there, unshaven, yawning, red-eyed, fully dressed. She suspected he had not disrobed or slept the night before.

"Where are you going?" he demanded sharply, fingers rasping over his stubbled chin.

"To – the post . . ." she faltered, instantly wishing she had said instead 'to the shops.'

"Give me the letter," he said, holding out his hand "I go to the post office myself a little later. I will dispose of it for you. No need for you to go out into the cold air. I heard you coughing just now. *Rest*, Essie, sit down, I bring you a Russian remedy in an instant."

"I'm all right," she insisted, but she sat down obediently. She had tasted his medicine before. Brandy, laced with something which would make her feel pleasantly relaxed, more inclined to put her feet up than to walk along the street, while Sergei did as he pleased and maybe posted her letter when he had determined its contents, or more likely, fed it to the stove. It was only a courtesy letter to the settlement regretting that she had not been well enough to help as usual. As for her gentlemen, they must have waited for her in vain, at the usual rendezvous. She could not write to them. That would breach unwritten rules. Nor would they contact her at home.

Fear rose like bile in her throat. He had been like this since he had an unexpected caller a few weeks ago; one who had questioned his reasons for, as he put it, lying low there . . .

Sergei must suspect that she had overheard that conversation.

"Learned any more about him, where he came from, his family, his past?" Polly asked shrewdly. They were by themselves in Polly's kitchen. Jerusha had popped over to tell her the news when she saw the cart arrive back with only Polly aboard. She could do without Bart's knowing grin, she thought.

She had to be honest with her good friend. "No, Poll. But then, I haven't told him – he hasn't asked! – about *my* past! All he knows is that I came from London, that I married Dan five years ago and that I have been a widow now for two."

"He could be married already—"

"He isn't. He says he never *wanted* to marry before." She was positive.

"Why has he changed his mind, then, have you considered that?

Does he know you have very little money, that you haven't paid off the loan on the holding yet, won't for another five years *if* you're lucky?"

"He came with me to the bank, he knows all that side of it. He's not marrying me for my money, Poll. Anyway, he insists that I retain all rights in the property—"

"Ah, we get back to 'no responsibilities', Ru, my dear. Well, it's your life and I can tell you've made your mind up. All I'll say is, I'll always be here for you . . ."

"Thanks, Poll. I know that."

"And I do know you're too young to have to live alone. I have to admit I like Joe. He's a charming fellow. And Goldie already seems like a little sister to you, doesn't she?" Polly replenished the teapot, pushed across the plate of shortbread. "So Boxing Day it is. I'll have to buy a hat! I'll be pleased to have you use the horse and cart. Bart can give it a fresh coat of paint! You really can't walk all that way to the church – suppose it's snowing by then, eh?"

"Thanks, Poll," Jerusha said again gratefully.

"You going to write to your London friends, to tell them?"

"I scribbled notes first thing, posted 'em off when we were in Maidstone this morning. Essie will be pleased, but I'm not sure what Oliver's reaction will be . . ."

"Stay in bed, Essie, you really don't look well," Sergei told her. He had brought up a tray with tea and toast for her breakfast. She pushed it fretfully aside.

Essie found it difficult to keep her eyes open. She must have had a bad night, she thought sleepily, but the last thing she could recollect was Sergei helping her up the stairs, she couldn't remember undressing or getting into bed. She focused her gaze on her attire. Her nightdress was on back to front, buttoned wrongly. She subsided on her pillows, mildly puzzled.

"You have a letter," Sergei told her. "Would you like me to read it to you?"

Essie nodded, eyes closed once more.

"It is from your young friend, the one who came to see you quite recently, Jer – Jerusha, that is it. She tells you she is to be married again very soon. She asks for your blessing—"

He screwed the letter into a ball, looked contemptuously down at her. She was snoring gently again. The rapping was repeated on the back door more urgently. He went swiftly down to answer the summons, though he knew of course who was calling. He had expected a follow-up to the visit when he had been challenged a short while ago . . .

Essie turned over, briefly aware of his departure. A vague memory stirred. There had been knocking on the door last night too. She must have imagined hearing Oliver's angry voice . . . A letter – where was it? The crumpled paper lay on the floor beside her bed, but she couldn't summon up the strength to retrieve it . . . *What* had he said about Jerusha?

"You'll have a room of your own now, Goldie, that's good, isn't it?" Jerusha said lightly, suppressing a little thrilling shiver at thinking why this should be. Since it had turned so much colder, Joe had moved the truckle bed into her room. She and Goldie talked and laughed late into the night and Jerusha knew how much Goldie enjoyed the sharing, even though Nibbles had to stay downstairs by the stove, which actually meant he was the most cosseted member of the household of course, for the bedrooms were never warm.

Joe had insisted that, as usual, he would clean and tidy the room that would become his daughter's. He had shifted his box out on to the landing space. Jerusha, feeling ashamed of herself, had tentatively tried to lift the lid but found it firmly locked. Joe was definitely keeping his secrets, she thought.

She was disappointed not to have heard from Essie, but Oliver had sent a brief letter of congratulations typed anonymously as always on the embossed hotel notepaper with a generous cheque enclosed. £100! The same amount he had given her when she married Dan.

> *'I shall be unable to attend your wedding Jerusha, due to the usual commitments at the festive season but I wish you well, both of you, and lasting happiness.*
>
> *My good wishes, too, for Christmas and your birthday.*
>
> *In return, I merely ask that you will keep in touch as always. O.'*

She had passed the letter to Joe to read. "A friend," she told him. The money would mean no worries this winter.

"A *good* friend," he commented, when he saw the cheque. But he did not question her about Oliver.

It was the day before Christmas Eve. Jerusha and Goldie were stripping her bed, remaking it with the best linen sheets and pillowcases. "Let's hope we can get the washing dry, Goldie. Don't want it all hanging about over Christmas—"

"I'll iron it for you later," Goldie offered.

Jerusha hugged her gratefully. "Well, let's hump it all down to the copper. Joe's chopping enough wood to last us for days, and he lit it first thing. Plenty more hard work ahead of us today, I'm afraid, and tomorrow, but that's mostly pleasurable, the Christmas baking and decorating the place—" She hadn't had the heart for it the last two Christmases, with Dan gone, she thought.

"And we'll all have another bath," Goldie said artlessly, "for Mother always said you shouldn't get into a fresh bed unless *you* were nice and fresh too."

"She was right," Jerusha agreed. She thought of her clothes for the wedding, her underthings smelling deliciously of lavender, the new stockings . . . She hoped Joe would not mind wearing more of Dan's clothes, she didn't like to suggest that she should give him money to buy replacements of his own. They had had little physical contact since the night Joe had promised to marry her, in fact, he had seemed rather remote, but she did not doubt that he would keep his word.

In the woodshed, Joe uncovered several sacks. The weight of them was suspicious. Bart was obviously into new ventures. There was a paper pinned to one sack.

> *'Don't say nothing, Joe Finch. You got the widow, what more do you want?'*

He replaced the barricade of logs, his mind in a turmoil.

As he emerged from the shed, Jerusha passed him with a basket of washing balanced on her hip. She hailed him cheerily, "Thank goodness for the wind today, Joe, this lot'll soon blow dry!"

The wind proved its strength by whipping the ribbon from her hair, so that her long locks danced on her shoulders, and her skirts blew around her knees. Laughing, she set down the basket and tried to quell both skirts and flying hair. He dropped the sack of kindling, went swiftly to her, caught her to him, nearly squeezing the breath out of her. "*I love you, Jerusha!*" he shouted fiercely.

"I'm *so* happy to hear you say that!" She flung her arms round his neck. "Oh Joe, I can't wait to be your wife!"

Goldie, coming up the path with another load of washing,

stopped, put her basket down too and did an excited little jig. Nibbles danced round her feet. She couldn't wait for Joe to marry Jerusha either, she thought, for she was so fond of them both. To her delight she saw Joe twirling the laughing Jerusha round in a dance of their own, stirring the crackling leaves and twigs underfoot. The bare trees sighed in the wind in the background.

"Come on, Nibbles," she said wisely to the pup, "let's beat a retreat. I reckon Joe's about to kiss her, and that ought to be private, eh?" Jerusha had been mistaken, she thought, surely she would change her mind now about it being romantic? And Goldie, of course, was right.

Chapter Twelve

There was a holly wreath on the front door and three pairs of mud-caked boots by the back doorstep. Woolly socks, gloves and scarves dangled from the airer over the stove. They sat at the kitchen table, with reddened cheeks and noses, numbed fingers warming up as they clutched large mugs of scalding tea. They had been busy all afternoon cutting boughs of greenery. Goldie had borne back mistletoe in triumph.

"You're coughing, Jerusha," Joe said, concerned. "We'll make you an inhalation, won't we, Goldie? Better safe than sorry. You must be well for tomorrow—"

"And the day after." Goldie was anxious, too.

Jerusha enjoyed their solicitude. "I'll inhale all you want, if it makes you both feel better," she agreed demurely.

While Jerusha and Goldie were rolling pastry for the mince pies and sausage rolls, Joe went up to the room he would soon be vacating and closeted himself inside. "Don't ask me what I'm up to, that's if you both want a surprise tomorrow!"

"You know what you're getting from me, Ru," Goldie said, "you've seen me pricking my fingers over it each evening. I hope there aren't too many blood spots among the french knots in my embroidery!"

Why did she have to say that, Jerusha thought, immediately recalling the stains on her dress, taken and burned by Poll after that terrible night . . . She made a conscious effort to clear her mind of the memory. A dreadful accident, an end but also a beginning. She would never forget Dan, but must think only of the happy times.

"There, that's the last tray. Now for the goose, Goldie." Jerusha rubbed the flour from her hands.

"Mother always let hers cook slowly overnight too. The *best* Christmases were—" she paused, biting her lip at her tactlessness.

"Yes?" Jerusha prompted curiously. It was good, she considered compassionately, for Goldie to talk of her late mother at this special time, to evoke happy memories.

"When *Joe* was with us . . ." Goldie finished slowly.

"I can believe that," Jerusha told her. She pushed the stuffing into place, heaved the heavy bird onto the baking dish. "There, when the baking's done, the bird can take its place!"

Goldie's arms encircled her from behind, as Joe's had that night she had realised she was falling in love.

"I shall *always* miss my mother, Ru, but you make up for so much . . ."

The knocking on the door startled them, for it was long dark and past seven o'clock.

"Who's there?" Jerusha called, glad she had turned the key in the lock and that Joe would come immediately if she called.

"Robey. Sorry I'm late, missus. can I see Goldie for a minute?"

Nibbles gave a belated yap. He jumped from his cosy basket and sniffed eagerly at the foot of the door.

Jerusha opened up, smilingly bade Robey come in. "There's flour all over the place, Robey—"

He put his head up like the pup, sniffed. "Smells like a real feast, missus."

"If you can stay more than five minutes, you can take back a few mince pies when they've cooled."

He looked chilled after his long walk. Goldie pulled a chair close to the stove. "Sit there, Robey." The pup instantly leapt on to his lap. The boy's rough, gloveless hand tickled all the blissful spots: behind the ears, under the whiskery chin, the tender pink tummy.

"Brought you a present, Goldie, you and the pup . . ." He fumbled in the pocket of the threadbare jacket, slipped something over Nibbles' head.

It was a soft collar, painstakingly plaited from strips of fine leather, stretching and retracting like elastic.

"You can fix on a brass curtain ring if you want to use it with a leash," Robey told her bashfully.

"Oh, *thank you*, Robey, it's lovely – I'm sorry I haven't got anything for *you*—"

"Seeing your pleasure's enough for me," he said gallantly.

The mistletoe was fastened just over his head. Goldie would never know what came over her: she pointed at it, and before he could escape, planted a shy kiss on his cold cheek. "Happy Christmas, Robey!" she cried.

He didn't pretend to object, as most boys of his age would have done. He grinned widely, showing off fine white teeth in that dark face. "Worth comin,' missus!" he said to Jerusha. "Can I take the pies, now?"

Joe came out briefly to wish them goodnight, and to take the heavy hinting from Goldie about the stockings waiting to be filled, suspended from the parlour mantlepiece. Entering into the spirit of it all, he wound his own sock round his doorknob.

While Goldie went into Jerusha's room to wash and undress, Jerusha gave him a quick squeeze and whispered, "I've hidden the bag of surprises, everything's named, behind the big plant in the parlour. You'll have to fill your own stocking, too!"

She wondered what he smelled of as he bent to kiss her. Later, as she undressed, it came to her. *Turpentine!*

Goldie rushed downstairs to make the tea, fetch their gifts to look at, back in bed.

This Place is Home
by Marigold Finch
Christmas, 1904

read Goldie's sampler, with a delightful little cottage not really resembling The Homestead, but somehow like it all the same.

"Happy birthday – happy Christmas, dear Ru!" Goldie told her. She had made a lovely card at school which repeated the sentiment, a red felt penwiper and a little box, painstakingly covered in a scrap of blue velvet, which she had filled with hairpins. "Will you let me put your hair up for you today – make you look really special?" she asked.

Joe had played his part. In the toe of the stocking was an orange, some of her cobnuts, a bright new penny for good luck all the year round. Polly's gift was touching. A tooled leather folder 'for photographs of you and Joe, dear Jerusha. With much love from your friend Polly.'

Jerusha was disappointed not to have heard from Essie, for she had always remembered her birthday and Christmas since they first met. There had also been no reply to her letter telling her about the wedding. She hoped that Essie was not ill. She did not expect to hear from Oliver again, and she had not. She had put the silver bracelet away in a drawer, it wasn't something she wanted to take out and show the others today. Besides, that would mean she would have to explain why and when.

"New boots!" Goldie exclaimed.

"I hope they fit. There's another present for you on the end of the bed . . ."

She and Joe had chosen the dress that day in Maidstone. It was a rich orange-red velvet – *marigold*-coloured, as Jerusha had exclaimed when she saw it in the shop window. The extravagant puffed sleeves were obviously perfection in Goldie's eyes. She had stockings from Polly and—

"Did you wonder where *my* gifts were?" Joe put his head round the door. "Thank you for my splendid shirt. I will, of course, keep it for tomorrow—"

"Come in, Joe – happy Christmas!" they said together.

"You'll need to get it framed – that's if you like it, Jerusha," Joe said diffidently, handing her a large picture, mounted on card. He sat close to her, on her side of the bed. "Careful, the paint's still damp in places. I finished it off this morning, just now, in fact."

There she was, with her basket brimming with nuts, her hair loose (artistic licence!) and a reflective smile just curling the corners of her lips; then she saw the cheeky goldfinch on the young nut tree behind her. It hung upside down, displaying the yellow and black pattern of its wings, and its bright red cap. Its fluttering was almost tangible, and Jerusha imagined the sweet 'switt, switt, switt' of its call. He had captured an uncanny likeness of herself, like a reflection in a looking glass.

"Oh, *Joe,* I never realised you were an *artist*! It's *beautiful* – I shall treasure it for *ever and ever*—" she exclaimed.

"I'm glad you like it," he said simply. Then he gave what was obviously a second picture, although wrapped this time, to Goldie.

It was not just a picture of Goldie, as both girls supposed it would be, but of a smiling woman with a golden-haired child in her arms. It was a smaller painting, but just as striking.

Joe's hand covered Jerusha's, pressed it warmly, as Goldie exclaimed: "Oh, *Joe*—" just as Jerusha had five minutes earlier. "Thank you! It's Mother and me . . ."

"I painted it when I first saw you, when I came back," he told his daughter. "I took it on my travels later. I think you should have it, Goldie, now I am to marry Jerusha."

"We will share it, always," Goldie said, wise beyond her years.

"Yes, you must," Jerusha said, returning the pressure of Joe's hand.

The spell was broken when Goldie exclaimed, "Oh, no! Nibbles must have sneaked in behind you, Joe. Look – he's done the most enormous puddle on the mat!" Nibbles hung his head. He had actually done rather more than that . . . They would realise that very shortly. But Goldie had neglected to put him out first thing as usual in all the excitement.

"Then I suppose it's up to me to mop it up," Joe said.

Chapter Thirteen

It was chilly in the church, the parson was tired after all the Christmas services, but the holly and other evergreen boughs, the scarlet berries still crowded in every niche proclaimed the happy season. It was lunchtime, the parson hadn't eaten, his stomach was growling, but he forgot his discomfort when he saw the radiant faces of both bride and groom.

The wheels of the cart were newly painted red, too, the boards thickly varnished. Jerusha's gift to Polly, a warm tartan rug, kept the little wedding party warm on the way to the ceremony. The horse wore red ribbons in his plaited mane. Tiny flakes of snow, blowing in the wind, fell on them like confetti, but melted as they landed.

Jerusha wore her sage-green, with the silver chain which Kathleen had given her tucked inside her blouse. Goldie, her marigold velvet frock with her mother's shawl, the warm stockings from Polly and her fine new boots. Joe looked uncomfortable in Dan's best suit, worn only once, on *his* wedding day, but Jerusha did not tell him that. She was glad she had bought him the expensive cotton shirt and cufflinks, her wedding gift to him, for the sleeves of his jacket were on the short side. His hair, like Goldie's, corkscrewed in the damp air. She felt full of love for him. She wore the kid gloves with pearl buttons he had somehow bought without her knowing that day they went to Maidstone, and they were precious to her because she knew he must have spent all his wages on them.

Bart held the reins, and his mother sat next to Ernest, for they were to participate in and witness the marriage.

It was a plain service, no music, no bells, no choir as there had been at her first wedding, even though Jerusha and Dan had thought that a simple affair, for the arrangements had been so hurried, and anyway, the choristers and bellringers were enjoying a day of relaxation after their busy Christmas. The only breath-catching moment occurred when the wedding ring was to be placed on the open prayer book. Quickly, Jerusha slipped off the gold band so recently transferred to her right hand, the ring which Dan had placed so proudly on her finger. She passed it quickly to Ernest, acting as best man, while Polly gave her away. So she was married for the second time with the same ring, something she certainly had not intended. She comforted herself with the thought that surely this was a good omen; her short time with Dan had been so happy. She must not think of the abrupt ending . . .

They were man and wife – somehow the whole event seemed dreamlike. Then they climbed back into the cart for the return journey. Goldie's excited, "Now you're Jerusha Finch!" in her ear, meant that they really were married.

The wedding breakfast had been as easy to provide as Jerusha predicted. Cold cuts from the goose and ham, potatoes, left simmering, just rescued from boiling dry when they entered the kitchen, like the Christmas puddings, plenty of the chutney Jerusha had laboured over in the autumn, more mince pies and great slices of fruit-laden Christmas cake. Polly had brought over a couple of bottles of her elderberry wine. Bart's face soon became flushed, his laughter raucous as he over-indulged.

"You can get some fresh air, it will sober you up if you come on my rounds with me, Bart," Ernest suggested, but not looking too happy at the thought. It was now late afternoon.

Polly squeezed his arm gratefully. "And I'll get off home, too, if you don't mind, Jerusha – Joe – thank you for a lovely time. It all went off very well, didn't it? You'll work up a good appetite again, I don't doubt, you two. Come back for supper, Ernest, do."

"Thank you for everything, Poll – I mean it," Jerusha whispered, hugging her hard.

The washing up and clearing took some time. Joe had the parlour fire roaring up the chimney by the time Jerusha and Goldie rejoined him, with the chairs drawn invitingly close to the blaze.

"I wish we had a piano," Goldie said wistfully.

"We can sing anyway," Jerusha said. "I'm sure we know most of the carols – how about 'The Holly and the Ivy'?"

A funny sort of honeymoon, with three instead of two, and a lively pup vying for their attention, but in the soft lamplight their happy faces were washed with gold.

It was near midnight when Jerusha and Joe went quietly up the stairs to bed. Goldie, afraid of feeling lonely in her new room, had taken Nibbles with her. There was no sound from there, no light showing.

They kept their lamp low, too, by unspoken agreement. Joe changed in a corner of the room, while Jerusha sat at the dressing table, still in her chemise, brushing her hair. Suddenly, she lifted her hair clear of her back and neck. "Joe, I want you to see this. *Don't* say anything, *please* . . ."

She felt the warmth of his lips moving along the cruel scars. His hands rested gently on her bare shoulders. Peace flooded over her instantly. It was as if she was a child, being kissed better. Dear Dan had sobbed when she showed him her back, then feared to hurt her with his loving. Joe had instantly understood. Although her shoulders were uncovered, she did not shiver as she usually did in the cold room after the heat of the fire downstairs.

"Come as you are," he said gently, taking her hands away from her hair, allowing it to fall, to conceal once more. Her pretty new nightdress lay forgotten under her pillow.

"Joe," she said, when she was in his arms, "I must tell you, Dan and I – we *never*—" Her voice was tremulous.

"I will be gentle, Jerusha," he promised. Again, he asked no questions, for which she was grateful, but he said, "Please don't talk of him tonight. I knew that there could be none of – *this*, without me marrying you."

"And – are you glad that you did?"

"I'll *show* you just how happy I am," he said.

Polly saw the light disappear from the window. She sighed, let the curtain fall. "A starry night . . ." she observed.

Ernest was drinking a nightcap, regarding her thoughtfully. She had not expected him to stay on after the late supper when Bart had sloped off to bed.

"Reckon the young widow's done the right thing, Poll, getting wed a second time?" he asked slowly.

She nodded. She cleared her throat, all this had made her feel choked, she realised. Joe mustn't let Jerusha down; the girl had taken far too many knocks in her short life.

Ernest took her completely by surprise. "How'd you feel, Poll, tying the knot with me? We get on well, being the same age, with children grown. It's lonely sitting on my own when I've got time off, time to brood . . . I wouldn't expect more of you than just, well, sharing my bed. What d'you think?"

"There's Bart—" she said helplessly.

"Ah. He needs a guiding hand. They say a good poacher makes a canny gamekeeper, don't they? He was quite handy to have around tonight. Reckon I'd like to have a go at putting him on the right road, the straight and narrer . . ." He rose and walked deliberately over to her, putting a broad hand on her shoulder. They were much of a height, so it was easy to plant a kiss on her cheek, to catch her with her guard down.

Polly felt suddenly impetuous, just as she had years ago. "Can't you do better than that?" she challenged him with a grin. "If I say yes – and I'm not sure if I'm even considering it – I'd expect to keep my independence, go on working, keep the name of Pepper for that, being proud of it like, Ernest Apps. You know I'm a good cook, and that I try to be a good mother, despite Bart's efforts to prove me otherwise, but I've never been a *wife*—"

"You'll soon learn, Poll!" he told her, with a wink. Maybe there could be more to marriage with this old friend than he'd imagined, he thought, surprised and encouraged by the gleam in her eyes.

Esssie had felt befuddled all over Christmas. She could remember lots of strange faces round her table, her glass being constantly refilled, and music, the throbbing, loud music of her childhood, with rumbustious shouting and laughter. There was much irate thumping on the wall from the neighbours, who had little to celebrate themselves. She remembered trying to light the brandy she had spilled all over the Christmas pudding, but she couldn't remember eating anything.

Late on Boxing night, someone – Sergei? – hauled her upstairs and heaved her on to her bed. The piece of paper still lay on the floor.

Her arm was dangling over the edge of the mattress. She reached down, smoothed out the crumpled ball, tried to decipher the writing. *Jerusha*! Her young friend had been *married* today!

She wept, then sleep overcame her. Downstairs voices were raised. An English voice was upbraiding the revellers. *Thump*, *thump*! came the exasperated message via the party wall. The din ceased abruptly. Then only the Englishman and the Russian were left.

Jerusha lay content in Joe's arms. He slumbered, but she didn't mind being awake. There was so much to think about. She was overwhelmed by the joy and passion of their loving.

"Darling Joe, don't ever leave me," she whispered.

"Mmm?" His arms tightened round her. Then, "Are you trying to smother me with your hair?" It was obvious he didn't mind being disturbed. Her fingers traced the outline of his smiling mouth.

"I'd tie you to me with it, if I could," she teased him, pushing her hair aside and waiting in delicious anticipation for his response . . .

Chapter Fourteen

The top field had been harrowed and the ditches cleared before February fill-dyke, but there was the promise of spring just around the corner, ready to blossom on the old fruit trees; meanwhile the catkins hung like fluffy lambs tails from the hazel trees and Goldie picked purple and white violets for Jerusha on Mothering Sunday and presented them shyly.

Joe worked from dawn to dusk, careful that Jerusha should not overdo the fetching and carrying, for he soon guessed that she was pregnant, although she was obviously reluctant to share her secret just yet, even with her husband. There was the bloom of spring on her too. Oh, she was pale-faced in the mornings, but her dreamy eyes sparkled and she stole kisses from him when he was weary and grimy, reaching up to hug him tightly, smiling as if she could not believe her luck when he hugged her impulsively in return. Yet, he was frustrated too, for there was no time for his painting and the box remained closed on the landing. When the cheque arrived at last for his pictures, he paid it into the joint account which Jerusha had insisted on opening at the bank with her wedding gift from Oliver. "He meant it for *both* of us," she told Joe. It was another shared responsibility, they were well aware of that.

They had been cocooned in their loving over the winter, with the short days, long nights and roaring fires. To Joe's relief the woodshed was left undisturbed. Bart worked with Ernest part-time now, for his mother still needed his help at busy times.

Polly was to be married to Ernest in a week's time, and Bart, believe it or not, was actually being nice to his mother and had even promised to give her away. Joe would return the compliment by being best man and Goldie was delighted to be the only bridesmaid, trusted to take care of Polly's bouquet during the service and to lift her skirts clear of the path when the bride arrived at the church. Polly wanted a day to remember, to look like a bride, "Even if I am fat and fifty!"

So Goldie was inconsolable, when she woke one morning, so close to the big day, to find herself covered in a pink rash, her eyes swollen and sticky, feeling decidedly out-of-sorts and itchy.

"It *can't* be measles, Ru, I had *that* when I was five, I can remember . . ." She wasn't at all grown-up today.

"German measles, I'm afraid, Goldie," Polly confirmed Jerusha's suspicions. "It's usually much milder than the other sort; you may ache a bit, but you might *just* be all right for the wedding." She put her lips to Goldie's hot, damp brow, the best way to test a temperature.

"*Might!*" Goldie wept. She felt too ill to rise from her bed. Aching a bit was an understatement.

Jerusha placed a cold flannel on her forehead, plumped the pillow behind her head, then, remembering the feathers, coughed. It was strange, she thought, she hadn't had a wheezing attack since Joe had come to her rescue that night, although he and Goldie sometimes made her inhale, just in case, when she was feeling stressed.

As she straightened up, she caught Polly's speculative glance. The curve of her stomach, the strained waistband had given the game away.

Outside Goldie's door she whispered, "I haven't told Joe yet, don't say anything, will you, Poll?"

Polly gave her a swift hug. "I'm thrilled for you, I really am!" She stifled a slight pang that it was too late for her to start a second family even if it was a relief not to have to worry in that respect. "When d'you think?" she asked.

"October, I believe. I'm so happy about it, but – I'm not at all sure how Joe'll take it, you see—"

"Tell him, then, and find out!"

"I'd like a little boy, I suppose," Jerusha confided, as she poured tea. "Girls seem to have a tougher time in life. I'm lucky that Goldie's mother was so open with her, Poll; there was nothing for me to tell her, blush over, she accepts it all as the natural way of things. I don't know how *I* would have coped at school without my good friend Millicent . . . But it won't be so easy for her to deal with the fact that she may not be well enough to be your bridesmaid on Saturday!"

"Oh, I'm sure she will, it doesn't usually last long, this sort of measles, does it? I had it around her age, thank goodness, else I might have been a rash bride in other ways!"

"You don't regret saying yes to Ernest, do you?"

"No – but – well, as I told him, I *can't* be just a housewife, any more than *you* can, Ru."

"Oh, I owed it to dear Dan to carry on, I've always been sure about that."

"You're still the boss?" Polly stirred more sugar in her tea. Blow the waistline – at least she'd look slimmer than Jerusha in the coming months, she smiled to herself.

"I suppose I am. Joe wanted it that way."

She had to tell him now she'd confided in Polly. She waited until she had settled a feverish Goldie for the night, having gently swabbed the most troublesome patches with a well-tried remedy, a cool solution of bicarbonate of soda dissolved in water.

"Joe—" He was already in bed, hands clasped behind his head, watching as she braided her hair, something she had taken to doing quite recently. Old habits died hard, she divested herself of the chemise under cover of the voluminous nightgown. She didn't mind his amused smile.

"Yes, Jerusha?" He never called her Ru, he'd told her that he loved her name, always thought of her as that.

She came slowly towards the bed, lay down beside him. He did not immediately put his arms round her, as he usually did. "Give me your hands," she whispered.

He allowed her to guide them round the gentle swell of her abdomen. Then he pulled her close and kissed the top of her head. "Did you imagine I wouldn't guess?" he whispered.

"You – don't mind? I'm tying a *stronger* knot, Joe—"

"D'you want me to yell again, like I did that day, and tell the world? *I love you, Jerusha Finch!*" But he said it this time for her ears alone, then cuddled her close.

I belong to this charm of finches, she thought, so does our baby. Surely he'll *never* leave us now?

On the day before Polly's wedding, Goldie did indeed seem her old self, delighted to be able to carry out her duties. It was Jerusha who felt tired and off-colour; concerned, Joe said sternly that she must rest.

She saw Goldie eyeing her speculatively and decided that it was time for them to spill the beans. "Goldie, how would you like a little brother or sister?" she asked casually.

Goldie squealed with delight, frightening Nibbles who had

grown into his paws as Robey said he would, and matched his mistress for leggy adolescence. He crouched under her chair, whining reproachfully.

Joe fetched a footstool for Jerusha. They were having toast for tea, round the parlour fire.

"Now I *know* it's true!" Goldie cried, seeing him lift Jerusha's feet and place them on the stool. "It's the best news since you told me you and Joe weren't at all romantic – but I just *knew* you were!"

"She has to take special care right now, things can go wrong in the early stages." Polly had told Joe that. He felt guilty that he hadn't been there for Margaret when she was expecting Goldie.

"Don't worry, I'm fine!" Jerusha interrupted Joe.

Following a restless night, when she requested Joe to open the window, even though it was blowing quite a March gale outside, she woke to see Joe, propped on one elbow, looking down at her flushed face with a rueful expression.

"What's the matter, Joe?" She tried to struggle up, but didn't seem to have the strength. She *must* get up, for it was dear Poll's wedding morning!

"Darling Jerusha, I don't know how to tell you, but I must. The German army of spots has invaded you, too, it seems!" The wretch was actually laughing!

"Oh, *no!*" she groaned. She felt tears welling in her eyes. "You two must go to Poll's wedding, even if I can't – oh, promise me you will, Joe!"

"We'll see. Goldie can go in any event. Fortunately it's usually a mild complaint, and if you rest the baby should be all right."

Despite the reassuring words she immediately felt alarmed.

"Joe, you don't really think he'll be affected, do you?"

"Don't you *ever* listen to what I say?" he asked her fondly. "It's just a childish infection. Look how quickly Goldie has recovered – and *you're* not so old, after all – just be glad you're not having to minister to *me*, I'm a tiresome patient! If you didn't look so awful, I'd say, wrap up warmly and go today."

"What do you mean, *awful*?"

"Exactly what I say! Now, stay where you are and I'll go downstairs and see to everything. Both my girls can have breakfast in bed this morning, eh? And it's time that hound was persuaded out of doors."

"*You* must go, Joe, you can't let Ernest down! Please! I promise to stay in bed all the while you're away."

She kept her promise and slept away the hour or so they were gone. Unlike their quiet wedding, Polly and Ernest had splashed out. The cottage opposite was packed with relatives and friends all eager to partake of Polly's generous wedding breakfast. Polly had got her way; she and Ernest – and Bart – would live there, not in the game-keeper's cottage.

"You stay as long as you like, Goldie," Joe told her, "but keep wrapped-up – you don't want a chill on top of that old german measles – I'll get back to our invalid and make her a bowl of broth."

"Give her our love!" Polly cried. She looked young and carefree today, splendidly curved in blue velvet with lacy collar and cuffs, pearl drops, the bridegroom's gift, hanging from her earlobes – it was obvious that the bemused Ernest could hardly believe his luck in marrying her. He'd had a teasing taste of what was to come in their goodnight embraces, now he hoped that the party would not go on too long. He, too, seemed to have shed years and cares, not seeming such a creature of the night as he usually did in moleskin trousers, heavy tweed jacket, greasy cap with feathers in the headband. Now he wore a smart grey suit with a canary-coloured waistcoat.

It was past eleven when Joe realised with a start that Goldie was not home. Jerusha was dozing on and off, and he had seized the opportunity to take out sketching paper and charcoal sticks. He was getting rusty, he thought with a sigh. He had re-read the letter which had come with the cheque a couple of months ago, which he had put in his box without commenting on it to Jerusha.

> *'I am willing to finance a trip to Canada as you suggested, subject to the following condition: that you pay for the outward bound journey yourself, thus showing your good intent. After all, this is much further than you usually venture. The fare would be repayable immediately I am notified of your arrival. Please arrange and advise poste-restante.*
>
> *I await your reply . . .'*

He was just opening Polly's gate when he became aware of a scuffling under the front porch. He heard Goldie's alarmed cry, "Let me *go*, Bart! I want to go home—!"

He wrenched Bart away from her. She had been trapped against the closed door and was obviously terrified.

"For pity's sake, she's twelve years old!" he raged.

"Well-developed for that, ain't she?" Bart taunted.

"That's got nothing to do with it, she's a child! *My* child! Keep your filthy hands to yourself."

"Wouldn't say *your* hands were that clean, would you?"

"Come on, Goldie, ignore him. If it wasn't a special day for your mother I'd—"

"Thrash me? Tell her? Oh, go home, Joe Finch, and take your silly little girl with you!" Bart turned and opened the door, but before he could slam it in their faces a firm hand grasped his collar and yanked him inside.

"You young turk," they heard Ernest growl, followed by the satisfying sound of a hard slap.

"Don't say anything to Jerusha," was all Joe could manage as he gave his daughter a convulsive hug.

Chapter Fifteen

"I haven't been so spoilt since—" Jerusha exclaimed, as Joe presented her with lunch on a tray. Then she stopped short, adding contritely, "I'm sorry, Joe."

"Sorry for remembering your first husband? Well, you shouldn't be. He must have been a good sort." Kind words, but Joe sounded hurt and offhand.

"Put the tray down, come here!" Jerusha commanded "There – doesn't *that* prove how much I love you?" She kissed him soundly, ruffled his curly crop affectionately.

He responded briefly, then pulled away, placed the tray across her lap. "Hope you enjoy my cooking – well, Goldie made the junket last night, it seems to have set nicely, she flavoured it with a little raspberry cordial. Polly brought over a bottle. I must get on, rain's in the air. You look much better today, Jerusha. I reckon you can get up for a while tomorrow."

"If my legs don't feel too wobbly, I might just come downstairs this evening, so you'd better tidy up, the two of you," she warned him with a smile. "Thank you for this, Joe, I do like a mixed grill."

"See you later then, but stay where you are, tomorrow is soon enough."

She did feel rather weak and trembly when she decided that she would be down in time to greet Goldie from school. It was too much effort to dress, so she reached out for her warm wrapper and felt slippers. Regarding her face in the mirror solemnly she was pleased to see that the rash had disappeared and that the puffiness had subsided. She stood sideways, observing with shy pleasure the curve of her belly. She patted the little mound. "That old german measles didn't get you then, eh, little one? I've rested up as Joe said I must, and now some exercise – well, going up and down stairs – will do us both good, I reckon."

* * *

Goldie was pleased to see her. "Did you enjoy the junket, Ru? I remember Mother always said it was good for you when you were poorly."

"It was delicious," Jerusha assured her. She felt just a trifle niggled. It was all right for Margaret's name to be mentioned, she thought, but since their marriage Joe seemed not to want her to talk of her first husband, which was hardly fair for none of them would be here, in this house, making a living, however precarious, if it weren't for Dan . . .

Nibbles, bounding in to see Goldie from up the orchard, where he kept at Joe's heels during the day, made muddy footprints all over the floor.

Jerusha seized the mop, only to have it removed firmly from her hands and to hear Joe say crossly, "What's this? Why ever didn't you stay in bed as I said, until tomorrow? We would have had the place tidied up by then." He had obviously taken her joking to heart.

She turned without a word, her eyes spilling scalding tears, and stumbled up the stairs, threw off her wrapper and fell back into her bed. She wasn't going to admit to herself that she felt weak and that tomorrow was soon enough to be up and doing.

He did not follow her as she thought he would, and she guessed that he was preventing Goldie from doing so too. Her pillow was damp and soggy, the room almost in darkness when Joe came quietly in to light the lamp. He touched her shoulder in passing, but she kept her eyes mutinously shut.

"Jerusha, are you awake? I'm sorry I upset you. But I was only thinking of your welfare, of the baby . . . Do you forgive me?" He sat on the bed, stroking her hair. "I'm not used to being a married man, I've always been a free agent. I appreciate that I was incredibly selfish where Margaret and Goldie were concerned but I have only just adjusted to being Goldie's father, let alone to this new little unknown one."

She opened her eyes, stretched out her arms, pulled his head down on to her breast and held him tightly to her. "You *must* love us, Joe, me, Goldie and the baby! Promise me you always will."

His voice was muffled. "That's a promise I can make, Jerusha. Whatever happens in the future, just you hold on to that."

Essie was feeling much more her old self. Sergei had stopped – she couldn't help thinking of it as *controlling* her – after that wild

Christmas party. It was obvious to her that he had been given a sound rebuke for his behaviour. He still wanted to know where she was going when she ventured out, though she certainly would never mention her gentlemen by name, for she believed he was not above blackmail. He came out from his room to see who was visiting when anyone called, which made them feel awkward, but the relationship of landlady and lodger was more or less restored. She was even more wary of him, though, than she had been in the beginning. She hoped he would eventually move on and leave her in peace. She no longer made him tea or bought extra sweet cakes with him in mind. And she certainly would never drink any more of his wretched Russian remedies, she thought wryly.

Another letter came from Jerusha, one asking anxiously after her welfare. The news of the coming baby made her happy. It was a long, long while since she had cradled a baby in her arms. She wrote back:

> *'I suppose you will be unable to come to see me so soon after you have had the baby, so I won't expect you at the usual time, but you must not leave it too long before you bring your little one to meet Aunt Essie!*
>
> *Have you told Oliver?'*

Jerusha had not, because she wondered if he would be embarrassed. However, at this prompting she wrote a short letter addressed to him at the hotel.

His reply was also short and to the point.

> *'Congratulations! Let me know when the happy event has taken place. O.'*

Yet another cheque to make her feel guilty because she imagined he might think that was why she had written. She would gratefully cash this one, she decided, for there was plenty to do in making ready for the baby – fine terry towelling, for a start, to be cut into squares and rolled-hemmed for the two dozen napkins required. That would occupy Goldie and herself for many evenings to come. She and Polly could also buy the soft flannel for the tiny nightgowns which the three of them were eager to sew, for these would be embroidered on the yoke and edged with narrow lace at neck and cuffs. And Joe, she hoped, would want to buy wood to fashion one of those simple rocking cradles. She'd drop an outrageous hint to him.

"Feel him kicking!" she winced, as they lay in bed that night. "Polly thinks he must be a big baby—"

"You're such a small person, no breadth to your hips," he sounded anxious. "You really should see the doctor soon, Jerusha, to make sure all's well."

"No need to spend money in that direction until we have to," she told him. "Dear Polly says she'll look after me here, and the old midwife who delivered Bart is still busy, it seems."

His reaction startled her. "Pity she hadn't smothered *that* one at birth!" he said bitterly.

"Joe! How could you say such a thing? Oh, I know he's a bit of a tyke, but he seems to have improved since Ernest has been keeping an eye on him. Polly's really relieved. Says it's the best thing that could have happened all round, her marrying Ernest at last."

Perhaps he should have warned her, he thought, that Bart had had designs on Goldie the night of Poll and Ernest's wedding. Still, Goldie gave him an even wider berth than she had before. She was a sensible girl but like all young women she was vulnerable. He was grateful for the presence of the stolid, vigilant Ernest. Also for the fact that now Jerusha was pregnant Bart never gave her a second glance, which was a relief. It had also become common knowledge that Bart had an obliging woman friend . . .

Joe was becoming restless, no doubt about that. The timing was wrong, but then it always was. Perhaps if the baby hadn't come so soon into their marriage, he agonised, for their love-making had been so fulfilling to them both, if it had been just the two of them, well, who knows? Maybe they would have left all this and gone travelling together. Their feelings were so strong for each other he believed Jerusha would have wanted that rather than lose him. He loved her, he was positive he always would, but the baby, when born, would naturally have to come first, for that was the way with women. It was all she talked of now, Goldie too, not meaning to exclude him, but doing so all the same. Sometimes he was glad to leave them to it, while he fashioned the baby's cradle, to Jerusha's specifications, in the old woodshed where he had cleared a space to work in. But there was another craft he longed to be busy with: his painting. He could not tell Jerusha how important it was to him, or about the opportunity he could have seized if the time had been right . . .

Chapter Sixteen

"Gettin' a big old dog, ain't he?" Robey had almost been bowled over by Nibbles when he came up the path. He had a brace of rabbits as an offering, in a sack. "Leave off!" he warned Nibbles. "No use your sniffing!"

Jerusha, looking weary, one hand supporting the small of her back, very obviously pregnant now, took the sack from him gratefully. "Saved my bacon, Robey! I don't seem to think as far ahead as tomorrow's meals nowadays." She opened Dan's old tobacco tin. "Florin, did you say? Same again, if you can get 'em, in a couple of weeks? Want to see Goldie? She's helping her father with a spot of hoeing up the top. The turnips and the potatoes are coming on nicely."

"Not long to go now, missus?" Robey was not shy to mention such a natural thing as giving birth.

"Not long," she sighed ruefully. "But *too* long for me! Goldie's a good girl, she does all she can now and promises more when school's out for the summer. Did you ever go to school, Robey?"

He shook his head. "Too late now, missus, I'm near sixteen. Our busy time o' year, all the fruit coming on but we're glad to stay put this summer as the farmer suggested, my mother expecting again so soon, and not carrying well, too. We've just begun picking the first apples."

"We are too, and we seem set for a good picking of nuts this season."

"Call you the nut lady, the gypsies do!"

"Well, I don't mind at all!"

"Think on this," he said shyly. "Should you need a hand like, well, I got time enough to spare for you, missus. It's cheaper to hire a lad, ain't it, though Dada says I work as good as any man. Come on, dog," he said, suddenly aware that this might sound like boasting, "show us where your young missus is then."

The baby's kicking feet, or maybe his thrusting elbows, she thought, caught her under the ribs. She subsided heavily into the old easy chair. Joe would have to skin and joint the rabbits this evening. Around the fourth month of her pregnancy, after she recovered from the german measles, she had been brimful of energy; now all she wanted to do was rest her tired legs and back. She hoped the birth would be at the beginning of October, rather than the middle. She heaved an enormous sigh. Time to get tea, but she must have five minutes sitting down. Probably, she thought ruefully, married life was proving more exciting for Poll and Ernest – all she wanted from Joe these days was a solicitious rubbing of her back!

And here was Polly, with a bunch of summer flowers from her garden, looking like a full-blown rose herself, with contentment written all over her. Not hot and perspiring like Jerusha with hair straggling down her neck, and about to burst, it seemed likely, out of her sack-like frock.

Polly instantly sensed how she was feeling: the pot was rinsed, tea made, cups set out and the workers called.

"I feel like – *like a lump of lard*, Poll, all melting and fat!"

"It'll all seem worth it, when the baby comes," Polly consoled her. "Here, you have the first cup, you shouldn't drink it so strong."

"I bet Joe wishes he hadn't married me, seeing me look like this."

"Now, just you stop feeling sorry for yourself, Ru, it's the heat as is doing it."

"The tea's making me sweat even more!"

"Let me pump you up a nice chill glass of water then."

"Sorry, Poll, I didn't mean to moan."

"If you can't let your hair down with an old friend . . . And as for Joe, he'll be besotted with that baby when he sees it, I know it. He's a gentle sort, you've always said so, I can just picture him with your little one up on his shoulder."

"I always feel better for seeing you, Poll," Jerusha said gratefully, "but I have to face up to the fact that Joe's not been exactly the perfect father in the past—"

She could have bitten her tongue when she saw Joe in the doorway. She knew he must have heard what she said, because the hurt in his eyes was all too revealing.

"Joe," she said helplessly.

"Would you pass me my cup please?" he said gruffly, "I haven't time to sit talking idly today."

They lay together yet apart in bed that night. He resolutely kept his back turned to her. She gulped back the tears. If only she could take back what she had said – even if it was true!

After a while he spoke, but did not face her. "Jerusha, are you awake?"

"You know I am."

"What you said – I can't deny it—"

"Joe, I'm *so* sorry!"

"So am I. Because I am going to ask you to let me go away, with your blessing, just for a while – at a time when any decent man would ask no such thing – but it was a promise you made to me when we married . . ."

She was endeavouring to stifle her sobs now, for Goldie might hear and be alarmed. "Oh, Joe, would you *really* hold me to that?"

He turned at last, reached for her. "*I love you*, Jerusha, you must believe that, and I will be back, that's a promise I won't break. Young Robey, he can take on my work – he'll have his heart in it – I must admit, I haven't right now. He suggested to me today that if we get really busy, his father could help out too. Goldie's got a lot of her mother in her, thank goodness, she'll be a great help with the baby when it comes, I'm sure of that, and you've got Polly, too, as good as a mother to you. I'll write to you as often as I can and I'll think of you and wish I was with you, holding you like this, I imagine—"

So, he'd already made his mind up. "Go then, dear Joe, with my blessing," and she clung to him as if she could not bear to let him go, ever.

It was not the time to ask him where or when. Every moment with him now was precious, to be counted, she thought. Maybe he would be back in time to see the baby born, but she knew in her heart that he would not.

Yet again, despite the reassuring presence of Polly and young Goldie, Jerusha Applebee, now Finch, was on her own once more.

Within a week he was gone, their joint bank account depleted with her permission, his patron having renewed his pledge to send funds immediately he arrived in Canada. She didn't tell Polly that she was paying the larger share of his passage money for she knew that Polly found it hard to believe that Joe could desert her at such a time.

Goldie wept bitterly while accepting the fact that her father had left her yet again: "It's hard to forgive him, Ru, for expecting you to have the baby on your own—"

Jerusha was surprisingly calm. "I'm not on my own; I have you, Goldie, and Poll!"

"Well, *we* won't let you down!" Goldie cried.

"Bart could help out," Polly suggested. She was taken aback at Jerusha's vehement "*No*!" quickly amended to, "Young Robey needs a job, Joe put him in the picture—" She did not notice the irony in these words. "I will oversee, naturally, and Goldie will be here all summer 'til school in September. Robey's dada can take on extra, he says, and glad of it, it seems. Thank you all the same, Poll dear!"

Polly was partly mollified. "Bart is much less of a problem these days," she insisted. "I should have provided him with a stepfather years ago, but then dear Ernest wouldn't have been available, eh?"

"Ernest wouldn't leave you like Joe has me, I know that."

Poll gave her hand a squeeze. "That's a fact and no mistake."

"Joe promised to write directly he disembarks—"

Polly shook her head. "Oh, Jerusha Applebee, what am I to do with you?"

"I'm Jerusha *Finch* now, Poll, and all I know for sure is I love him and when his baby comes I'll have something to link me to him, *always*."

"Take care of her, young Goldie," Polly sighed.

"I will, Auntie Poll," Goldie promised.

Chapter Seventeen

It was August 22nd, St Phyllida's Day, the day on which traditionally the first nuts, perhaps called filberts in her honour, were picked and tasted.

This was also the day the letter arrived from Canada. It was written in pencil on cheap paper. There were several pages of it to decipher. Joe, it seemed, was in a spot of trouble.

'I have moved on from Vancouver to Montreal. The money I was expecting was not forthcoming, despite my cables. The journey over was a nightmare, like being on a cattle boat. There were some problems with my passport, but these are now sorted.

Have to find work as I am pretty broke. There are hundreds, maybe thousands in the same situation: all seeking employment in the lumber business. It would help to speak French! I met a Canadian of English parents who told me the English do not hit it off here, because we are not navvies at heart. He would have laughed if I told him I am really an artist, and came to this beautiful place to paint, not to load timber on the railroad. It is all Saint-this, and Saint-that here, due to the French influence.

Which reminds me of what you told me about St Phyllida's day – I shall picture you delighting in picking your nuts in their frilly green, dear Jerusha.

I hope to have an address for you to write to me soon, but everything seems so uncertain here. The only thing I am sure of is my love for you and for our unborn baby. Tell Goldie, too, that I love her.

Keep well, think of me sometimes, your loving husband Joe.'

Jerusha passed the letter to Goldie to read at the breakfast table.

"I don't really know what to make of it. 'Think of me sometimes' – doesn't he realise I think of him all the time, Goldie?"

Goldie held the basket while Jerusha picked the nuts. "Don't stretch too high," she warned anxiously. "You know Auntie Poll said that if you did, the baby's cord would tie in knots."

Tie in knots, Jerusha thought, parting the green to hold the perfect first nut in the palm of her hand. That's what I tried to do to Joe and I failed. Where are you, my darling? On the map, it all seems so far away.

There was a sudden sharp pain low down in her body; she gasped, dropped the nut and looked down. To her horror, she saw a stain spreading on her skirt, felt something warm trickling down her legs. She seemed to be rooted to the spot. She realised that her waters must have broken. She was unaware that she had cried out.

"What is it, Ru?" Goldie's eyes widened as she saw what must be happening. "Here, sit down – rest against the tree – *Robey*!" she yelled. He was not far away, picking the early ripening apples, The Beauty of Bath.

"Don't call him," Jerusha said faintly, "he shouldn't see this—"

But Robey was already there, taking in the situation at a glance.

"I'll fetch Mrs Apps, missus, saw her come in the gate a while back. You stay there, like Goldie says, moving'll make it worse." He was a practical young man, and he had, after all, seen his mother when her labour pains began, even though it was still taboo for gypsy men to be present at the actual birth. "C'mon, boy!" he called to Nibbles.

"His mother's had eight, he's not shy about such things." Goldie told her. She took off her apron, rolled it loosely and slipped it behind Jerusha's head. Then she squatted beside her and held her stepmother's hand. It was a warm, reassuring clasp from a girl of such tender years. It should, of course, have been Joe, not his daughter, who said simply, "Don't worry, I'm here, hold on to me."

"Thank you, Goldie, I do love you," Jerusha murmured faintly.

"I know you do," Goldie said. "I was *meant* to come here, to look after you, just as you care for me, I was sure of that, right from the beginning."

* * *

They couldn't move her. Under the canopy of the trees, Polly comforted her in her distress. Goldie, at Polly's behest, dashed to fetch towels and blankets from the linen press. Robey had gone tactfully out of sight, but within call.

There were birds singing, Jerusha thought, as the pains lessened, then washed over her forcefully again. She was only half aware of what was happening to her, lying on the bed of straw which Robey had fashioned, a bed such as he had seen his own father make for his mother under their wagon for a summer birth. Goldie was holding her hands again, and Polly urging and encouraging her to get the baby born. It was barely an hour since she had proudly picked that first nut.

She felt as if she was being torn apart as Polly delivered her tiny baby girl. Polly held her by her heels and gave her a slap. There was a thin, mewling cry, the baby was alive! Polly heaved a heartfelt sigh of relief. "You'll do, darling! Scissors, thread, Goldie dear, you were so sensible to think of those without my saying. We have to cut the cord now. Here, my dear, you take the baby, wrap her up and go with care – sit near the stove and cuddle her up. In a hurry to enter the world, weren't you, little one? Now, despite the summer heat, you'll need to be kept warm and cosy."

Polly carried Jerusha easily in her strong arms, for she guessed this was something they must not ask of Robey. Jerusha was wrapped well as the baby had been, but she was shivering, teeth chattering uncontrollably. "Shock, Ru, that's what it is, we'll soon have you tucked up in bed, with your little, early blessing!"

The midwife came half an hour later, rather ruffled at being caught out. They left the cleaning and examination of the baby and mother to her.

"Well done," she told them, when she was finished. "Got the afterbirth? I'll need to make sure it's all there. All right, young mother, are you?"

Jerusha, big-eyed and pale, but calm now, nodded.

"A very small baby, my dear, but breathing normally. Still, she'll need watching for a week or two, these eight month babies sometimes cause more concern than the seven month ones."

"I thought – that's all it was – seven months—" Jerusha managed.

"Maybe five weeks early, perhaps a little more – she has her finger nails, see, even if they are soft and curved. She's too small to weigh, but I reckon four pounds. What are you going to call her, had you thought?"

"I thought – it – she was a *boy*. I don't really know—"

"St Phyllida's day," Goldie put in, for she'd been allowed to stay throughout, being a sensible girl and knowing what was what, after witnessing the birth, as the midwife rightly said. "Why don't we call her that? Phylly for short!"

Jerusha looked down at the tiny face resting against her breast. How heavy she had felt with the baby inside her, she thought, and how small and light the baby seemed now it was here.

"Phylly – yes – I think Joe would like that . . ."

He should be here, was the look Polly gave Goldie.

"I can't even let him know 'til I hear from him again but, Poll, would you send a telegram soon to Essie in London for me?" She'd write to Oliver herself later, she thought.

"You know I will."

Jerusha glimpsed the rocking cradle which Joe had made for the baby. Goldie had made it up with the bedclothes they had sewn together. The nighties and napkins were too big; Phylly was wrapped in muslin and soft flannel for now. Silent tears ran unchecked down her cheeks, dampened the baby's dark, downy head. She closed her weary eyes. She would keep the baby with her, in her arms, for now. Her tiny face already bore a strong likeness to Joe. That scalded her heart.

"She should rest now," the midwife said, gathering up her things.

Downstairs, Polly talked to the nurse, while Goldie went to call Robey in for his tea and to tell him all was well.

"Perfect little soul," the midwife confirmed.

"I was a little worried, you know, though of course I didn't tell Jerusha, that illness she had, early on, they do say it *sometimes* afflicts the baby like—"

"Perfect," the nurse repeated. Then she added, "She can see, I'm sure of that; the eyes, I've known them to be affected. Depends how far gone Mrs Finch was when she caught it, I believe. The baby might be a little – *slow* – perhaps, or maybe *deaf*—"

It was Polly who was shivering now.

"Now, don't you worry, Polly, she's just an early bird, that's all, your little Phylly Finch."

Joe had moved on. He was blazing the trail, as they called it, where the endless barbed-wire encircled vast acres. There were trackless swamps, with dire warnings of rattlesnakes lurking in the marsh grass.

He travelled in a wagon to a camp built beside gigantic trees, tall and straight, timber for ships' masts and great beams. There was wildlife in abundance, some of it familiar: foxes, bullfrogs, wildcats and even goldfinches. But there were also great bears and snakes.

There was also dust, sweat and sheer physical exertion such as he had never known before. It was a man's world. He had learned to ride a horse, to wield an axe. Food was cooked in bulbous pots over open, fiercely-crackling fires of chipwood.

He could earn money here, there was little to spend it on for he was not a drinking man. His hands were blistered, but when they hardened, he determined that he would unpack his painting materials. He could not help feeling excited at this thought. Coming to Canada might not prove to be a disaster after all. His patron had died. That news, received at last, had seen him in despair – this was the only way he could see out, if he was ever to return back to England, to Jerusha, his wife; Goldie, his daughter; and to the baby which would be born before long.

Part Three

1907–1909

Chapter One

Little Phylly Finch, at twenty months old, appeared to be an enchanting child, with hair which curled like her sister's, but was darker in colour like her father's. She resembled Joe so much that sometimes Jerusha found it difficult to look at her without sudden tears. Joe had betrayed her trust, she thought sadly, for the last letter she had received had been the day Phylly arrived so unexpectedly. The hardest thing to bear was the knowledge that Joe did not know he had a second daughter. History was repeating itself. She knew now exactly how Goldie's mother must have felt, bringing Goldie up alone for the first three years of her life.

Goldie, of course, had been a bright and loving child. At fourteen years old she had not lost these characteristics and to Jerusha, she had been the greatest comfort and, despite her youth, as steady as a rock.

Jerusha thought, I would have gone under long ago, if it had not been for Goldie . . . The girl had insisted on leaving school last Christmas and, with the faithful Robey shouldering all the work which needed greater physical strength, she had taken on the day-to-day running of the smallholding, while Jerusha cared for Phylly.

Phylly had been a fretful baby and was now, as a toddler, prone to exhausting tantrums, high-pitched screaming and wilfulness. Occasionally she held her breath when she was in one of her paddies until she was blue in the face and then lapsed into unconsciousness. These episodes had terrified Jerusha at first, but she had learned that Phylly would just as suddenly revive, limp and pale but now, mercifully, quiet. Jerusha thought dully that she couldn't remember the last time she had a good night's sleep.

There was a reason for all this, of course. It had been a terrible shock when Jerusha discovered that her baby was deaf. To what extent she still did not know. On a sunny April day last year, when Phylly was eight months old, at Polly's suggestion she spread a rug under the trees and they watched, smiling, as the baby made a determined effort to crawl towards them. At that moment, Nibbles, tired of trailing after Goldie and Robey in the field, came racing back down the orchard, barking shrilly and excitedly at the unfamiliar: Phylly's rounded back view, as she pulled herself up on to her knees.

Even as Jerusha reprimanded the dog, she realised that Phylly had not even flinched at the noise Nibbles had been making. That because she had not seen the dog, she was unaware that he was there.

"*She can't hear, Poll*!" she cried.

Polly said quietly, "My dear, I was afraid of that . . ."

It was April, 1907. Over seven years since Jerusha Finch came to this place as Dan Applebee's bride. Two years and four months since she married Joe and this summer it would be two years since he left her before Phylly was born. She didn't need to look at the dates she had written in her diaries, a habit she had kept up since Kathleen gave her the first little book before she went away. In those early days, she had found it helped to write down her worries and later, happy days with Essie and then with Dan, when she noted down her discoveries as she settled into a farming life. The last full entry she had made was on the day she faced the truth about her daughter's disability.

Now she watched from the path as Goldie came romping towards her with her little sister on her back. Phylly was crowing with excitement, her hands tight round Goldie's neck, almost throttling her. They had gone up to the field to watch Robey at work with his hoe.

Jerusha smiled to see Phylly so happy, so animated. She was beginning to talk in her own way now, which was a great relief, for as Polly said, it was possible that she might be able to hear some sounds. Jerusha was not so sure; sometimes Phylly's lips would purse, her throat would pulse, her eyes spill frustrated tears as she tried to communicate. Polly did not tell Jerusha that these baby babblings were unlike the first sounds which she remembered her own child making, at an earlier stage.

Goldie really was a golden girl now, Jerusha thought, with a rush of affection for her. She was tall, carried herself well, unselfconscious about her full bosom, her neat waist and her smooth, serene face. She was mature for her age, in mind as well as body. Jerusha's secret worry was Robey, so obviously adoring: would he, at eighteen, be prepared to continue his long wait?

"Phylly's come to wish her mummy a lovely day out and not to hurry back!" Goldie cried.

"I'm still not sure I ought to leave you, you know. Phylly is a real responsibility—"

"I can manage, honestly, Ru! You do so need some time to yourself. I'll keep an eye on her all the time, I promise. Robey will see to everything else. Look, Auntie Poll's at the gate – your conveyance is here, madam! Off you go."

Jerusha kissed them both, then hurried down the drive, so that they wouldn't see that she was crying just a little, torn between going to London and seeing Essie and Oliver and staying with Phylly. She had never left her before. Essie had visited them last spring, but Oliver had not come, although he kept in touch and was generous with his financial support as always. She was only going to London at his request. She had been saddened a few weeks ago to learn of Valentine's death. Oliver, as her cousin's executor, wished to tell her personally of a bequest. She and Valentine had corresponded faithfully over the years, but, in fact, they had never managed to meet since Jerusha left Copper Leas. Jerusha had been so hoping that this would change, when Valentine wrote to say that her companion had died, that her years of faithful nursing were at an end. But Valentine's own frail health had precluded that.

"Don't worry, Ru," Polly said perceptively, as they journeyed toward the station. "Goldie won't let you down. She'll have her hands full with the baby and Robey won't take advantage. I will be around today and will look in from time to time, I promise."

"How well you know me, Poll! I really do think those two were meant for each other – but not yet, of course. And, later, well, there could be opposition from his family, I suppose—"

"They haven't stopped him working for you regular like, have they? As long as he lives in the gypsy camp and follows their way of life, and marries a girl, according to their custom, who's prepared to do the same, Robey won't be cast out, I think.

"Talking of casting out, Ernest has been grumbling lately that it's time I gave my Bart a push. After all, he's twenty-one now and has never bothered to get a regular job. Ernest reckons he'll never be reliable, we've done our best, and that should be *it*. The wretch always seems to have money in his pocket, and *that* worries me; another thing, I hear that girl of his is expecting again and her father's finally put the finger on Bart. Two little boys already, and that red hair telling a tale, he says, but both taking after their mother in being slow on the uptake. She's generous in her favours, they say, so there's a chance it's not Bart's responsibility . . ."

Jerusha thought that she would be more than glad if Polly did harden her generous heart and push Bart not just out of her home, but a fair distance away. She still feared him, not only for herself but for Goldie, because she was positive that, in certain circumstances, he could be dangerous, *ruthless* in his dealings with any woman he desired.

She kissed Polly goodbye at the station.

"Now don't worry," Polly repeated, "I will be here to meet the last train, as always."

"Oh, darlin'!" Essie exclaimed. "There's nothing of you, never was much, eh, but now you're so thin . . ."

Jerusha held on to Essie as if she would never let go. The perfume of frangipani almost overwhelmed her as usual but for comforting the lost souls, the heartbroken, there was only one Essie, she thought, as she sobbed, "I'm *so* glad to see you!"

"Sit down, let me make the tea. And dry those eyes, darlin', or I'll believe the end of the world has come. You can tell me all about it later."

The inner door opened and Sergei appeared. He did not bother to smile at or greet Jerusha but addressed Essie briefly: "I go to my friend's now. I may be back late. Leave the door unlocked." He went out of the back way, carrying a bulky parcel under his arm.

Essie released her breath in a whistle of relief. "Now we can talk without interruption, darlin'."

"I'm surprised *he's* still here," Jerusha accepted her cup of tea gratefully.

Essie's reply startled her. "*Oliver* brought him here, Jerusha. *He* will tell him when it is time to go. He does his best to see that Sergei does not upset me."

"Oliver? I don't understand; whatever d'you mean?"

Essie drained her cup. She looked very serious. "I think it's time to tell you what I have kept to myself. Oliver, Jerusha, is my son. I imagined you would have worked that out long ago –

it was only a secret in the beginning because, well, I was a *spy* at the Mastersons', working there because Oliver asked me to. It was because he was worried whether he was doing the right thing for you. We never intended to keep up the pretence, I assure you. As I said, I thought you would have guessed. Browne – *Bronski* – he changed his name as little as possible when he went to work for his father."

"He didn't disown you, then?" Jerusha asked urgently. She would, herself, feel betrayed if that was true, she knew.

"No, darlin', he's *always* looked after me, I had no need to work, it was my idea, in fact. Shall I tell you the rest? Oliver's father, you could say, was the first of my gentlemen. I was still 'Little Essie Bronski' then. He was long-married, he had to be discreet. When Oliver was born, he sent me money, he's a very rich man, so that was the easy way out, but he kept away, from that time. As soon as I could, I wanted to make a living for us both, to accept no more from him. I knew where he was, of course, that he owned the hotel. When Oliver was sixteen, he wrote to me. He wanted the boy to work for him, to one day take over the hotel, if he proved himself. He said he would now also let it be known that Oliver was his son. Naturally, he expected me to stay in the background, although his wife had passed on, but he had three daughters, disapproving, I suspected. They were much older than Oliver and they had all married well. At the time I thought he was taking my son away from me, that things could never be the same, but Oliver has never forgotten me, *or* who he is."

"Essie, that explains a lot," Jerusha said softly. "But not about Sergei—"

"You know, of course, that I – we have Russian blood? I never pry into Oliver's affairs, but I think, I guess, that he has my nature for wishing to, well, change things for the better. Perhaps – and this must be our secret – *perhaps*, he has certain sympathies with whatever cause Sergei believes in. But I have never asked. He is a good man, I trust him to do right."

"So do I, Essie."

"Now, darlin', it is your turn to talk."

"It's my baby, my little Phylly. There's something wrong with her. *She can't hear*, Essie! I loved Joe so much, but he let me down. *Why* is life so cruel to me?"

"I can't answer that one, darlin', I really can't . . ."

Chapter Two

Oliver hadn't changed, but Jerusha was sure that he would see the differences in herself.

They greeted each other politely, as if they had met only the other day. He looked at her for some time without speaking, while they awaited their first course at their usual table in the hotel. Because it was so mild out and she had lost weight, Jerusha had despaired of finding something she could wear which would look reasonably smart for London. At the last moment she had remembered the dress Valentine had sent her when she was not much older than Goldie was now, just before she left the Mastersons and went to live with Essie. She had already retrieved it from the press, wondering if it would fit Goldie. Of course it had not, so she thought of cutting it up to make something for Phylly. She sat opposite Oliver looking almost as she had all those years ago, in that simple moss-rose frock with the silver chain round her neck, but with her hair swept up and almost concealed by Polly's burgundy-coloured hat, which she had trimmed with a new ribbon. She was twenty-five years old yet Oliver was still painfully aware of the gap between them, for he would shortly reach his forty-third birthday.

"Something is troubling you, Jerusha?" he asked at last.

She toyed with her food, her lips trembling. "Yes. I will tell you later, Oliver. You wanted to see me, to tell me about Valentine? I was very sad to hear the news. I thought she would go on for ever, she was such a strong character. I'm sure you won't remember, but this dress – Valentine sent it to me, years ago. She knew I must be growing up and out of all my clothes. She never made a fuss about the nice things she did; she was always so thoughtful in a quiet way. I will miss her letters very much."

"You are wrong, Jerusha. I *do* remember you in that dress. It was the day I became aware that you were a young woman." He paused, pushed aside his own half-eaten meal. "Valentine has left everything to you, Jerusha. I must tell you that her estate is a very modest one, for her house must be sold and the proceeds divided between you and the family of her late friend, who owned a half-share. There is some money which can be released soon, and I shall need your signature on some documents from the bank. I also need to know whether you wish Valentine's personal effects to be sold, or whether you would like to keep particular items. These are all listed, and if you could look at these today and decide, it will simplify matters considerably. Is this all too much to take in right now? When we have finished lunch, we can go to my study and discuss things in detail."

"I don't know what to say, Oliver. I suppose, if I had thought of it at all, I would have imagined that Valentine would name my *mother* in her will."

"I am sorry to give you another shock, Jerusha. The truth is, neither Valentine nor I have heard from Kathleen in several years. Please don't jump to the conclusion that anything awful has happened, I am almost sure that is not the case. I think that Kathleen decided that she had burned her boats as far as you were concerned. The letter she sent you before you married Dan: that is the last time we heard from her, too."

"I knew that must be it! I was too afraid to ask you, Oliver, I suppose. I really can't eat any more, I'm sorry – do you mind if we go to your study now, and have our coffee there?"

He rose instantly. "Valentine often said that she thought you were a wonderful girl, Jerusha. Hopefully, her bequest will help to ease things for you at last. You could pay off your mortgage, perhaps. Yes, it's time to talk."

They sat in comfortable leather armchairs, with their backs to the book-lined wall, their coffee cooling on the tooled top of Oliver's desk.

"I discovered today the real relationship between you and Essie," Jerusha began.

"Is that why you are upset?" Oliver asked. "If it is, then I ask your forgiveness. After a while, I thought you would be happier not knowing. You and Essie got on so splendidly, there were no constraints as there could have been if you had been told she was my mother. You might have thought that she only took care of you, treated you as a daughter, because she felt obliged to. Perhaps you would also have believed that your every move was reported back to me, so that, in turn, I could communicate with your mother. Essie loves you for yourself, Jerusha, you must be sure of that."

"I am, Oliver. I, too, have kept something from you both, but I finally told Essie this morning. My little girl, Phylly, is deaf. This makes her a difficult child. It is hard for both of us to bear, particularly as I do not have the support of a husband," her voice was bitter now. "I have to rely on a young girl, Joe's daughter, who does far more to help me than anyone should expect from one of her age. Did I tell you, Oliver, that Joe abandoned Goldie's mother? He didn't even marry *her*!"

"You never discussed his background with me, with Essie, before you married him so suddenly. Nothing would have changed your mind, I could tell how much in love with him you were, the last time we met. Did he treat you badly, Jerusha?" There was anger in his eyes now at the thought.

"Not in the way you mean – *no*! I loved him passionately, Oliver. It was very different from the way I loved Dan. I can tell you now about *that*, without embarrassment, I hope. It was a fulfilling partnership in every respect except *one*. I *have* to believe that Joe loved me too, and wanted me every bit as much as I wanted him. But he is a man you can't tie down. Perhaps that part of him is like my father – except that Joe promised me faithfully that he would come back. There must be a reason, and I'm so afraid what that might be, because I was so sure he would keep his word. *I need him*, Oliver – so do his daughters!"

Oliver rose, pressed the bell. "I will order fresh coffee. Would you study the list I mentioned now, please? When we have finished the paper signing, we will go for a walk, and talk some more. Just bear this in mind, Jerusha. I shall have plenty of time to spare shortly. My father is selling the hotel and insists that he gives me a generous settlement now, rather than later. I could stay on here, but I have been considering a complete change, not only in where I might live – I already have somewhere in mind – but in my career. Seeing you today, realising just how worried you are, has made up my mind for me. I need a home, yes, but there is no need for me to rush, with regard to earning a living. I intend to help you in any way I can to solve your problems. You see, you have always meant a great deal to me, and that will never change." He cleared his throat, smiled reassuringly at her.

Jerusha jumped to her feet, flung her arms round him and hugged him. "Oliver," her voice was muffled against his shoulder, "you and Essie, you are very dear to me. I really don't know where I would be without you!"

Perhaps it was fortunate that she did not see the way he looked as she whispered that.

"All's well back at The Homestead," Polly said, as the horse turned out of the station yard and headed for home. "I advised Goldie to bolt the back door and to open it only when she heard your voice. Phylly went to sleep quite quickly tonight. You see, you didn't need to worry after all, did you? Goldie is a second mum to your little girl."

She shouldn't have to be that, Jerusha thought. She said aloud, "Valentine has left me some money, Poll. I've talked it over with Oliver and he agrees with me that Valentine would have been happy for me to use some of it for Phylly. I'm going to take her to London to a doctor who specialises in deafness, to see if there is anything to be done about her hearing, and how we can help her to overcome her handicap as much as possible. Oliver is looking for a house in London now, he tells me, because his father is selling the hotel. He says we will be able to stay in his new place any time we need to, even if he isn't there, because he is planning to travel abroad for some time.

"It may mean that I will have to leave Goldie in charge again from time to time, or take her with us and trust that Robey can cope on his own—"

"Don't try and sort all that out tonight," Polly said wisely.

"You're right, Poll, I won't!"

The door knob rattled violently once again. Goldie stood by the sink, candle wavering in her hand, with Nibbles pressed against her legs, hackles up, growling softly. She was sure the unwelcome caller must hear her heart pounding. She hadn't pulled the curtains quite to. Was his face pressed to the window? Could he see her?

"I know you're there, and I know you're alone, except for the baby, and she don't matter, and I ain't afraid of that soppy dog! *Let me in!* I won't hurt you, I only want to talk. I'm fed up of you ignoring me all the time. Chitter-chatter to your gypsy boy, don't you? You're driving me *mad*, Goldie—" Bart's voice went on and on, slurred with drink but insistent.

She wouldn't have come into the kitchen in her nightdress if she hadn't thought it was Jerusha at the door. Now, she seemed incapable of moving. How long was it since Poll called and told her she was just off to meet the train, and to lock the door? Half an hour? Bart must have been lurking and listening. She'd been so pleased with the way the day had gone and now he'd spoiled it all. She was sure of one thing. She would have to make some excuse if Jerusha asked her to hold the fort again.

She strained her ears. Was that the sound of the horse and cart approaching? Bart was quiet now. It must be! She took a deep breath, waited to hear Jerusha's welcome call. When it came, she couldn't help herself, she began to sob as she thrust back the bolt. Nibbles immediately shot out, barking and searching in the dark, but returned, whining, to greet Jerusha.

"Goldie, dear, whatever's the matter? It isn't Phylly, is it?" Jerusha cried, instantly concerned.

"No, I'm just so glad you're back!" Goldie choked. She didn't want to cause trouble, upset Polly, who was so kind to them. Nothing had happened, after all. But she would need to be even more on her guard where Bart was concerned. "Can I come in with you tonight?" she asked, for she knew it would take a long time for the fear to fade.

Chapter Three

It was time to plant the early potatoes in the top field. Jerusha and Goldie had been responsible for the chitting, the sprouting of the seed potatoes indoors, while Robey had prepared the land. Chitting was one of the first tasks Dan had taught Jerusha in the spring after they were married. She always thought of his patience, his slow way of talking when she placed the small seed potatoes eye-up in the seed boxes. 'They must be kept warm, Jerusha, but not too warm, and in a darkish place, but with a little light . . .' she remembered him saying. They were ready for planting when the time came to rub off the weaker shoots with a deft caress of the thumb, leaving two or three strong shoots to flourish.

Robey had fashioned the shallow drills with his spade yesterday. As Goldie moved slowly along the rows, placing the potatoes about a foot apart, Robey covered each one with a little mound of soil, to protect them against any late frosts.

Jerusha and Phylly watched their progression for a while. She found it a calming scene. When Phylly tugged at her hand and began to grizzle, Jerusha actually felt a rush of relief that she had unburdened herself yesterday and that with her friends' support, she would now be able to do something positive regarding her daughter's disability.

"Come on, then, let's go and see how Mummy's nut trees are getting on." She mustn't stop talking to Phylly, even though it seemed unlikely she could hear. She was sure that was important. Polly's latest advice had been to lift her up so that their faces were on a level in order that Phylly might watch her lips moving. Now, Phylly stopped moaning, and put out one hand, touching Jerusha's mouth with her fingers.

Jerusha hugged her tightly. "Oh, darling, this is a beginning, *I know it*!"

*   *   *

Robey had grown into a broad-shouldered young man. Not as tall as Bart, but more powerfully built. He was darkly handsome, and his Romany looks contrasted with Goldie's fairness. Following her along the field, he watched her graceful, seemingly tireless dipping down as she mentally measured the distance between each seed potato. He shouldn't really be alone with her like this, but how would Dada know? She was not a gypsy, even though, like her mother before her, she was a trusted friend. If they should marry, Goldie would have to learn their ways . . . She enjoyed such freedom here, it might seem hard.

Sometimes the longing almost swamped him. Unlike his contemporaries he had not indulged in swaggering horseplay to impress the pretty girls on the camp. He knew what happened when a young couple lay together for the first time, of course. But there were courtship rules among the gypsies to be observed, a strict moral code. Gypsy girls were invariably chaste before marriage, their parents made sure of that. One day, too, he would be expected to 'jump the broomstick', to go through the age-old ceremony of the gypsy wedding. Sooner or later, his father would speak to him regarding this.

They had reached the far end of the row, the hedge. Goldie straightened her back with a sigh. She had placed bottles of water, bread and cheese tied in a cloth, in the shade before they began. It was time for a rest. The panting dog was already waiting for them there.

They stretched out on the rough grass after they had hungrily eaten and drunk the contents of one of the bottles of water. They filled Nibbles' dish at the same time. Propping himself up on one elbow, Robey gazed at Goldie's flushed, dirt-streaked face. Her eyes were closed, but he knew she was not sneaking a nap. There was an ant crawling on her neck, where she had undone the top button of her blouse. She had rolled up her sleeves at the same time, and he saw how smooth and pale her forearms were above the grubbiness of her hands, her broken nails. He daringly brushed the insect away with a roughened forefinger, and she opened her blue eyes and smiled at him.

"I wondered what was tickling me," she murmured, then shut her eyes again.

The temptation was too great. He planted a clumsy kiss on her mouth, still damp from the water. She instantly sat up, pushing him away. She tried to sound indignant, "Robey! What *do* you think you're doing?"

He stood up, gave a little whistle, then picked up his spade. "Better get busy again, afore missus calls us for lunch, eh?" he said nonchalantly.

"No more of that," Goldie warned him. Then she added, as she chose the first potato, "All right. I'm your girl. I always have been, and you know it. But I'm too young for what I think you had in mind—"

"I did not! I will marry you first, you must know that. But *one day* . . ." he said, with confidence now.

"Yes, one day. I promise," she said. She had been trying to pluck up courage, when she closed her eyes first, to tell him about Bart, last night. Now, she thought, how could she spoil the wonder of that first, innocent kiss?

The village bobby was, frankly, fat. He was puffing when he dismounted from his bicycle outside Polly's house. He lifted the heavy knocker, let it thunder, twice. He did not expect to see Polly, or Ernest, for the latter came and went between the keeper's lodge and here, and Polly, naturally, would be out on her rounds.

Bart opened the door eventually, bleary-eyed and yawning widely. "Mum's not at home," he said.

The bobby kept his huge boot in the open doorway to prevent Bart from shutting the door in his face. "I guessed that. It's *you* I want to see. Tired, are you? Out and about last night?"

"Better come in, then," Bart said ungraciously. Amazingly, this was the first time the bobby had called. He'd become complacent, sure of his mother's protection and he thought he'd kept one step ahead of Ernest, despite his stepfather's recent suspicions. It helped, being an inveterate liar.

When Polly returned at teatime, Bart had gone. He had taken all the cash from the old teapot and some of his clothes in a canvas bag which usually dangled from a hook on the back door. Tonight's supper, cold meat pie, a hock of ham, a loaf of bread and a whole pound of cheese were missing from the larder, also a bottle or two of her homemade wine. She did not discover the loss of that until some time later. He had not bothered to write a note for his mother. She would have been even more frantic if she had known that with him was Dan's shotgun.

The bobby knocked again when he judged that Ernest would be home for his supper. He braced himself to impart bad news. He had come, this time, armed with a warrant for Bart's arrest on suspicion of burglary.

The three of them waited, aware that it was in vain. Polly had to submit to questioning herself. Was she aware that her son was in trouble? Did she know where he went at nights? Had she been back at home before he left? Did she know it was an offence to aid and abet someone in evading the law?

When their visitor had left, promising to return next morning, Polly put her head in her hands on the table.

"I ought to go," poor Ernest said helplessly.

"I ought to have known," Polly said dully. "I *did* know, if I'm truthful, I just shut my eyes to it. Why didn't I tell him to go a week or two ago, when you first brought it up? Did you guess something like this would happen, Ernest?"

"Yes," he had to admit. "I wanted to save you from all this, Poll. You've been a good mother to that young devil – you don't deserve this."

"I even refused to believe at first he'd fathered those children, got that poor, simple girl into trouble; you're right, Ernest, he *has* got the devil in him! He hasn't got a conscience, that's a fact."

"We're well rid of him Poll. The police'll catch up with him in good time. I must get off to work, old girl. Will you be all right?" He added, just as she had to Goldie the other night, "Lock the door and bolt the windows. And don't answer the door to anyone but *me* . . ."

Chapter Four

When Polly came over next morning to tell them the news, red-eyed and still in shock, Jerusha couldn't help noticing the relief on Goldie's face. She felt guilty herself, for how could she commiserate with poor Polly like this when her initial reaction had been exactly the same?

She jigged Phylly up and down on her hip. She was aware that there were struggles ahead to be faced in bringing up her own child, but she prayed silently that she would be able to cope with all this. Bart had a bad core to him, she thought, he was a rotten apple all right. Polly had deserved better.

"Must get back home, Ru. Sorry to unburden myself like this—"

"Who else would you tell, Poll? That's what friends are for. You've always been there for me. If there is anything we can do, just tell us, won't you?"

"Silver and jewellery, small pieces, that's what the bobby says is missing from houses here and about – things he could pocket, Jerusha. I haven't dared check my own things yet," Polly confided sadly.

Jerusha suddenly thought of her mother's solid silver snake bracelet which she kept in her handkerchief drawer, which seemed to have mysteriously disappeared. A few weeks ago she had thought of selling it, as Oliver had suggested, for she had outstanding bills to pay. That was, of course, before she heard about her legacy. She had tried to convince herself that she must have misplaced the bracelet. However, she hadn't left her bedroom window open since, as a precaution. Now, the thought of Bart, for who else could it be? climbing up into her room and carrying out a daylight robbery, made her blood run cold. How could she voice such suspicions to Polly?

Bart was already quite a distance away. He was resting up in a barn eating his breakfast. He had been walking most of the night, which was no hardship to him; that was the only thing he had in common with his mother's husband, boring, upright Ernest, he thought contemptuously, working undercover, in the shadows . . .

The only thing he missed now was a mug of his mother's good, strong tea. There was furious resentment bubbling inside him too: at being caught out after so long; at being thwarted by Goldie that night he had decided to seize his chance . . . It was Jerusha's doing, warning the girl of his intentions, he decided. He'd get even with *her*. She'd quake in her boots if she knew what he was thinking. He fingered the silver bracelet hidden with other valuables in the poacher's pocket. Still waiting for Joe, still hoping, was she? What if she were to learn his version, not Joe's, of what happened the night Dan died . . . ?

"You must inform me if you hear from him, or he comes home at any time," the bobby warned Polly. He had searched the house but found nothing.

"I really must get out on my rounds," Polly told him. "My customers will wonder where on earth I am—"

"Some of 'em will have a good idea why you've been delayed, Polly, I'm afraid. I feel I should tell you, unofficial like, that he probably did a bit of snooping when he went out with you, and your customers may well be among the losers."

Somehow, that fact was the hardest to bear, Polly thought. She prided herself on her honesty. Would folk she considered friends now tar her with the same brush as Bart? She would need all her courage to face them today.

Jerusha spread the unpicked pieces of the pink frock on the kitchen table. She had cut a simple pattern from brown paper, reminded of the sewing lessons at Copper Leas. The girls had been encouraged to make do and mend, to adapt, lengthen, shorten garments. This experience had been invaluable, she mused now. She had to snatch precious moments when Phylly had her afternoon nap. She thought that Valentine would have been pleased at her thrift; to know that she was making her daughter a pretty outfit for her first visit to London.

There was an unexpected knock at the door. A letter by the afternoon post! As always, she felt a sudden rush of hope, as she thanked the postman. Would it be, at last, a letter from Joe? But a quick glance told her that it did not bear the right postmark.

The postman looked tired, careworn. "Would you tell Mrs Apps, please, for I don't like to, that my Pansy had a baby girl early this morning? I know she's got her troubles, but so have we, not that I'm not glad that – *beggar* – has gone, and I hope he don't *ever* come back . . ."

"I'll make up a parcel of Phylly's outgrown things, would that help, Ted? See, I'm making her bigger clothes now, she's grown out of so much," Jerusha offered sympathetically.

"Thank you, Mrs Finch. Pansy'll be grateful. Silly girl keeps moaning about losing him. *I'm* the loser, I tell her – *who's* had to support her, all along? I have to be father and mother to her, *and* to them little lads."

When he had gone, she sat down to open her letter. She didn't recognise the pencilled writing on the envelope. The single sheet of paper, torn from a notebook, bore no signature, but she knew then, at once, who had sent it.

'Your wasting your time waiting for Joe Finch. He was around that night old Dan got killed. Did he ever tell you that? I saw him with that chain. He got blood on his hands. Your well rid of him. Do Ma say the same about me I reckon she do. And you look out for that girl of yours with that gypsy boy. She lifts her skirts for him. She's no good like her father.'

She sat there, shocked, at the cruelty, crudity of the message. She didn't even hear Phylly's demanding yells from upstairs, the bars of the cot rattling. She sat unmoving until Goldie came in for her tea.

"The kettle's boiling dry—" Goldie began, then she saw Jerusha's face. "*What's wrong?*" she asked urgently.

Jerusha couldn't speak. She held out the paper. Goldie took it, read it. She guessed it was from Bart, it couldn't be written by anyone else.

"It's *spite*, Jerusha! *You* know Joe like *I* do – he'd *never* do anything terrible like that! Oh, he's hurt you, and me, so much, by going away as he did, but I believe, as my mother always did, that he'll come back, and *you* must too. He hurts people in that way, yes, but he's *not* a *violent* man—"

Jerusha seemed to come to, at last. She tore the note into shreds and fed it to the stove. They must keep this from Polly. "I know that, Goldie. Bart's lying, he must be. But if Joe was here now, as he should be, he could tell me so himself. And, Goldie, I'm so sorry, but, I *must* ask you, he was trying to make trouble for you, too, wasn't he?" she appealed.

Goldie flushed deeply. "Robey and me – Jerusha, we've done nothing to be ashamed of – but I've got something to tell you, about the night you came back from London, *then* you'll understand why Bart wrote that . . ."

Chapter Five

In June, they boarded the London train in some excitement.

"I've never been to London before, there's so much I'm longing to see," Goldie whispered in Jerusha's ear, for they were not alone in the carriage. "Four days, a real holiday, Ru!"

"Thanks to Robey, and his Dada, we can stay away without worrying, Goldie. I didn't like to ask too much of Poll, she's still so down. I'm glad you are thinking of it as a holiday, but remember there's a serious side to this too: the visit to the specialist tomorrow with Phylly."

"I hope Nibbles will be all right, sleeping in the woodshed—" Goldie suddenly thought.

"Of course he will. It's not cold at nights, after all. He can guard the place for us, can't he? And Robey will make sure he doesn't go hungry and that he has plenty of water, as he promised."

The welcome cheque from Oliver, the first money from Valentine's estate, had swelled Jerusha's bank account last week. There had been another trip, to Maidstone, to buy more summery clothes for Jerusha and Goldie, and new shoes for Phylly.

The little girl looked solemnly around her from the safety of her mother's lap. She looked very bonny, Jerusha thought fondly, in her pink dress, matching bonnet and long white socks. Goldie was quite the young lady, in a creamy muslin blouse and long cotton skirt in pale green. She had placed her straw hat beside her on the seat, and the sun streaming through the windows of the carriage haloed her curly golden head. She had pinned her hair up and Jerusha fancied that she resembled a Botticelli cherub. Robey had looked lingeringly, admiringly at her earlier, when he bade them goodbye. Jerusha told herself she trusted the young couple implicitly, but she couldn't erase Bart's cruel taunts entirely from her mind. It was a responsibility, looking after a girl of Goldie's age, particularly one so pretty and bright. She certainly wouldn't leave her on her own in the house again.

Jerusha, too, wore a blouse and skirt. A coffee-coloured top with pin-tucked bodice, billowing sleeves and a neat little velvet bow at the neck, matching the dark brown of her skirt. Like Goldie, she had a new straw boater. She was taking no chances, even though there were no clouds visible in the sky. In her capacious bag she had a rolled umbrella.

Essie was there, waiting as the train steamed in, among the crowds on the platform, but easily seen because of her startling hair.

"Oh, Essie dear, isn't this wonderful, seeing you again so soon!"

Essie held out her arms for Phylly. "How you've grown, you little darlin'! And Goldie, why you're quite grown up! Follow me, girls, I've got a cab waiting."

She's got a wonderful way with children – with people! Jerusha thought, as Phylly laughed at them over Essie's shoulder and threaded her fingers through the thick magenta coils.

"Oliver's away, I'm not quite sure where, but the house is at your disposal, he says. You must think of it as your London home. He wanted me to come and live with him, but I thought it over and decided I was comfortable where I was – if only my lodger would take the hint and go. However, I'm very happy to keep you company there right now, that's if you'd like me to, of course—"

"You know we would!" Jerusha assured her.

"A secret destination!" Goldie said dramatically. "How much further, Essie?"

"Not far." The cab turned and they were bowling along a street which somehow looked familiar to Jerusha. They stopped outside a square three-storeyed house behind ornate railings coated in shining black and gold. The front door and window frames, too, gleamed with new paint.

Jerusha stepped down and walked between the trees that lined the pavement. They were leafy now, but still tall and spindly. She was back at her old house, which she had left when she was just seven years old.

The reception rooms downstairs were still empty and echoing. Uncarpeted, but smelling of paint. Someone had hung curtains on the poles. But the big kitchen was furnished and the latest gas stove had been installed. Essie opened the cupboards with a flourish. "Oliver asked me to get in supplies!" She added, "He has plans for the other rooms on the ground floor, but I mustn't spoil any surprises. There's a woman comes in every day to see to what needs doing, she'll cook breakfast for us tomorrow, but I'll get the meal tonight. Oliver won't need more staff until he's actually living here, which could be quite a while yet. Come upstairs; your old rooms are ready for you, Jerusha! The nursery for young Phylly, and the bedroom off, for you two, and Goldie and I are to share, in the bedroom by the new bathroom. Aren't you going to say anything, Ru? Or are you just too surprised?"

"Something like that," Jerusha murmured. "It's all so familiar, Essie, and yet it's different, too. Whatever made Oliver buy this particular house?"

"Needs a family, not a single gentleman, eh, but he did it for *you*, Jerusha, I'm positive of that."

"It seems impossible," Jerusha cried, when they walked into the old nursery. "The same nursery frieze, it must be! Look, Phylly," she carried her daughter over to the wall and pointed out Little Jack Horner. "And the window seat's still here, but, of course, the rocking horse has gone. I can still imagine it nodding up and down."

"It's a *very* grand house," Goldie said in awe.

A grand house full of ghosts, Jerusha discovered, when she sat up, wheezing, in the early morning. Essie had remembered about the pillows, so it couldn't be that, but there was a creaking sound, faint but unmistakable. The dream had seemed so real. Valentine sitting, writing, and the little girl who was herself, rocking up and down on the dappled horse. She just stopped herself from calling out for her mother. Kathleen, of course, was not there . . .

Phylly, lying beside her, for she had had to lift her from the cot when she came to bed, made a strange utterance. Jerusha wondered if she had heard aright; the sound was not repeated, but surely it was, "Ma-ma!"?

Jerusha eased herself down in the bed, slid her arms round the warm little person she loved so much, but despaired over, and lay awake until dawn, remembering days long past.

The doctor had a fierce moustache and glinting, gold-rimmed spectacles, but he was patient and gentle with Phylly. This was a hospital for the deaf and dumb and Doctor Howell told Jerusha that he had specialised in this branch of medicine because, "My own parents were deaf; as a child, I was their ears . . ."

He was, Jerusha discovered, from the very start of what would be a lengthy association, not only dedicated but inspiring. For the first time since she had realised that Phylly's hearing was seriously impaired, she felt hope for her daughter's future.

Doctor Howell did not agree that those who were deaf were inevitably dumb. There had been what many regarded as a miracle more than three hundred years ago in San Salvador in Spain, when a Benedictine monk, Pedro Ponce de Leon showed that many deaf children could be taught to speak, that the deaf were not incapable of learning because of their disability. The doctor told of the many schools for the deaf which now existed; he spoke of wonderful teachers who had paved the way and the missions for the deaf. "I will give you a list of books which you should study whenever you can find time. Now we must talk of your daughter and what can be achieved. I favour a strong mixture of both the oral method and the signing – the language of the deaf. You, Mrs Finch, will be learning constantly, alongside your child."

"Will she be able to lead – a near normal life?" Jerusha ventured. Phylly, tired after the tests, snuggled on her lap, thumb going into her mouth. Jerusha's arms tightened round her.

"The most important gift you can give her is independence, whenever possible and practical," Doctor Howell said perceptively. "It is difficult, at this early stage, to diagnose the degree of deafness. You will come to see me so often that you and Phylly will think of this clinic as your second home. We have to gain her confidence and that is a slow process.

"There is a special church for the deaf here in London. St Saviours in Oxford Street. You might go there; if you do, I think you will be both comforted and fired with optimism for the future. I will also give you the address of the British Deaf and Dumb Association, a wonderful institution, formed some seventeen years ago . . ."

Essie and Goldie, who had been window shopping, arrived to escort them back to the house so that Phylly could have her nap after they had eaten lunch. Then Essie proposed to take them sightseeing, if Jerusha felt up to it.

"Let's take another cab," Jerusha said recklessly, "but we'll do our sightseeing later from the top of a bus, eh?"

Essie took the sleepy child into her arms. They walked along a lengthy corridor, down the steps, out into the sunshine and fresh air. Goldie tucked her arm in Jerusha's. "We're *longing* to know how you got on, Ru?"

Jerusha took a deep breath to dispel the odour of carbolic, which seemed to linger. She smiled happily at them. "Dr Howell believes that Phylly has some hearing in her right ear, that's why she is beginning to make sounds we can recognise, at last. She is also learning to watch our lips as we speak, that is the start of lipreading. And I am just beginning to understand that *anything* is possible if we work together with Phylly."

"There's a church," Essie began.

"The doctor told me. St Saviours. We'll go there, won't we, before we go home? I've neglected my prayers, been full of doubts and sorry for myself ever since Joe left us—"

"Joe will be back, Jerusha, he promised," Goldie gave her arm a squeeze. "But we'll pray hard for *that* to happen, too!"

No dreams for Jerusha that night, cuddling Phylly close. She was positive, as she closed her eyes, that having reached a crossroads in her life, she had chosen the right path ahead.

Chapter Six

Polly couldn't prevent an involuntary trembling when she heard the knock on the door. She had answered too many knocks recently and learned more unwelcome facts about Bart.

She went slowly to the door, opened it and stared at the caller. She had known Pansy as a small girl, of course, and she had been friendly with her late mother. She couldn't lay blame on the girl for her encouragement of Bart; he should have known better, or done the decent thing and married Pansy, for *he* had the sharper wits of the two of them, she thought. She felt a rush of guilt that she had chosen to ignore the evidence that the two little boys were her grandsons. When Ernest tried to broach the subject in his concern, after Bart had disappeared, she had said, unkindly and out of character for her, that the girl was likely accommodating other fellows beside Bart. This was possibly true, but Ernest sighed reproachfully and said no more.

Pansy's two little lads clung shyly to her skirts, peeping now and then at Polly. In her arms, the girl carried her new baby, wrapped tightly in a shawl, despite it being a summer's day.

"Come in," Polly managed. She had a tray of scones cooling on the table. It helped to keep working. She busied herself splitting and spreading the scones with butter and placing cushions on the hard wooden chairs so that the little boys could sit up at the table. "You're Peter, are you? And you must be Jimmy – would you like a drink of milk?"

She made tea for the girl and herself. She had not long been in from her rounds. A few of her regulars mysteriously no longer had any need of her services, but most had been very loyal.

"Father tell you, did he, that baby had come?" Pansy, pale-faced and slow-speaking, looked, Polly was now aware, as if she had not recovered yet from this event. Pansy continued, "Mrs Finch, she send me some clothes. Father fell off his bicycle, right on his head, this mornin'. Mr Apps find him, later on. He've been took to hospital. He've not woke up yet. Mr Apps say, 'Pansy, when you see my wife goin' home, like, you come on down to her house and *she'll* look after you.' I still got bad troubles, see, from when she got born and the doctor say I'm not to do anythin', I'm to rest up. Will you take her, missus?" She held out the damp bundle to Polly.

Such a dear little face, Polly thought, fingering aside the shawl. Knowing eyes, too: *this* one looked bright enough. Anyway, what did it matter if she wasn't? She knew she could love her all the same. Bart had been too clever by half, after all. "What's her name?" she asked huskily.

"I called her for *you*, missus, seein' as Bart left us – you *and* me. Polly-May, seeing's that was the month she was born," she added hopefully.

"Well, Polly-May," Polly said, "and you boys, I'm your grandma, and I'm going to look after you all until your grandad comes home. You just sit tight, Pansy, and rest up like the doctor said, while I sort out – Bart's room for the lot of you. Then I'll harness up the horse again, and we'll go back to your place for your things, eh?"

She was going to be really busy again, and that was good, *so* good, Polly thought.

Jerusha had neglected her letter writing of late. Catching sight of Valentine's writing slope, as she always thought of it, she decided it was time to write to Millicent. Her friend must think she had forgotten her! She had last contacted her when Phylly was born, but it had been a short letter because she had found it too painful to write about Joe leaving her. Millicent had replied to say she was delighted to hear about the baby, that she had qualified as a teacher and was looking for a permanent position.

> *'I don't think I will ever marry myself, I could not give up my career. As for children, I often have* forty *to care for, not just one! It's strange, because when we were at Copper Leas I never really appreciated how kind our teachers there were, how* fortunate *we were . . .'*

Nor did I, Jerusha thought, re-reading this letter. She dipped her pen in the ink. The words spilled out of her and she covered several pages.

It was ten days before she received a reply. Her letter had been forwarded, for her friend, too, had changed direction, moved to another school.

'It must be meant, that you should write to me at this particular time, Jerusha! Last year I attended a mission service for the deaf. I found it so inspiring I decided there and then that I would undertake further training and become a teacher of the deaf myself. I seized the opportunity when it arose to join the staff of this special school in Surrey, to continue with my studies as an assistant to a qualified teacher.

When it is possible, I would like you to visit my school with Phylly, to see how much the children can achieve, how happy they are when they can communicate and move beyond their closed-in, silent world.

It would be wonderful *if you should decide that, in time,* this *should be the place where your daughter could receive the education she deserves, and that I might be privileged to be one of those to help her! I was sad to learn that you have not heard from your husband for so long. You and I both know too well, from our childhood together, what it is like to be parted from those we love.*

Let me know next time you are in London to visit the clinic. I will endeavour to take a day off to meet you then.

With my love, Millicent.'

Jerusha showed the letter to Goldie. "I would love to see Millicent again! Yes, I too think this was meant to be."

Oliver could smell the frangipani growing. He had disembarked from the boat a day ago, and gone straight to the hotel in Port of Spain. The formal gardens were brilliant with colour, splashing fountains. He found himself reluctant to seek Kathleen out, although his exhaustive enquiries had brought him back here.

It was very hot. He wore a linen suit, a panama hat. He was a fastidious man; he disliked the thought that he couldn't avoid sweating here in Trinidad. He mopped his face with a large cotton square. He would delay his visit until the evening, when it was cooler.

It was a squalid area, near the docks, it did not smell sweet, heady, here. Oliver was forced to hold the handkerchief to his nose, pretending to wipe it. *Drains*! that was it. Worse than the sour odours which assailed him when he approached Essie's house.

The door was open, hanging almost off its hinges. In the darkened room beyond, with blinds drawn, he saw Kathleen, lying limply on an unmade bed, in a crumpled, flimsy frock, shoes kicked off, eyes closed.

"Kathleen . . ." he said, uncertainly.

She opened her eyes, looked up at him, unmoving. "Oliver?" There was no surprise in her voice. "I knew you'd come!"

Edwin was dead. Oliver was already aware of that from his enquiries, but he allowed her to relate all the sordid details. Kathleen was destitute. A woman she had met had taken pity on her, allowed her to stay in this shack. She did not go out, her friend advised against it. She had not eaten properly for weeks.

As she rambled on, she slowly sat up and close to he could see how low she must be. Except for the dark hair and eyes, he would not have recognised her.

When the woman who had helped her returned, Oliver talked briefly to her, thanked her for what she had done for Kathleen. Money discreetly passed hands. The woman went away. She would send for a carriage of sorts, she promised, so that Oliver could take Kathleen back to the hotel.

He helped her to gather together her few possessions, fetched water in a leaking basin for her to wash her face. He knelt to put her shoes on her feet. She was passive, allowing him to take charge.

"Are you ready, Kathleen?" he asked gently, supporting her with an arm around her shoulders.

The small crowd which had gathered to see their departure, parted to allow them through. A girl darted forward, thrust a red flower in Kathleen's hair. "Goodbye, pretty lady!" she cried. "Be happy with your man . . ."

Guarded explanations were made to the proprietor of the hotel. He was assured that Mrs Carey was a respectable widow, despite appearances to the contrary, that she had been ill, that, as soon as arrangements could be made, Oliver would be taking her back to England. The proprietor drew his own conclusions and gave Kathleen the room next door to Oliver, which had a communicating door.

Kathleen had bathed, put on the borrowed nightgown and gone straight to bed. When Oliver brought her a tray with a light supper, his knock on the door was answered with a faint, "Come in."

She was hungry, but he could not coax her to eat much. He looked at her with pity and a stirring of affection. Now that she was clean, her hair brushed out and her thin body concealed by the fullness of the nightgown, he could recognise something of the old Kathleen.

She began slowly: "Oh, Oliver, how can I thank you? Knowing you loved me has kept me going all through the worst times. I'm free to marry you at last, if you still want me. With you to help me, I can try to wipe out Jerusha's memory of my desertion. I am so longing for our reunion, but apprehensive, of course, at the thought of seeing her again! Tell me about her, is she happy?"

"There is too much to tell tonight," he said evenly. He rose from the chair by her bed, removed the tray from her lap to the bedside table. "You should sleep now, I think." He turned the lamp low.

She stretched out her hand, caught at his sleeve as he bent to this task. "Oliver – *please* don't go – I want you to stay, I don't *ever* want to be alone again . . ."

He sat down again, patted her hand gently, then tucked it under the covers. "I won't leave you, Kathleen," he said.

Sergei had gone out to his club in Jubilee Street. Sometimes he came back the worse for wear, having drunk and no doubt argued too much with his comrades. Essie left him completely to his own devices nowadays and hoped for the best.

She had been out with her favourite gentleman tonight. When she returned, she noticed that the parlour door was ajar. She called out, but there was no reply. She looked inside. The room smelled fusty, of stale tobacco and other odours which she could not put a name to. It was still light, being midsummer, and the curtains were undrawn. There were untidy heaps of papers on the table. She could not read them, of course, for although she spoke a few words of Russian and could understand more, the written language was to her incomprehensible. She recognised the newspaper, *The Workman's Friend*, however. She felt suddenly sick, frightened. Some said it was directed at anarchists . . .

Sergei's hand descended heavily on her shoulder from behind. "You are interested, Essie? You care to borrow it, eh?"

She thrust it at him. "No! I—"

"You wondered what I do in here all day? I write letters, articles, for the cause. Is that a crime? You should not concern yourself with my affairs, Essie. Oliver would not like it."

"He was sorry for you, that's all, that's why he brought you here! *He* is not involved in politics—"

"Not directly, no. But soon I may have to go away – he will help me then. He would be foolish to refuse."

She summoned courage, pushed past him and went into the back room. She turned, and he was still there, standing in the doorway, regarding her with a faint, mocking smile. "Yes, Essie, your Oliver would be forced to comply with my wishes; you have heard of *blackmail?* It should not be necessary, I think. I wish you goodnight," and he retreated, closed the door.

She hoped fervently that Oliver would return home very soon.

"Oliver!" Kathleen exclaimed, when the cab stopped outside the house. "Darling, what a *wonderful* surprise!"

She looked so much better, he thought, in her new clothes and with her hair in the latest puffy style. Her expression was animated, her eyes sparkled and she was about to relish her role as lady of the house. It was obvious that she thought he had bought the family home for her return. How could he tell her that he had done all this for Jerusha's sake?

They would be married as soon as they could arrange it. "I owe everything to you, Oliver, and you have waited so patiently for me," Kathleen said.

Wasn't this what he had always wanted? Privately, he wondered if it was too late . . . He tried to suppress thoughts of Jerusha. He really would be like a father to her shortly, he thought wryly.

Once inside the echoing hall, when the cab driver had departed, Kathleen flung her arms round him. "I do love you, you know, Oliver, I always have, I was just blind to it before, I suppose. Has there been anyone else in all these years? Oh, I wouldn't blame you if you had looked elsewhere, you'd be a *saint* if you hadn't!"

What would she say if he replied, "I fell in love with your daughter – but maybe it was because she was part of *you* . . ." Instead, he said, "Well, I *am* a saint then, if you say so, Kathleen." And he held her close, because they would be together from now on and he hoped very much that his love for her would be revived.

Chapter Seven

"We're going to London again, Phylly," Jerusha told her. "To stay in the big house. Oliver will be there this time, and he has a surprise for us. We're going to see nice Dr Howell too."

"O-ie," Phylly mouthed, looking at her mother, but pulling at Goldie's hair as she sat on her lap.

"Yes, Goldie, too. And Millicent hopes to meet us if she can get away."

"Do you think Phylly understands?" Goldie wondered.

"A little, I'm sure of that. We must keep on talking to her, but we must never forget it's very frustrating for Phylly when she can't make much out."

They were sitting in the kitchen waiting for Polly. Robey was already busy in the top field.

"Polly's not so punctual nowadays," Jerusha said ruefully, "with the little ones to see to. But it is wonderful how it keeps her mind off Bart and what *he* might be up to, eh, Goldie?"

Polly was in her element with a baby to cuddle and care for. Polly-May, to save any confusion with two Pollys in the house, soon had her name shortened to May.

She passed her reluctantly back to her young mother to feed. "You be a good girl for Grandma, May Pepper, while I take our friends to catch the train. Then I have a delivery or two," she said to Pansy, "but I should be back by midday. Perhaps we might stroll up and see how your father's doing now he's back home, and take him a few bites to eat to save him cooking."

"I oughter be there to look after him—" Pansy worried.

"Now you just be sensible, my girl. With a bad head, who wants children making a noise and larkin' about, eh? And you've got to keep resting up 'til the doctor says otherwise! Well, goodbye for now, all of you."

So Polly was away when the bobby called again. Bart had been caught thieving in his new haunts and, worse, had threatened one householder who bravely confronted him, with his shotgun, indeed he had pulled the trigger, deliberately blasting a lamp and causing a fire before he was tackled and disarmed by neighbours. He was now locked up, and likely to be for some considerable time, with all the previous offences taken into consideration too.

When the bobby had gone, saying he would be return later when Polly was back, and unsure whether he had passed on good or bad news, Pansy gathered up her little tribe and went home to cry on her father's shoulder. She didn't leave a note for Polly because she didn't know how to write anything other than her name.

They were becoming quite blasé about taking cabs. An hour and a half after boarding the train, they arrived at Oliver's house. It was nearly three months since they had been there last and a transformation greeted their gaze when the housekeeper opened the door to them. The hall was now furnished with oak settles, with an imposing desk facing the entrance. There were cards, beautifully lettered, with arrows pointing left and right to: GALLERY ONE and GALLERY TWO, the erstwhile reception rooms.

The door to one room opened and Oliver came out, smiling. Behind him were revealed white walls, polished wood flooring, more settles, placed back to back in a rectangle in the centre. A man in a white overall was up a stepladder carefully positioning a picture on the wall to one side of the white marbled surround of the fireplace. More pictures were stacked ready for hanging.

"You look *amazed* – not aghast, I hope?" Oliver asked. "It's good to see you. Take a deep breath or two before we go upstairs! Yes, this is my new venture. *The Oliver Browne Gallery.* I wish to promote promising new artists. What d'you think?"

"I think," Jerusha said in awe, "I think – how *enterprising* you are, Oliver! It's *just* what this house should be used for."

"It will help with the upkeep, I hope, too. Let me carry young Phylly, if she will allow it," Oliver said. "Leave your bags in the hall, I'll bring them up later."

Phylly permitted him to pick her up, but hid her solemn face against his shoulder.

"I wonder what changes we will find upstairs," Goldie whispered to Jerusha as they followed Oliver up the wide stairs.

Jerusha wondered if Essie would be waiting for them in the nursery; she hoped so.

Oliver opened the nursery door, ushered them in. The room was flooded with September sunlight. Someone sat on the window seat, had obviously been watching out for their arrival.

Jerusha saw a small woman, slender and dark-haired, wearing a blue dress, high-waisted with the modern hobble skirt. The creamy lace insert in the bodice showed off the silver necklet set with sapphires, which was matched by screw-on earrings. The styling of her hair, although just as dark, was very different to Jerusha's, which was tied back today with petersham ribbon; the eyes could have been her own, large, deep brown, fringed with extravagant lashes. She knew instantly that this was her mother.

"Aren't you going to say anything, Jerusha?" Kathleen asked, after a long minute of silence, broken only by Phylly going over to the toy cupboard and rattling the doors so that Goldie would know she wished it to be opened. Oliver, advised by Essie, had filled it with toys before their first visit and Phylly had not forgotten!

"Hello – Kathleen." How could she call this stranger anything more intimate?

Oliver took her hand, led her to her mother. "It's a shock for you, I'm sorry, Jerusha, but—"

"I wished it to be like this," Kathleen said softly. "Oliver wanted to write and tell you he'd found me, that he had brought me home, don't blame him, please. This is a moment I had come to believe would never happen."

"I thought that too," Jerusha said simply.

"Kathleen and I were married last week," Oliver said. "Your father died some months ago, in Trinidad. Kathleen was ill when I arrived there. She didn't want to see you until she looked—"

"Until I looked more like the person you remembered, Jerusha," Kathleen finished.

She wants me to put my arms round her, to say how wonderful this is, we two meeting again after so long, Jerusha thought. She turned instead and beckoned to Goldie, who, having summed up the situation, was tactfully emptying the cupboard of toys to keep Phylly happy and occupied.

"These are my daughters," she said, knowing that Oliver must have enlightened Kathleen as to her relationship with Goldie. "Marigold and Phyllida. Girls, this is your grandmother, my mother, Kathleen Carey—"

"Kathleen Browne," she corrected swiftly.

Jerusha felt a sudden pang at these words. Surely she couldn't be jealous? But Oliver had cared for her all these years and naturally she was closer now to him, and to Essie, than she might ever be again to her own mother. Still, wasn't this outcome always what Oliver had hoped for? She must be generous, show forgiveness even if she did not feel it.

"Freshen up," Oliver suggested, "And then come downstairs to the dining room for lunch. Essie will be joining us shortly, I hope. What time is your appointment at the hospital, Jerusha?"

"Two o'clock," she said.

"I could come with you—" Kathleen offered.

"It is better if Phylly and I go on our own," Jerusha replied equably. "But thank you all the same, Kathleen."

She saw the appealing look Kathleen directed at Oliver, then she turned and began to coax Phylly away from the clutter of toys.

"We will see you when you are ready to eat, then," Kathleen said, and she and Oliver went out of the room.

Jerusha was tired, rather dispirited, for the session at the clinic had not gone as well as the last time. Phylly must have been affected by the tension between herself and Kathleen at lunchtime, she thought. She looked forward even more now to seeing Millicent tomorrow. She regretted having disappointed Oliver in her reaction to her mother's return home. Essie had been subdued too, hardly referring to her son's marriage, although she had made the afternoon out enjoyable for Goldie, which was good.

She knew immediately who was tapping on her bedroom door. Should she pretend to be asleep? Instead, she called out, "Yes?"

"It's me, Kathleen, Jerusha. Can I come in for a few minutes, please?"

"Yes." Jerusha did not sit up, but turned on to her back, after making sure that Phylly, slumbering beside her, was well covered up. The lamp burned low, for Phylly was afraid of the dark.

Kathleen perched nervously on the edge of the bed. With her hair hanging loose and her satin wrapper tightly tied round her waist, she looked young and vulnerable, not like a woman in her mid-forties at all. "Jerusha, I just wanted to tell you that I still love you, I always have. I don't expect you ever to really forgive me, because I can see how much you love your own little daughter – you'd never desert *her*, would you?"

"*Never*," Jerusha said vehemently.

"Oliver told me – he *had* to, don't be cross with him! – that *your* husband went away, too, that you were heartbroken—"

"I still am!"

"Then I believe that eventually you will understand why I had to see your father again, but I never dreamed it would lead to such a long separation for *us*."

"Do you love Oliver?" Jerusha asked abruptly.

Kathleen's words were an echo of those spoken in the past. "I feel great affection for him, yes. I am so grateful for all he has done for you, and for me, but Oliver is, well, an ordinary man, and your father, flawed as he was, was an exciting man, a real adventurer. He was my passion – I really couldn't help myself—"

Even as Jerusha wanted to protest that Oliver was far from ordinary, she realised that Kathleen's final words mirrored exactly the way she felt about Joe. She thought carefully before she spoke now. "It will take time, Kathleen, for us to become close again. But I am beginning to understand . . . Just make Oliver happy, return his affection, that's all I ask. Goodnight."

Kathleen moved, bent to kiss her cheek. "Goodnight. I will, Jerusha, I promise!" Daringly, she planted a fleeting kiss, too, on the damp head of the sleeping child.

Kathleen and Oliver had not yet shared a bed. She guessed that he must be waiting for her to ask him to do so. Now, she went through her room into his dressing room and touched him on the shoulder. She was sure he was awake. She did not turn on the light.

His bed was narrow but comfortable. She slipped in beside him, put her arms round his waist. "Oliver . . ."

He turned slowly towards her. "Have you made your peace with Jerusha?" he asked.

"I *think* so, well, we've made a start."

"And you want that from me too?" His voice was muffled now against the warm pulsing of her throat. Did he imagine the scent of frangipani?

"Oh, Oliver, my darling, *of course* I do . . ."

"Now, Polly dear," Ernest advised, "dry your eyes and think about things. Sooner or later, we were bound to get news like this, and it could have been worse – that boy, loose with that shotgun, it makes me shudder. At least we know where he is now, and perhaps he'll get straightened out, you never know—"

"I do know, Ernest! He's a bad lot, and always will be. I've got to face up to that. I didn't want Pansy to go, especially now—"

"Think of her poor father, Poll. He needs his family. You got me, we've got each other. And now you've shown you care about the girl, and those little innocents, 'specially young May, you've got plenty to carry on for, haven't you? Pansy said she'll be glad for you to have the children here, or for us to take 'em out, and we can help in lots of ways, I do believe."

"You're right, Ernest, you always are! That was one thing I did right in my life, marrying you!"

"That cuts both ways. And Jerusha and her family need your friendship, too. What would we *all* do without our Poll, eh?"

Polly smiled. "I do love you, Ernest Apps, you know! I wonder how Jerusha's getting on in London?"

Chapter Eight

Millicent was very much the same. Tall, angular, careless in her dress. Jerusha couldn't help noticing that the top button of her jacket was missing. Her hair, which had darkened to a pretty chestnut colour, was pulled back off her face into a tight bun at the nape of her neck. She did not greet Jerusha with a hug, but gripped her hands warmly.

There was a trace of shyness between them at first, as they sat together in the nursery and watched Phylly, who was absorbed with undressing a doll. They were on their own in the house, for Oliver and Kathleen had gone to the hotel for lunch, and Essie had collected Goldie this morning and taken her over to her house for the day. They were all being tactful, Jerusha thought, really appreciating this, because she and Millicent had so much to catch up on. This was a different kind of reunion to the one with her mother: that this would take much more time was already accepted by them both.

"She's a lovely child, Jerusha," Millicent observed.

"She looks like Joe. To think he's not seen her—"

"That's sad, not right, I agree. But you mustn't condemn him before you know the reason why he hasn't returned. As Phylly grows, you might look out for all the *positive* traits she has inherited from her father – perhaps she might be artistic? Those with her disability often express themselves through painting. You must be strong for her; because you don't have Joe with you at this time, you are able to concentrate your love and determination on Phylly. She can have your undivided attention."

"Do you think she really will be able to lead a near-normal life?"

"What is normal? Phylly needs you right now, but as Dr Howell wisely told you, she must also be encouraged to be independent later on. I know what the right school, dedicated teachers, can do for deaf children. At some point you will have to decide if you should send Phylly away for her education. It will be hard, but you are always so brave—"

"I don't think I was brave before I met *you*, Millicent! You taught me how to cope with life, and I've been grateful for that ever since . . ."

"You taught me something very important too, you know. I was a lonely, miserable, self-centred child. Through you, I learned to care for those more vulnerable than myself. Maybe that's why I have taken up my profession."

Phylly came suddenly hurtling across the room, thrust the naked doll in her mother's hands. "O-ie!"

The doll possessed a rippling wig of soft gold hair. Jerusha ruffled Phylly's own curls. "Yes, she looks like Goldie, doesn't she?" And she smiled happily at Millicent.

"You don't mind birds, I hope?" Essie asked Goldie, as Perry swooped to greet the visitor.

"Oh, no, I love all creatures! I wish I could have brought Nibbles with me, but London and dogs, well, country dogs, don't really mix, do they? I like your cat, too." The cat looked apprehensive, wondering if she was going to be turfed out of the chair, as she always was when Jerusha was visiting, but Goldie tickled her under her chin and left her in situ.

"Oh, she's a bit moth-eaten, a real alley-cat, you could say. Ever tried green tea, Goldie darlin'? Ooh, must just slip my shoes off. I try to look smart when I go over to Knightsbridge, but my feet do swell up in this tight pair. Do you mind if I put a match to my copper? I left my sheets soaking when I came away this morning, and there's a bit of a blow out if I can get them on the line in a while. Then I'll fry up a nice gammon rasher or two for our lunch, shall I?"

"That sounds tempting, Essie!" Goldie glanced over at the door to the front room, which remained firmly shut. She had rather been hoping that the mysterious Russian, whom Jerusha had told her about, would appear. He was in, that was obvious, from the occasional noise, movement from within the room.

The washing was heaving, the water bubbling, and Essie poked it with the copper stick, before she dished up the delicious bacon and fried eggs, with frizzled edges. They seated themselves at the table, where Essie sawed at the bread and refilled their cups with tea.

"Would you like to come to the settlement with me this afternoon, darlin'? I usually go on Saturday afternoons. Dip your bread in the egg, if you want to, we don't stand on ceremony here! I guess that Oliver and Kathleen are eating in a more genteel fashion, but what could be better than gammon and eggs?"

"Not much," Goldie said through a mouthful.

"You're a *very* pretty girl, do you know that? I bet you've got lots of lads beating a path to The Homestead door—"

Goldie grinned. "Only one. Robey – has Ru told you about him?"

"The young gypsy, is it? I used to know a troupe of 'em once, from Romania, I think. So full of talent they were, dancing, music, and so handsome, too! I was *Little Essie Bronski* then, you should've seen my contortions – I can still do a cartwheel as easy as ever, but there's not the room in here for demonstrations!"

I can understand why Ru loves her so much, Goldie thought. She's always so happy and kind. But it's hard to believe that Oliver is her son, he's so different, except, of course, *he's* very thoughtful too, in his quiet way. I did feel a bit worried at one time, that he was hoping to take Joe's place with Ru, but it's plain now that he was just longing and waiting for Kathleen, just like Ru is for Joe.

They were rinsing the washing in the sink when the door opened and Sergei appeared with an armful of papers. Without a word, he opened the stove door and thrust it all on the fire. Instantly there was a roaring up the chimney as the paper flamed.

"Whatever are you doing, Sergei? Trying to set the place alight? That chimney needs sweeping, for a start! Close the damper—" Essie exclaimed in alarm.

"*Close your mouth*!" he said crudely, his brows beetling, his face red with temper. He turned on his heel, returned almost immediately with more bundles of paper which he fed to the stove.

Essie was goaded into action; she seized his arm with her soapy hand and shook him. "I said *stop it!* Or we'll have to get the fire-engine out."

He thrust her aside. "Get out of my way! I've got to get rid of all this, you silly old woman. *Who* is this girl?" he demanded, suddenly aware that Essie was not on her own.

Goldie was still standing by the copper, stick in hand, as if mesmerised.

"That's none of your business!" Essie flashed at him.

"Should she talk, it is." He was back in his room now, which Essie, following him, could see was in complete disarray. "The police, I expect them shortly. A friend was arrested last night. I learn this while you are out this morning . . ."

"You're getting rid of evidence, is that it?"

"I have done nothing wrong! I merely write—"

"*To incite*!" Essie cried.

"You wish your Oliver to be involved? No, of course you do not. But *he* brought me here, so he can see me away. He must make arrangement for tonight. You go, *now,* and tell him that—"

"*I will not*!"

"You shall. For the girl will stay here with me, until your return."

Before she could stop him or shout to Goldie to run outside, he was behind the girl, hands gripping her shoulders. "You see? I mean what I say, Essie. Tell Oliver. *Go*!"

"Goldie, forgive me! I'll be back as soon as I can," Essie wept, as she thrust her feet in her shoes and snatched up her bag. She prayed that Oliver would still be at the hotel.

"Now, you must help me, Goldie, is it? Tidy the room, as if it is not my place of work. I am strong, I do not hesitate to silence you if you should scream. But you need not fear I would – *violate* you – women are nothing to me. It must all be normal when they come to try to catch me out. You do the talking, if Essie is not yet come. Today, you are Essie's granddaughter, come to see her, but you find her out. *Work*, now!"

Silent from shock and fear, Goldie set to her task.

Kathleen sipped her champagne, raising her glass to Oliver. "To us, Oliver . . ."

"To us," he repeated. He smiled at her, remembering last night. How could he forget it? He had thought, when he married her, that it would be a marriage of convenience, of old friends on his side perhaps, with silent regret at what might have been if Kathleen had never met Edwin. But then, of course, there would have been no Jerusha, who was so dear to him . . .

Kathleen had been warm, exciting, just as he had so often

imagined she would be, in the past. This really was a new chapter in both their lives.

She smiled back, leaned forward. "You surprised me last night, Oliver."

"I'm glad," he said simply.

"At the end, you know, I felt contempt for Edwin. He let me down so badly. I want to make you happy, you so deserve it."

"You *have* made me happy, very happy," he told her.

A waiter coughed discreetly, passed a folded message to Oliver, waited for a reply.

Oliver rose. "Please excuse me, Kathleen. I am wanted in Reception. Will you escort Mrs Browne to the lounge, please, and serve our coffee there? I will be back as soon as I can."

They could not retreat to Oliver's study, for the hotel was no longer his domain. He moved to a quiet corner, sat down next to Essie. "What's wrong?" he asked gently. It was very obvious that she was upset.

The story came bursting out. Oliver was shocked, for a few moments indecisive. Then he went to the desk and requested paper to scribble a note. "Please will you see that my wife has this? She is in the lounge, having coffee. I would be grateful if you would call a cab, immediately, and another, later, when she is ready, to take Mrs Browne home. Thank you." He took out his wallet.

"Try not to worry," he told Essie, as they waited on the steps for the cab to arrive. "I have urgent arrangements to make now, but I will come tonight, after dark."

Goldie had worked like an automaton. When the men in bowler hats, dark suits arrived, she told them that her grandmother would be back in a while, and that she would answer any questions on behalf of the lodger who had little English. As far as she knew, he had lived here for more than two years and paid his rent regularly, and that was that.

The men went away after searching Sergei's room, but said they would return. They had others to call on. Goldie wondered if the men saw the flicker of fear in Sergei's eyes when they stated that. It gave her renewed courage.

When they had gone, she said boldly, "I must wring Essie's sheets, hang them out. If we don't behave normally, the neighbours will be suspicious."

"I will watch you, all the time," he stated ominously.

She was pushing the pegs down when Essie opened the gate. She was out of breath for, of course, the cab had dropped her off at the top of the alley.

"Is he—?" Essie mouthed.

"I am here. Come in, Essie," he said from the doorway.

"You'll let Goldie go home now?" she pleaded anxiously. "Oliver will come for you tonight." If only she hadn't brought the girl here today!

"Sit down," he said roughly. The police will be here again in an hour or so. "The girl should be here. How can I trust her? Call her inside now. I don't wish her to run off."

"Goldie! Here, darlin'. She knows nothing, why keep her here?"

He suddenly yanked her head back by her hair. She exclaimed with pain.

"So proud, so vain you are, old woman, of your hair. I shall *pull it out, like this,* see? Until you say the truth." He dangled a clump before her eyes. "Was it you betrayed me, Essie?"

Goldie had been transferring the last of the washing to the sink, lifting it out of the still boiling water with the stick. Outraged, she rushed at Sergei, copper stick in hand and raised it threateningly. "*Leave Essie alone*!"

"Give it to me," he commanded. "You are a stupid girl."

She hurled the stick at him instead, and turned to flee, at Essie's scream, "*Run, Goldie, run*!"

The missile caught him on the side of the head and he dropped like a stone, striking his head again on the stove as his legs buckled.

"He's *dead*, isn't he?" Goldie whispered, feeling horribly sick. Essie, hearing approaching footsteps, snatched up the stick and flung it back into the bubbling copper water.

"Let *me* do the talking," she hissed. "Sit down over there."

The police were sympathetic. They carried the unconscious man into the other room, laid him on the couch. He was bleeding, but the fall had not been fatal. Would madam like to tell them what had occurred?

A heated argument, she said. She had told him that this was a respectable house, despite the neighbourhood, that the constabulary were not regular visitors here. "'I want you to pack your bags and go,' I said. He got very hot under the collar and grabbed me by the hair – the pain was such, I shoved him, and he slipped and hit his head—"

"You were within your rights, madam, to ask him to leave. We can't pin anything on him at present, but he has the wrong sort of friends, who could get him into trouble. When he comes round, he won't be in any fit state to continue the argument. We suggest you pack his bags for him, and tell him if there is any further trouble you will call us to evict him for you. Can you manage that?"

"I certainly can," Essie told them.

When at last they had gone, she sat down limply beside Goldie, who was still in a state of shock. "Oliver will come. He'll get rid of him. I'm *so* sorry, darlin', *I really am* . . ."

The docks were never deserted, even at dead of night. They were expected: a small boat was bobbing on its moorings beyond the looming bulk of the cargo ships.

Two figures, one supporting the other, came slowly and stealthily down the steps. One, the weaker, was assisted into the boat. There was a sudden burst of strident laughter from a boat nearby, then just the lapping of the deep, dark water.

Oliver retraced his steps, quickly this time, nervously shading his face with the collar of his coat. He had seen too much of docksides, both in London and Trinidad in the past few months. He had been a fool, he realised, helping Sergei because he had been persecuted for his beliefs in his home country. He had believed him to be idealistic, not anarchistic. He would never know the truth of it now.

Essie and Goldie were back in Knightsbridge. Goldie requested that she might be allowed to tell Jerusha what had happened in her own good time. "I don't want to spoil her happy day with Millicent, Essie, and I don't believe Oliver wants to tell the others anything at all, do you?"

"Your Joe can't be as bad as he's painted," Essie said softly, "if he fathered a grand girl like *you* . . ."

Chapter Nine

"I was worried about you," Kathleen murmured, as they lay side by side in bed. He seemed remote tonight, with his hands clasped behind his head.

"You mustn't worry about me, Kathleen," he said wryly. "After all, haven't you always thought me so dependable – dull even – compared to Edwin?"

She caught her breath. It was unlike him to be sarcastic. It was, however, the truth. She had to admit that to herself. "Dependable, yes," she said softly, "but never dull – think of last night . . ." As his arms went round her, she added, "I'm very glad I married you, Oliver, I really am."

Essie and Goldie were talking quietly, too, in their shared room.

"Oliver wants me to think again about coming here to live. Kathleen is going to be working with him in the gallery, she fancies being at the reception desk, and entertaining guests – think of all the smart new clothes she'll need! I could be in charge of the house; after all, I know all the wheezes the servants get up to, having had experience, as you say! After that business with Sergei," she rubbed at the sore patch on her scalp, "maybe I should give in gracefully, and let my son look after me, after all."

"You wouldn't have to keep dashing backwards and forwards either, Essie, when Jerusha and Phylly and I come to visit."

"I wouldn't have to worry about wet washing hanging about, either, with others to see to the laundry, eh?"

"You'd still be able to visit your settlements – oh, I never got to go with you after all, did I?"

"Next time, darlin', next time."

Jerusha cuddled her daughter and thought back to Millicent's visit with pleasure. She vowed never to lose touch with her friend again. When Kathleen arrived back unexpectedly without Oliver she had chatted to them for a few minutes, then went tactfully to her room.

Later, after Millicent had left, Kathleen joined Jerusha and Phylly in the nursery for tea. It was then that she asked, "Why don't you come and live here permanently, Jerusha? There's plenty of room, we wouldn't get under each other's feet. It would make it so much easier for you, with the clinic appointments, for a start. I know Oliver would be as pleased to have you – your stepdaughter too, of course – as I would."

"I have my own place, Kathleen. My own life," she said bluntly. "I know how much you want to put things right between us, to make life better for me, but I love the country ways, and most of all, I want to be there when *Joe* comes home."

Now she whispered to Phylly, "I don't know why, darling, but all of a sudden, I'm full of hope again. We'll see your daddy *soon!*"

Joe had been in the hospital for many months. That first winter in the camp, before the snow lay thick, deceptively soft and white, before the lakes froze solid, he painted furiously whenever he had the chance. While the others drank and smoked and cursed the cold, he made thumbnail sketches on any paper to hand, before the blood drained from his fingertips. It was a testing time, but also exhilarating, and he was sure that this was the best work he had ever done.

He had no memory of the accident, the felling of the first tree that spring. He knew, of course, that he had been badly injured, that the concussion had been severe and the gash on his head had required many stitches. The blow to his back had cost him a kidney and temporary paralysis. He was in a plaster straitjacket which kept him immobile, on the flat, hard bed of the mission hospital of St Anne. As a casual worker, he had not been insured, but the Company had paid for his transportation to the hospital and for the initial, vital treatment. Now that he was convalescing, he was aware that he was a charity patient.

The nursing sisters brought him paper, pencils. They even provided a portable stand on which he could fix the paper at an angle, so that he could draw; it could be used as a prop for reading books, too. His precious box, which contained the lumber camp sketches and paintings, had been brought with him to the hospital; his other possessions, few as they were, were in a cupboard at his bedside.

"You would like to write a letter home?" he was asked one day. He shook his head. Not until the plaster cast was cut free, not until he was sure he would be mobile again. He was no use to anyone as he was. He might never see Jerusha or Goldie again. He didn't know whether he had another daughter or a son.

Sometimes he dreamed that he was back in Kent. He saw Jerusha, laughing, stretching up to pick the nuts. He danced her round, as he had the day he told her he loved her, her black hair streamed in the breeze and she was warm and pliable in his arms. How long ago was that? Two years or more . . .

How could he blame her if she had turned against him?

They cut him free of the plaster as the leaves changed colour on the maple trees. Gazing out through the hospital window he thought how beautiful they were, orange, red and gold, that soon they would fall and scatter in the first bitter winds.

He had no strength to speak of. He had to be taught to walk again, like a baby. It took two strong men to get him on his feet, to hold him upright, support each painful step forward. Often he felt despair. Why couldn't he have been killed outright, like Dan, that dreadful day? He was in constant pain.

"Won't you write to your wife now you are getting better?" a young sister asked, as he subsided gratefully on to his bed after one of these sessions.

"*No!* Not until I can walk unaided across the room," he said.

"That may be some way off, Joe—"

"I know. I *do* know that."

He lay awake that night, tired from his exertions but unable to sleep. Quite suddenly, the anxiety and depression left him. Despite the pain in his back, he felt peaceful. She's thinking of me at this moment, he thought, she *knows* we won't be parted too much longer. Sister was right, I must send a letter soon.

Jerusha held the letter for some time in trembling hands before she opened it. Goldie looked at her curiously, as she buttered the toast for breakfast, but said nothing.

"It's from Joe . . ." Jerusha said at last.

"Aren't you going to open it?" Goldie cut Phylly's toast into strips and decapitated her boiled egg. "Where's it from?" She couldn't conceal her excitement. "Oh, please, Jerusha!"

"From Canada. It's his writing, so that means—"

"He's *alive!* Do read it!"

'My darling Jerusha,

I must begin by asking you to forgive me, if you can, for the long silence between us. You will see from the address that I am in hospital.

What happened before I came to this place is a long story. I don't feel up to writing it all down. I was wrong to leave you, but I hope you will have me back. I injured my back eighteen months ago. I have been in a plaster cast, unable to move. I am slowly improving, but the doctors are unsure how long it will take me to regain full fitness, if ever. As soon as I can, I will come home to you, Goldie and the baby. I hate to ask you, but if you could arrange for some money to be sent to the hospital here, I would be very grateful.

I love you very much, all three of you. Believe me. Joe.'

Then they were both crying and hugging each other, and Phylly was banging her spoon on the table, which usually made them spring to her service. Her lower lip was trembling, but when they parted and looked at her, their happy faces made her smile.

"Phylly, Joe's coming home! We don't know when, but he still loves us! *All of us*!" Goldie told her little sister.

Naturally, they had to share their news with Polly. She had been quiet and drained of her usual colour since she had learned of Bart's imprisonment.

"I'm so glad for you," she said. She was minding her grandchildren today, while Pansy went with her father to the hospital, hopefully to be told he was fit to return to work.

They sat round her table, while the boys showed Phylly how to build a tower of coloured toy bricks and little May dreamed and dribbled against Polly's shoulder.

"I suppose you would expect me to say I wish it was Bart, but I don't. The children give me so much comfort; they're much more loving than he ever was. They may not be as sharp, but better kind than crafty, eh? I do write to him, Ru, for I don't forget he's my son."

"Of course you don't," Jerusha consoled her. There was so much she had to do. Write to Oliver – he would advise her regarding the transfer of money to Canada, for one thing. But first of all, she and Goldie were going home now to write to Joe. "Come on girls," she said.

Chapter Ten

It was 1908. The year of the Franco-British Exhibition. A great 'White City' was built in London's Shepherd's Bush. There was a fair, chock-a-block with amazing amusements including the Flip-Flap, which hoisted sightseers in its cars far above the ground and whirled them round.

The capital was crowded with visitors from home and overseas. *The Oliver Browne Gallery* almost burst at the seams. Kathleen and Essie were in their element. The wariness in their relationship had long since evaporated: Essie was disarmed by Oliver's obvious contentment in his marriage, and his enthusiasm, encouraged by his wife, for his new venture.

Oliver was planning a very special exhibition. When he heard from Jerusha last autumn that Joe was in hospital in Canada and that he was, to put it plainly, destitute, he had insisted on sending funds himself. He told Jerusha that she would need all her resources when Joe at last came home, as he would obviously still need medical care. It no longer hurt him to realise that to Jerusha he really was now a father figure. The most important thing he could do for her was to ensure that Joe came home to her as soon as possible.

Phylly would be three years old on her saint's day. Jerusha's trees were bearing a magnificent crop of nuts. Letters had gone back and forth between Kent and Canada. Joe was painting every day in the hospital. Oliver had been very generous in making sure that he was well supplied with art materials. He had suffered some problems in regaining mobility. It really was a case sometimes of the frustrating, 'one step forward and two steps back'.

Jerusha, Goldie and Phylly travelled up to London on a summer's day. Because Joe had said that was her colour, Jerusha wore a tunic top and skirt in light leaf-green, with a belt in a darker shade to match the saucy tricorn hat. She felt cool and comfortable. She had hesitated over her hair: wasn't she getting too old to have it hanging down her back, even if it was tied back with a ribbon? Goldie had decided for her. "You must look just as you did when Joe went away! In *my* case, that's a bit difficult," she added, with a grin, "'cause I'm all grown up! D'you think he'll know I'm me?"

"He will!" Jerusha assured her. "Same golden hair, same smile, same Goldie!"

"D'you think he'll have changed much?" Goldie sounded anxious now.

"I don't know, Goldie, I hope not. But we mustn't expect too much."

Jerusha wondered how Phylly would take to her father. She had told him, of course, about Phylly's deafness, but dwelt much more on how beautiful she was, how intelligent, and how she had found a wonderful school for her to go to, in a year or so. She had also mentioned briefly what had become of Bart, but she did not tell him about the dreadful slur in the letter she had destroyed. Joe would tell her the truth, she believed stoutly, when he was ready to do so.

Essie met them at the station. Oliver had already left to meet Joe off the boat.

"You've only brought one bag," Essie said, leading them to the waiting cab.

"We're only staying one night, Essie, we want to take Joe home tomorrow."

"You know best, darlin', but Oliver thought—"

"I know what Oliver thought! That you could all help to make it – easier – for us, being together after so long, but he needs to go home, to *our* home, you see."

"We thought it best to put you in our room tonight, Jerusha. The stairs to the nursery quarters might prove difficult for Joe." Kathleen looked anxious. "How do you feel?"

They were in Kathleen and Oliver's bedroom. Essie and Goldie had tactfully whisked Phylly upstairs to her usual ceremonial emptying of the toy cupboard. "You'll want to be on your own, you two, tonight," Essie had conspiratorily whispered. "Goldie and I will enjoy having Phylly with us, and she'll have to get used to not sleeping in your bed!"

"I feel," Jerusha said slowly, "as if I'm dreaming . . . This day has been so long in coming, and now it's here I suppose I'm a little afraid that we'll be, well, strangers, Kathleen."

"Like you and me?" Kathleen suggested wistfully.

It was time for another true reconciliation. They held tight to each other. Then they turned and smiled at their reflections in the mirror on the dressing table.

"You're still beautiful, Kathleen," Jerusha said softly.

"So are you. We *are* alike, aren't we?"

"Yes, we are. I suppose that you, more than anyone, know exactly how I feel, now I'm about to see Joe again . . ."

It helped that Goldie and Phylly were with her when Oliver ushered Joe into the hall. The gallery was closed today, but the desk and furnishings made the greetings impersonal.

"Hello, Joe," she said.

He came slowly towards her, leaning on his sticks, his face revealing his apprehension, his fatigue. His hair was newly cut, his clothes unfamiliar, but he was *Joe*.

Jerusha stood still, Phylly clinging to her skirts.

"Hello, Jerusha, Goldie," he said.

Goldie kissed him first. "It's wonderful to see you, Joe! This is Phylly, she's a bit shy, as you can see—"

Jerusha scooped her up, hid her face in Phylly's curls. "She's been practising, haven't you, Phylly?" Her voice was muffled.

Goldie mouthed the magic word to her sister.

"Da-da!" Phylly said suddenly, loudly. Then she repeated it, joyfully, over and over.

Oliver, busying himself with Joe's luggage, turned away from the sight of Joe, dropping his sticks and enfolding them both in his arms.

"If you prefer, Joe, you could have the bed to yourself, and I could sleep in the dressing room," Jerusha said hesitantly.

He was resting on the bed in the pyjamas and dressing gown Oliver had unobtrusively laid out for his use. They had eaten dinner early and when they had kissed Phylly goodnight, they had by unspoken agreement retired themselves.

"Is that what you want, Jerusha?" he asked.

"No – I was thinking – your back, I wouldn't like to – you might need more room—" she floundered.

"But we'll have to share a bed at home, won't we?" he sounded almost teasing.

"Of course! Oh, Joe, I wanted us to be there, our first night together after so long!"

"It doesn't matter, Jerusha, really, the important thing is I am here, and you are here. We need each other, don't we?"

There was no talking, no love-making, but there was all the time in the world for that, Jerusha thought. She was contented just to lie close to the man she loved, to put out her hand every now and then to touch him, so that she was sure he was still there.

"I know you're anxious to go home," Oliver said, "but I have a business proposition for you, Joe. I just need a yes or no. Kathleen and I would very much like to stage an exhibition of your Canadian paintings. All you would need to do would be to leave the pictures here with us and we will see to the rest. We would time the exhibition to when you feel you could come here, to stay, to meet prospective buyers, to perhaps talk about the experiences which led to these works . . ."

Joe could not hide his surprise. "I don't know what to say, Oliver—"

"Say *yes*!" Jerusha interrupted.

"Yes! And thank you. It would perhaps be a chance for me to repay you for all your generosity – d'you really think the paintings will sell?"

"I'm convinced of it. They are full of colour, vitality . . . Kathleen will start work on the catalogue immediately, won't you, darling?"

"I'm dying to do so!" Kathleen smiled. The partnership with Oliver was proving to be fulfilling in all senses.

Essie and Goldie had taken Phylly for a walk in the park. "A happy day for all of us, isn't it?" Essie observed. "You just do your best to make sure that father of yours stays with our Jerusha this time."

"I *know* he will, Essie. They've got Phylly, haven't they, and *she* needs both parents."

"So do *you,* darlin', so do you," Essie said wisely.

Goldie gave one of her happy grins, then ran to prevent Phylly from stepping into an ornamental pond. When I get married to Robey, she thought, even if he wants to travel around with his folk, I'll go wherever he goes. And if Joe ever dares to step out of line again, well, I'll remind him of how he feels right now, I really will . . .

"You've got your shoes wet," she scolded Phylly fondly. Whether she could hear or not, Phylly knew she was being daring. "Da-da," she said obligingly, well aware how that pleased everyone.

They walked slowly round the orchard, looking at all the trees. Phylly made a face, for the apple she had made Goldie pick was not sweet enough for her taste. Nibbles bounded after the fat core to crunch it up.

Robey proudly showed off the vegetables in the top field, and Joe congratulated him on his hard work.

"He's a good lad and no mistake," Polly said, for of course, she had rushed over to see them.

"I am sorry to hear about Bart," Joe told her.

"Not unexpected, was it? No one could ever call *him* a good lad, eh? Seen all Jerusha's nut trees?"

"We were leaving those 'til last . . ."

It was still a slow process for Joe, getting undressed. He sat down on the edge of the bed, waiting for the niggling pain to subside. He watched Jerusha brushing out her hair, then dividing it to plait it.

"D'you remember how I showed you the scars on my back, Joe, on our wedding night? You didn't ask me why or when, you just kissed the marks and made me feel it didn't matter after all. Can I look at *your* scars, Joe? I'd like to do the same for you."

She lifted his jacket carefully and looked for some time at the scars, so much deeper than her own.

"I had my right kidney removed, you know. It was crushed, and I had a bad infection. But I got over that well. I will always have the weakness, pain in my lower back. I won't be much use to you on the smallholding, I'm afraid."

"You're going to be a famous artist, Joe! Oliver says so. You do want to go on living here, don't you? I know it was Dan's house first, but—"

"There is something I should tell you about Dan," he said quietly. "I should have done so before we married – forgive me for not doing so."

"You were there, weren't you, the night Dan died? You tried to help him, didn't you? Unlike Bart. I know he was there, too. It was a tragic accident Joe. *That's the beginning and end of it.* I do wish you had trusted me enough to tell me, but we must promise not to keep secrets from each other, ever again. Dan would have liked you, Joe. He wouldn't have been able to understand why you left me like that, but all he ever wanted was my happiness, and I've got that, now you're back." She pulled back the covers. "Into bed now, and let's make the most of it, before Phylly starts crying in Goldie's room."

"You're wheezing a bit, Jerusha," he worried, as their lips met.

After some time, she replied. "You took my breath away – that's what loving *you* does to me, Joe!"

Chapter Eleven

There was a gypsy wedding in the spring following Goldie's sixteenth birthday. She would never sleep under the roof of a house again, not even The Homestead. Sometimes she and Robey would return to work there, but they had their own vardo: Goldie would travel, if not as far, like her father before her.

"Don't let her see you crying, Jerusha," Joe said, as she put on her own wedding finery.

"She's so young, Joe."

"She's very wise already—"

"Like Margaret. I don't mind you saying it, you know! Because it's true. They are deeply in love, I can see that."

There was no actual jumping the broomstick but a pricking of thumbs and mingling of blood; the bride and groom ceremoniously drank water from the same cup and then that was solemnly broken.

Jerusha and Joe were at the wedding, but Polly looked after Phylly at home. They sat a little distance from the other wedding guests, privileged to witness but not actually take part.

The golden hoops in Goldie's earlobes which Robey had given her flashed in the firelight as night came swiftly down, transmuting the bright colours of the gypsies' clothes. There was music from the fiddlers, exuberant dancing, showers of sparks from the fire, which floated down rather like falling stars, or so Jerusha imagined. The guests ate and drank, sang and laughed and cried. Nibbles, that faithful hound, hid under the nearest wagon, gazing out anxiously at the unfamiliar scene. He, of course, was leaving home with the bride. Other dogs, lurchers mainly, fought over scraps, and the ponies, tethered, shifted and blew down their nostrils. Children played hide-and-seek.

"We should go home now, I think," Joe said at last. The straw bales on which they were seated seemed uncommonly prickly and hard. His back was throbbing.

Goldie came to kiss them goodbye: it was an emotional moment for all three of them. Robey gripped their hands firmly in turn and told them he would love and take care of their daughter. But his simple words made Jerusha feel a little sad: "*She's one of us now, missus.*"

Jerusha shivered a little, for it was chilly now they had moved from the aura of the fire. Joe's arm went round her shoulders. It would be a long, slow walk home under the stars, with Joe still using one stick, but hopefully, Polly would bundle Phylly up and they would come in the horse and cart to meet them along the way.

Goldie wore her mother's shawl. Robey held her close to his side. "We go away tomorrow for a few days by ourselves. It is our tradition," he said.

"I can't believe this is all ours," Goldie said, as they climbed the steps and closed the vardo door firmly. She blushed as she saw the bunk bed ready made. There were fine turned bedrails, with curtains for privacy, but these were pulled back. "What *are* you doing, Robey?" she exclaimed as he jumped on the bed with his boots on and set the wagon swaying and creaking.

He continued without answering for some minutes. Goldie was aware of smothered giggling. It seemed to emanate from the floor, over the hubs. "Turn the lamp low," he said finally, stepping down. He listened intently for a moment, then, "It's all right, Goldie, they've gone, don't worry—"

"What do you mean, *gone*?"

"The young people, they hide under the wagon, they climb on the wheels, listen for—"

"How *awful*!"

"It's no problem. Dada told me what to do! Now they will leave us in peace, I think." He looked at her lovingly. "Tomorrow will be better, Goldie, I promise. We will travel to a quiet place. We can learn to love in peace. Tonight, we will just lie here and dream of our future together."

In a few years time Goldie, like her mother Margaret before her, would be known as 'the wise woman' by her gypsy family, but on her wedding night, she shed just a few tears for the family and way of life she had left for ever.

The first exhibition of Joe's paintings had been exciting, nearly all had been sold. Now he was busy with more pictures for another show. It was still a precarious living, but they could afford daily help on the smallholding.

They missed Goldie very much at first. Robey had worked as hard as the man and the boy together whom they employed during the busiest times. "We'll get that new plough next spring," Joe pledged, "and a team of horses. They won't be kept near the house. I don't think you'll be troubled by asthma. We must move with the times."

Jerusha was unable to do much for, to their delight, she was expecting a December baby. "It won't be born out in the open this time, I hope!" she said to Joe. "And don't worry, I'm not fretting and nor should you, the doctor says, that the new little one will be deaf. It will all tie in very nicely, for soon Phylly will be home from school for the holidays, so she'll feel part of it. Oh, I'm so happy, Joe, aren't you, that she's taken to the school like a duck to water? Of course, we miss her terribly, but because Millicent is there we know she's all right!" She and Joe practised their signing, the communication between fingers and palm of hand, every evening.

"I don't think we should risk you travelling up to London for Kathleen's birthday, Jerusha—"

"I won't have to! They are all coming to us! Oliver, Kathleen and Essie. D'you think we can fit them all round the table? And whatever can we give them to eat?"

"I don't know what to suggest for the main course, but you must make one of your apple pies. I used to dribble when I dreamed of those in Canada—"

"You weren't supposed to dream of my pies, only *me*, Joe Finch!"

"Well, you're not easy to separate," he teased. "Except that you look like an apple *pudding* right now!"

There was one thing Jerusha hadn't taken into consideration: that the baby might come early, as Phylly had done. She had been on her feet far too long, that evening, Joe reproved her, when after she had made the apple pie on her biggest plate for the family party the next day, she then insisted on stirring and wishing on the Christmas puddings before putting them to boil.

"Now, do remember to take them off the stove at eleven o'clock, Joe," she persisted, as he propelled her firmly upstairs to bed. She wouldn't admit it, but she felt rather odd, which might account for all that restless activity, she thought.

At some unearthly hour in the night, she was rudely awoken by the first sharp pains, coming far too quickly, one after another. It was not easy for Joe to hurry nowadays, so he did not wait to get dressed, but went over the road with his jacket over his nightclothes, and his boots unlaced, to fetch Polly.

He got back just in time to hear Jerusha shouting for him, to see his third daughter born and to lift her clear of the bedclothes. Another small baby, but lively and wailing.

"Well," Polly said, "do you *always* have to do things in such a rush, Ru, dearie?" She shooed Joe out of the room. "Make some tea! Bring hot water! And drag out the tin bath and fill it with cold – there's all this bedlinen to soak! I'll see to the rest here. Not much point rousing the nurse until dawn!"

Some time later, Jerusha lay, bemused, looking at her new baby. "I can't believe it, Poll! It's my mother's birthday, and they are all descending on us later today!"

"Not if I can help it, they're not!" said practical Polly. "Joe must send a telegram first thing and put 'em off for a few days!" She wouldn't give Joe away and tell Jerusha that he'd let the Christmas puddings boil dry. She'd make some more herself and replace them, she thought. First things first. "Has this one got a name? It's not a saint's day, as I recall—"

"Well, if Joe doesn't mind, she'll have a saintly name, anyway. I'd like her to be Valentine, after someone very special to me. And Goldie must be her godmother, of course. She should be round this way again soon, I hope. She'll be thrilled, I know. I wonder what Phylly will think of her too? Who do you think she looks like?"

Joe kissed the baby's dark head, then he kissed her mother. "*You*, Jerusha . . ." If only he had been there for the birth of his other daughters, he thought. This was a night he would never forget.

"What did you say?" Joe yawned. "You really *must* try and get some sleep, Jerusha." He put out a tentative hand. Yes, the baby was still there, snuggled in her arms.

"I said," she said very softly, "we really are *a charm of finches* now . . ."